Benjamin Gott

Matilda of Canossa

An Historical Drama in Five Acts

Benjamin Gott

Matilda of Canossa
An Historical Drama in Five Acts

ISBN/EAN: 9783337376963

Printed in Europe, USA, Canada, Australia, Japan

Cover: Foto ©Andreas Hilbeck / pixelio.de

More available books at **www.hansebooks.com**

MATILDA OF CANOSSA

AN HISTORICAL DRAMA

IN FIVE ACTS

BY

BENJAMIN GOTT

AUTHOR OF 'A POETICAL ENGLISH TRANSLATION OF ARIOSTO'S ORLANDO
FURIOSO, FIRST AND LAST CANTOS' 'AN ENGLISH VERSION OF
THE POEMS OF GIUSEPPE GIUSTI AND GIOSUE CARDUCCI'
AND OF 'TANCRED, A TRAGEDY OF SALERNO'

Printed by
SPOTTISWOODE & CO., NEW-STREET SQUARE, LONDON
1885

PREFACE.

VICISSITUDE is the touchstone of Character. In Mediæval Europe principles were untried, and before the result of their application could be ensured dynasties passed away, and still speculation offered more advan-tages, and still speculators were credulous. The eleventh century, convulsively portentous of solutions, was an extra-ordinary crisis. To its rapid development of new views we may trace the germ of all present, all future events. Experience sanctioned the intervention of Chance, while hitherto the chief candidates for. approval and success had only trusted particular principles, which methodically appeared to bring them out right or wrong in subservient obedience to half-visible operations, which they distantly observed and which were regularly either infallible or delusive. But now this simple organisation broke up into practices contrary to these obvious causes. Why was this? The process was too exact, and admitted of improbabilities unreasonable enough at first sight, and almost unaccountable. The boldest drew back in dismay. Men of equivocal abilities and correspondingly inferior theories gained on them, and disposed of their sagacious prudence and cautious routine. Trust and confidence disappeared, and it was not until success was permanent here and there that they were restored. The element Chance presents and sanctions unexpected and profitable moments, and raises despair to hope. If we rely upon it it deserts us ; if we implicitly trust regularity and method, unappealed to, it ignores us. But in a grand heterogeneous complication, when beacons are unlit or out, and signs and symptoms are confusing, when the past is no more oracular and the future more than indefinite, Chance rules Life.

The drama of *Matilda of Canossa* discloses the state of Europe at this particular period. Congresses and Diets were continually resorted to to settle otherwise endless disputes. But their affirmative or denunciative verdicts were not of long duration. The conflicting feeling which they caustically treated preferred to disentangle itself in some other form. Its champions challenged impartial opinion, and for a time chaos prevailed. An unsuspected rival menaced all contending parties, and civilisation halted till a battle or marriage terminated prodigal animosity and intolerant passions.

If Dionysius of Halicarnassus declared that History is Philosophy teaching by Examples, how much then we owe to the Drama by emphasising these examples and girding them with all the importance they should truly possess! Combining in his simulation all arts and sciences, and appealing to every accessory, the dramatist calls out impulses with a vehemence that is not pomposity, and regulates, if possible, their application without ungenerous insinuation. Whether he addresses the judgment or the feelings, the head or the heart, aims at enforcing principle, recommends practices, or overturns prejudices, his influence on mankind for better or worse has no equal. Vindicating his views without tedious expatiation, and illustrating them without effort, he is capable of conveying in an indirect way constitutional manifestoes, creating or subverting dynasties, calling out or disposing of character, and suggesting to the social world and the domestic circle points for the most desirable deductions, the most admirable examples.

'Dramatical or representative poesy,' says Bacon, 'is, as it were, a visible history, for it sets out the image of things as if they were present, and history as if they were past.' For useful purposes and to inculcate certain yet unfixed principles the Drama supersedes all design. The incidents and events do not weary; cause and effect are not insisted upon, but accompany deeds indistinctly, not pressed into the narrative to impose ceremonially on the judgment. Weaker characters are worked up into connection with stronger ones, while these last are so placed as to enable the reader or witness not only to study them on their account, but to place other people in similar positions, themselves for example, and so realise all time at intervals.

The period I have selected for my drama is beyond all others voluminous in parallel events. In Ireland Brian Borohainde was struggling patriotically against the Danes, whom he ultimately defeated at Clontarf. In Scotland its hereditary monarch, unable to cope with refractory malevolence, succumbed to the iniquitous Macbeth, who was in his turn defeated by Malcolm III. at Dunsinane. The Eastern Empire from Romanus IV., who was poisoned, to Nicephorus, who was illegally dethroned, was a succession of treasonable conspiracies and perfidious plots. Bolislas, King of Poland, killed Stanilaus, Bishop of Cracow, and was himself assassinated. William I., Duke of Normandy, put himself at the head of his troops, and invaded England, defeating the Saxon monarch at Battle. Halstein and Olaf advanced the already discernible interests of Sweden and Norway, bringing new fields for civilisation to the front. Philip I.

ruled France, and Solomon, a magnate of superior intelligence and precocious views, Hungary. And it is interesting just at this period to observe the cabals and intrigues presaging a sudden general movement here west, there east.

Canossa was founded by Diomede, but antiquaries trace its origin to the Pelasgi. In passing through it on his road to Brindusium Horace makes remark that the wheat of the locality was gritty, and the supply of water was scanty. Its inhabitants had certain peculiarities of dialect, and also of pronunciation.

This bud of a rare flower, and yet richer fruit, was then just disclosed. Emancipated from the condition chastening its spring, the surrounding district has produced more famous characters than any other. Dante, Petrarch, Ariosto, Galileo, Machiavelli, Alfieri, Michael Angelo, Correggio, Giotto, and Tassoni, born on this territory, have raised it to the highest estimation of lovers of genius, and given it a deathless reputation. Yet what convulsive throes agitated its earlier years! Struggles faithless to origin, dubious of futurity, clouded the scenes over which the star of triumph was to rise, but a race of superior comprehension watched for this, and gave character and point to energies yet unborn.

Henry the Fourth, who became emperor in 1056,

was of short duration, for he was slain at the siege of Antwerp in 1076. In a troublesome period of the middle of her career in order to strengthen her cause in the North, as it was ably supported in the South, a fresh alliance suggested itself between Matilda and Guelfo d'Este, son of the Duke of Bavaria. On this point, however, discrepancy of years produced difficulties which were not so easily overruled. When united, settled domestic happiness was not immediately productive of continuous political security, and the future of Matilda's life was characterised by alternate reverses and success following on each other so closely that but feeble support was accorded to the permanency of her reign. In 1080 she was defeated by Guibert, the anti-pope, at Ravenna. Henry IV. laid waste the territory contiguous to Mantua in 1082. In 1084 she repulsed him at Sorbara in the Duchy of Modena. He attacked Canossa with a large force in the year 1092, but a dense mist pervading the region round precluded his success, and his standard was captured and hung in the Church of St. Apollonio. Matilda died at the age of sixty-nine, in 1115, at Bondeno di Ponaro, and was buried in the Convent of St. Benoist di Polerone in Mantua.

B. G.

Bath, Somersetshire :
June 18, 1885.

MATILDA OF CANOSSA

Errata.

Page 3, line 2, *after* Canossa *read* Interior of Hall in the Castle
  ,, 29, ,, 5, *omit* Soldiers—Barons
  ,, 175, ,, 13, *after* Vallombrosa, near Florence, *read* A Forest
  ,, 352, ,, 1, *after* The Castle of Canossa, *read* The Council-Room

B

was of short duration, for he was slain at the siege of Antwerp in 1076. In a troublesome period of the middle of her career in order to strengthen her cause in the North, as it was ably supported in the South, a fresh alliance suggested itself between Matilda and Guelfo d'Este, son of the Duke of Bavaria. On this point, however, discrepancy of years produced difficulties which were not so easily overruled. When united, settled domestic happiness was not immediately productive of continuous political security, and the future of Matilda's life was characterised by alternate reverses and success following on each other so closely that but feeble support was accorded to the permanency of her reign. In 1080

BATH, SOMERSETSHIRE :
June 18, 1885.

MATILDA OF CANOSSA

B

DRAMATIS PERSONÆ.

HENRY THE FOURTH, *Emperor of Germany*
GODFREY DE GOBBO, *Duke of Lorraine*
THE KING OF SAXONY
THE DUKE OF BAVARIA
THE PRINCE OF THURINGIA
THE DUKE OF SUABIA
THE DUKE OF CARINTHIA
CONRAD, *son of Henry the Fourth*
GUELFO D'ESTE, *son of the Duke of Bavaria*
AZZO, *Duke of Brunswick*
THE COUNT OF PIEDMONT
ODONE OF SAVOY
THE MARQUIS OBERTO
EPPONE OF ZEITZ
BUONVICINO, *Prime Minister to Matilda of Canossa*
GANGARELLI, *Minister to Henry the Fourth*
COUNT HOFENSTAUFEN
COUNT RINALDINI
COUNT GEOFFROI DE FACUNBURGE
BARON VALERIEN DE ST. CHEVEROLLE
CHEMNITZ, *a Tyrolese Lapidary*
TARCHETTI, *a Banker in Florence*
SASSELLI, *a Florentine Jeweller*
BONNIERES, *a Jeweller and Goldsmith of Rouen*
MATILDA, *Countess of Canossa*
BERTHA, *first wife of Henry the Fourth*
ADELAIDE, *second wife of Henry the Fourth*
THE COUNTESS HOFENSTAUFEN
ETHELGA HOFENSTAUFEN
SIGNORA SASSELLI
THERESA SASSELLI

Barons, Soldiers, Shepherds, Citizens, Jailors, Courtiers

SCENES : *Florence, Wurzburg, Canossa, Turin, Vercelli, the Brenner Pass, Milan, Rouen, Pforzheim, the Mont Cenis Pass, Nuremburg*

PERIOD : *between* A.D. 1000 *and* A.D. 1100.

MATILDA OF CANOSSA

DRAMATIS PERSONÆ.

HENRY THE FOURTH, *Emperor of Germany*
GODFREY DE GOBBO, *Duke of Lorraine*
THE KING OF SAXONY
THE DUKE OF BAVARIA
THE PRINCE OF THURINGIA
THE DUKE OF SUABIA
THE DUKE OF CARINTHIA
CONRAD, *son of Henry the Fourth*
GUELFO D'ESTE, *son of the Duke of Bavaria*
AZZO, *Duke of Brunswick*
THE COUNT OF PIEDMONT
ODONE OF SAVOY
THE MARQUIS OBERTO
EPPONE OF ZEITZ
BUONVICINO, *Prime Minister to Matilda of Canossa*
GANGARELLI, *Minister to Henry the Fourth*
COUNT HOFENSTAUFEN
COUNT RINALDINI
COUNT GEOFFROI DE FACUNBURGE
BARON VALERIEN DE ST. CHEVEROLLE
CHEMNITZ, *a Tyrolese Lapidary*
TARCHETTI, *a Banker in Florence*
SASSELLI, *a Florentine Jeweller*
BONNIERES, *a Jeweller and Goldsmith of Rouen*
MATILDA, *Countess of Canossa*
BERTHA, *first wife of Henry the Fourth*
ADELAIDE, *second wife of Henry the Fourth*
THE COUNTESS HOFENSTAUFEN
ETHELGA HOFENSTAUFEN
SIGNORA SASSELLI
THERESA SASSELLI

Barons, Soldiers, Shepherds, Citizens, Jailors, Courtiers

SCENES : *Florence, Wurzburg, Canossa, Turin, Vercelli, the Brenner Pass, Milan, Rouen, Pforzheim, the Mont Cenis Pass, Nuremburg*

PERIOD : *between* A.D. 1000 *and* A.D. 1100.

ACT I.

SCENE I.—*Canossa.*

MATILDA.

The game is mine, and all posterity
Will wonder at this reckoning !

           [*Enter* MESSENGER.
           What news ?

MESSENGER.

Henry the Emperor halts upon the brink
Of Life's unequal precipice : grim, shadowless,
Distinct stand out against the Future sky
Gaunt warnings of a grave disparity
That guide him to a cavern of Despair,
Wherein Reproach will thicken round his head
From out cold steel to shake timidity.

SECOND MESSENGER.

Rumour replies that he respects your name,
Congratulation adds to your success,
Extends forgiveness to cupidity,

Embarrasses his Fortune with your Pride
Assumed or ostentatious, and suspects
A lateral resolution to be true
To all old Rome has left us of Renown.

GODFREY DE GOBBO.

A venturesome attachment !   What if faults
To their redemption have bequeathed a debt
Already payable in Flattery
And easy of disbursement that redounds
To his own credit first?   A man of parts
Skilful in enigmatical disdain
Of what he has and has not !   This is yours !

MATILDA.

Godfrey ! the World is mine, not in its parts !
Invalid portions of assisted dreams
That shelter a fulfilment anywhere
For plain ambition to put on new sleeves
And breathe a finer and remoter air,
Till pampered dignity betrays their stock
Of heedless fit with hazardous relapse,
Attached to every blatant principle
That threatens Fame but fortifies Romance,
Cannot attach my banners to their soil.
But in this age, rounding an universe
I seek a home and find a happier heart,
That in the spirit claiming what it knows

Adorns the age that qualifies all Time,
And captivates it, and acquires the world.
Henry let us disclaim, and ratify
Fresh treaties with fresh temporalities
That, not absorbing with a thrifty glaive
Good gifts, seek larger with a larger mind,
And venture into onsets for a pass
To join Futurity at its earliest bidding.

      [*Clamour without.   Drums and Trumpets.*
         Matilda goes to the window.

Enter party of Soldiers.

CAPTAIN.

The Marches and Romagna in revolt
Your majesty defy, your outposts vanquishing
They drive for succour to Spoleto first
And then to Forli.

GODFREY DE GOBBO.

          Gird on your armour quick !
Spoilt and insipid danger fright with might.
Gird on that faculty your ancestors
Proved and applied to every precedent
And instance imminent as prominent
Uneven, harsh, and unripe Fortune sent
To be a step to your prosperity
Till Time had burnt out all its vanity.

MATILDA.

Canossa in remembrance of itself
Will some day its presumption realise,
If provocation be not petulance,
In that it gages not for its own self
The wager of defiance and attack
That in the whirlwind of vicissitude
It may discern the Haven of Success,
Conciliating the oracle of Hope,
Which yet shall serve me now better than these
Whose vague ambition is not satisfied
But with repletion as its monument,
Whose urgent call on Hope destroys false Health,
Contaminates Discretion with a curse,
Releases to infirmity their cure,
And to dissemblance gives priority
Which strength had fostered for decrepitude,
For a base humour true sagacity,
But in fulfilment and accomplishment
Of hopes Futurity shall justify
Solidity from shadows shall burst forth,
And in the whirl of real and unreal work
Retrieve confusion !
                       But 'tis idle here
Within a circle of extravagance
Assuming a responsible domain
Bound by no limit but an easy law
Of sensible reduction to itself,

Itself its only enemy because
Unworthy of a vulnerable past !
What is Rebellion but a blessing then,
Bequeathing all commotion for all gain ?
Its rapine but a rescue from a foe
That lives upon a threat but never strikes.
Gives Rome no sword but a despondent heart,
Gives Germany no cross-bow but an ache.
Then let us save ourselves from sordid views,
And give Italian blood a character
That hopeless Romans can no longer give !
And give Italian arms a preference
That jealousy shall burn with like the torch
That Parma lights to be extinguished thus.

       [*Puts on her armour.*

A woman has the spirit of a man
When manly deeds have made her what she is,
And when man falls into desuetude,
And lingers on the fragment of a cause
By treachery from tyranny evoked
She leans upon the sword a conqueror.
So few will learn the sacredness of Life !
So Life once more to man reanimate,
By Hope sustained, fresh nurtured from Decay,
Deducted from all origin once more
To its effect committed once again,
May stay and still Destruction's envious wand
Entangled in a centre of its own,
Tumultuous elements sad and immature

'Till the whole mass disorganised retreat,
And from experiment man a spirit pluck
Enough to guide him to Prosperity
And Happiness. His again who knew it not,
Yet lived to find the secret is myself,
Who in dissemblance wakes it from the ground
And speeds discovery to the same result.
Our cause is then to succour what we love,
And realise as we may frail Happiness.
If succoured Love demolish what we save,
Twice worthless in remote unworthiness,
I wake a vengeance they supported thus
Whose dreams are balked by infidelity,
The fruit of too procrastinated power
That quitted earlier might have blessed pursuit,
Space and all time held captive in the chase.

So Parma is in arms, sufficient food
For rule that feeds upon Rebellion
But perishes of Harmony, because
Ill combinations rectify good laws.
A willing votary is a working Pope !
My own then his who knowingly compels
As knowingly repels the sycophant.
His danger is desertion of success
As never quite enamoured of itself
But from dissatisfaction plucks dismay,
And gorges to repletion of the Fruit
Timely misfortune has not tasted of.

SCENE II.—*The Palace in Turin.*

HENRY *the* EMPEROR, *and his Minister* GANGARELLI.

EMPEROR.

No fiend so subtle as a surfeited Monk !
His actions dark from bright resplendencies
Through which he looks upon generalities
That he can never technically solve,
But finds some atom sooner than the whole
And drinks the nauseous compound, and becomes
The very serpent, long misunderstood,
From which he might have learnt to draw the tooth.
        [*Enter* GANGARELLI.
Be seated : I am anxious, and I know
Deception is no medicine for an ache
That in susceptibility out-chants
That filcher of improbable surmise.

GANGARELLI.

My liege, there is in mystery no charm
To those whose Life has been a sacrifice
To disentangle mystery of its gloss.
And if to others it is manifest

To be sound policy our plans to shroud
With that impenetrable barrier
To all the shafts of Man's inquisitive mood,
Claiming your love I leave the mask outside.

EMPEROR.

Explain the attitude of Germany,
A race that halts between the slave and seer,
And in the vortex of disquietude
Uncertainty from the balance must create.
A patriotic spirit is evoked
The essence of devotion without cause,
Perfection of adherence to a creed
That in the declaration of its rights
Celestially illuminates their earth
With all that fallen earth can elevate,
Until refinement dedicates pure gold
An offering where the Gods expected brass.

GANGARELLI.

Bad news! Their half-accomplished crimes have met
And have elected an accomplishment
Of many crimes in one disunion
With your designs. Repudiation this
Of each and every treaty with my liege,
In cool disinclination to combine
In fair affection for the common cause.

EMPEROR.

What is the origin of this ?   A void
Of all profession, of all principle,
All rectitude, all conscience, all respect
To obligations full of innocence,
And unaffected purity of mood,
And every boasted sacrifice of self
In sufferance of self where else it be ?
Is this the essence of the Teuton brood
Nurtured in forestry by the margin broad
Of the blue rolling Danube's eddying flood ?
Their spark has been exalted into flames,
As once the sacrificial single torch
A thousand years since lit their altared Gods.
Then superstition stood them in more stead
Than with deserted and abandoned homes.
Embodying in their spirit a tenderer air,
They might have now joined issue with old Rome
Against more reckless, more ambitious foes
Than could be guessed of in their desert wilds.

GANGARELLI.

What if your Majesty, descendant sage
Of Otho, first united Emperor,
Should view this question in a different light.
You are not of a profligate origin,
But therefore are to them a profligate.
These times are rapid emanations now

Of a pure spirit quickly essentialised
Before all virtue they appreciate.
They breathe in discord in dissembling mood,
Vested with emblems of mysterious hate
And multiplied in endless interchange
Of attitudes that the true facts misrepresent,
The end and cure of all our misery.
Esteem then what you see and what you know
With rare concern and rarer gravity.
Is there a point the Future may decide,
Decide it now at once upon the spot.
Is there a lull that beckons you to sleep,
Sleep not, but measures swift consolidate
Into a practicable harmony
Lest sudden understanding intercept,
Waylay, and seize upon and slay your plans
And make all your prosperity its own.
It is no time for following Fortune's nod,
She is decoyed by many a clever head
Into acceptance of wild overtures
Themselves the heralds of new Destiny
Which we must close in with if we would thrive.
Strike out a line your own !   Defy the Pope !
Your plans by treachery to undermine
Who with the Countess of Canossa has
A fond agreement lately signed and sealed,
That so to trouble you in Italy
Will make you fly from your false feudatories
Transalpine to recover Italy.

EMPEROR.

'Tis very well for you to calculate
What should be done, and what should not be done.
I as a soldier know how to disarm
Before I struggle with my adversary.
From Italy to Germany I advance:
Their twofold union shall be understood
Through all the curious eye of Christendom
To be the secret object of my heart.
Reining my furious German coursers in
I will all Italy carve into a car,
Tuscany, Rome, Naples, and Lombardy,
And call on all creation to admire
An image of Triumphant Victory.

GANGARELLI.

You will have troubles in your glass of Time
Concurrent, and continuous, and complete.
Each grain of sand a separate difficulty.
Think you Matilda and the Pope will rest
On temporal and spiritual base
Their fort of opposition springing up.
First having injured you they will affront,
They will suggest a Diet be convoked
Of all the ruling Powers in Germany.
Matilda hates the badge of Servitude,
She will announce your incapacity,

Which means your want of popular support :
He will domestic differences expose
And with a shrewd but not quite slanderous hint
Place you in that position in their eyes
So faulty, yet so far from odious
That in their dubitation of so good,
So virtuous, discreet, and sensitive
So moderate a summary of ills,
That if enlarged would hazard all their homes
And place their hearts at variance with their heads,
They will elect a monarch in your stead
And send you in despondency to Rome,
Where they dislike the shadow of a name
And will not bear fresh insignificance.
You know the Normans are a venturous race,
Skilled in the pastime and pursuit of war,
Your own domains at home consolidate,
Canossa seize with all you have at arms,
Gregory the Seventh with his furious hate
Depose, and nominate another Pope.
Have yourself crowned upon the Capitol.
Germany has neither artifice nor descent,
You can enclose it in the iron grasp
Of Reputation and armed Energy,
And as for all that ever Otho did
In close amalgamation of the realm
United Germany and Italy,
In ignorance of tares that spring unseen
To choke the wholesome wheat he would have sown,

His valour your ability will shame
To put a point upon his headless spear
To check the nations he thought to control,
Which otherwise will do more than rebel,
More desolation and destruction breathe,
Nay leave you simply a recorded name
And him the object of all calumny.

EMPEROR.

Rome without Germany is only Rome !
A falsehood as it utters the word Home :
A modest, prudent mediocrity
That you would have in vision of itself
Of admiration like Narcissus die.
No ! I will venture all upon the cast
And win my German feudatories first.
They, as the victims of a strange despair
Which none can ever style ambition, yearn
To celebrate the thousandth anniversary
Of a dominion to be founded now
Upon the ashes of all natural gifts,
A massive fortress built upon the flood,
The walls and buttresses of Corinth mould,
Their base the shifting and irresolute sand.
What can avail us yet if we desert
That which is a desertion of itself?
Then what we know they now will soon discern
And subject it to a hot crucible

Wherein all the deposits turn to Gold.
No !   Universal empire is mine aim,
And I am bound to study it more near
Than gazing on that ancient mirror Rome,
Whose name is but a type of things to come,
Whose words are oracles it cannot use,
Whose deeds are but to lay the sword in rust
That Germany will brandish on all round
And prove the verity of Roman words.
Union is strength, and let us join the two ;
You say that moderate measures seek to die,
Time will not wait for truculent designs
To foster cowardice by cowardice.
Thought springs triumphant from its dew-dry bed
And summoning each one with a trumpet call
Announces that we cannot compromise
By long allegiance to a threadbare creed
The duty which we owe to its surmise,
But by the acceptance of more manliness
It will be changed into a suit of mail
That every martial soul would gladly wear
And all its liabilities endure
Provided he could see with eager ken
From out the shadows now dispersing fast
The beacon that you know of and I see : -
Creating satisfaction out of risk,
Maturing purposes of costly note,
Enriching poverty no longer ours,
And to discernment of a dubious kind,

Hardly more welcome than a wandering guest
Without an introduction or a friend,
Lending the proper succour long desired,
Sealing with Victory extended Hope,
Giving encouragement to the forlorn
Exhausted spirit, oftentimes renewed,
As often bent beneath unheeded care,
And rescued by the loneliness of woe
That talks of meritoriousness to itself,
And thinks not of discredit or distress.
To-night for Germany I shall depart
To seek a Fame that they shall register
As surely as you prophesy my name
Unworthily, unprofitably risked.
To draw into my banners in support
Of aims they know the value of too well
An element of monstrous origin
In singularity of dissonance
From all that dignifies the Southern race,
That has from Glory so distilled their soul,
That in the Essence of Perfection lost,
They must be reanimated hastily
By Teuton imperfections, vitalised
By poison, otherwise strangled by gold,
Steeped in soft languor, thence, swift to arouse
This prodigy, into ruin unbetrayed,
Ourselves, Rome, and the world alone shall save.

SCENE III.—*A Palace in Florence.*

CONRAD, *son of Henry IV.*   BERTHA, *his mother.*

CONRAD.

Your Honour vindicated elevates
My own severer Life.   Since I was first
A guest within these old parental walls
Enough we both have suffered and endured
To blot out all I loved of Italy,
To blench the shades of earlier renown
That hover round its ancient Capital,
To wither every laurel that they wore
That Time could not have touched with envious
    stamp,
To banish into exile what survives
Of joy and satisfaction at my lot,
To cool all ardour for predominance
Into a spirit of intolerance
Not of its enemies, but of itself,
This base criterion of false rectitude,
Till discontent my fortitude supplants.
Methinks Rome's Eagle has become an Asp,
And it has bitten you with hateful tooth.
But this is glorious news from Germany !

BERTHA.

If all be true it is most fortunate !

CONRAD.

Nay ! it is more than true.   At length amazed
At endless deviations from all right,
At moral waste of great munificence,
At wilful misconception of all creeds,
The one that points to blind Divinity,
The other that enjoins domestic rights,
A third that limits such parental rule,
And leaves Posterity to feel its way
With jealousy enjoyed by Hannibal
When frenzy urged him from the arid South
To plant his legions in the Capitol
And subjugate too vulnerable wealth
To binding lines and superstitious laws,
Cramping such broad and boundless energies
Within the compass of a subtlety
That never fostered half that it observed,
Since unaware of that criterion
Which measures all to each and each to all,
Germany has renounced Henry's unworthy sway,
Review our blessings past and present, then !
Watching the requirements of prosperity
In our attachment joyfully fulfilled
And with your eye recovering in the glad
And permanent accomplishment of all

That by our ancestors scrupulously decreed
Brightened the doubts of all futurity
With swift accomplishment of its designs
Haste to perform the part which I advise.

BERTHA.

Matilda should be but a vassal though,
Not independent as she seems to be.
And is she Henry's friend or enemy?
It would conform into a parodox
This distribution of our Italy
Into so many various elements
That none can make so many parts a whole!
Some malediction sheds its vicious blight
Upon Earth's secret store of excellence
All its prospective value to denounce
Before the budding of its second reign.
Is hesitation then fatality?
To scruple at its execution Death?
This absolute no imperative decree?
This ladder to Renown based on the Stars?
And we must climb at once into the space
That seasons Life with the infallible,
Or fall at once into the common track
And boast our admiration of ourselves?

CONRAD (*reading a manifesto*).

The token of this declaration here
And now before us vividly proposed

In both a common principle replies
And negatives dissension, binding us
In the strong link of unity, designed
First for all rightful purposes within
The steel-formed ring of nationality,
Next for the valorous extravagance
Of fury, should it be our lot to rage
In positive establishment of Right,
Turn out the cavern of accustomed ills
For evils that are therefore curable,
And in security uphold ourselves,
Borne out by every happy counterpart.

BERTHA.

But if Matilda of Canossa stands
Herself at issue with our Infidel,
Again a traitorous vassal menacing
All natural harmony with discordant thrill,
What then ?

CONRAD.

    Then she will recognise myself
As one more worthy of Italian rule.
There is another bond of union :
Her Father Bonifacio lorded it
In the same spirit of intolerance
Which forced us out in exile from our home,
Adventurous spirits of a rebel mould.

Enter Deputation from Parma.

DELEGATE.

Good Prince !   Your dignity is compromised
And cordiality and sincerity
In your unqualified and strong support
Of our opposed secession from a wrong
And ruthless regulation of a State
As worthy Italy as it the World,
The World of all Creation.   It were'vain
To call Canossa Parma's Capital
If from the verdict of all sober minds
We cull the insulation of divorce :
To Rome success, if it approve the deed,
Fatal to all the world our union.

CONRAD.

Say who attacked your independence first ?

DELEGATE.

The Duke of Parma long reigned undisturbed
And hoped to reap the harvest of the Po
And tribute rivers' offerings, just then
Unclaimed and uncemented, therefore free
And common to the avaricious grasp
Present inadequacy furnishes
To guide dissimulation to the rest,

In token of fulfilment of some view
That harmonises regency with right.
Matilda of Canossa at that time
Claimed all her ancestor Fedaldo held,
Ferrara, Brescia, Mantua, and Modena.
Now she annihilates well-fostered hopes,
And Parma, with its fortresses and fruits,
Becomes a stranger's seizure and escheat.

CONRAD.

What chance has Italy with such perjured oaths?
What room for the expansion of a line
Disseminating to expectant sycophants
What virtuous expectation vainly seeks,
If on the virtue of its plundered stars
It loses in debarred philosophy
The recompense and ransom of its fears?
Its integrality itself is wrong,
For now unsound, uncertain exigence
By perfidy and jealousy stirred up
Acquires the basis of more villainy
Untrammelled by the councils that proscribe
The ray sublime of a superior light
That had dispersed irregular energies
And lit solution through its grievous path
Till satisfaction echoed all that Hope
Anticipating already had announced.

BERTHA.

The prospect is most serious and sad !
That we desert our Father it is well :
He will be put to straits to make this good.
Can he to any formal body appeal ?
Assemble it to adjudicate all rights,
Administer reproofs, weakness coerce,
Infidelity restrain, treason forbid,
And quell the unforgiving spirit of man
That, tempered to the dictates of the hour,
Obeys the hour and disappoints all else ?

CONRAD.

How can these reconcile blood with strange blood ?
How can they re-unite these tattered shreds
Once the imperial garment of old Rome ?
Endue it with fresh majesty and might,
Endow it with perennial dignity,
Surround it with imperishable steel,
Enlarge its influence, yet contract it still,
And in consistency so mould the whole,
That Rome that was might stare at what Rome is ?
No longer broken with its gravity ;
No more by its out-spaced extravagance
A pointless principle, a random shot ;
And as it thundered from the Capitol
A million orders to a million slaves,
So felt the crushing shock of the recoil

That it drew back alarmed at its own mood,
A prey to its ambition falsely poised,
Heralded by the symbols of deceit
That vaunted conquest made a conqueror,
Till it became unworthy of the age
Of which it was the worthy paragon,
And hated all success.   I, if I had my way,
And you been fairly treated as a spouse,
Caressed and honoured in our equipage,
Though unimportant items in this train
That fails with all the chosen sons of man,
And vanishes unknown Life's pilgrimage,
Would throw aside all probable consequences,
And in fulfilment of a quoted law
Would quickly realise a prophecy
Mistaken in this miserable result ;
But if we do not yet exert ourselves
For theirs and our own re-establishment
What will futurity not exercise
Upon events of these escheated rights
In the reversal of true Destiny,
The undistributed aim of centuries,
Intended to enrich with endless store.
Italy, Germany, and us for evermore ?

Enter MESSENGER.

MESSENGER (*presents a letter*).

Good Prince ! I do enjoin your confidence
In this communication brought by me
Straight from Canossa.

> [*Conrad reads.*

BERTHA.

Permit not hesitation to defer
Counselled adherence to our common cause.

CONRAD (*holds up the letter*).

If point is Death and Life a pointless shaft
Then my proud breast has further cause for fear,
If fear can penetrate a royal heart.
Matilda rules Canossa all alone ;
Her will the sole restriction on her deeds,
Which may be prejudicial to our cause
Unless an angel's conscience guide her will.

Enter Deputation from Canossa.

DELEGATE (*offering gifts*).

Good Prince, we bring you in all deference
These presents from our mistress, sending which
She tenders you her wishes that all joy,
Matured by time into real happiness,

May gild the wreath which now adorns your brow,
Made up of antidotes to poisonous care
That so, reaching your great inheritance,
Matilda of Canossa you may greet
With every proof of confidence and trust.

CONRAD.

Italy has no fairer spot on Earth
So sanctified with opposite design
For moderate ambition to do good,
And dwell on all the good it has within
And all the virtue that grows from its root
Than fair Canossa.   With prophetic care
No sooner had it perfected our aim
And sealed our problem with a rare success
Upon the basis of a broader view,
A structure taller and more elevate,
Than the same magic wand drops paralysed
That from the wilderness a paradise coined,
The state penurious to a palace changed,
And as it spread in grandeur to the eye,
Albeit by unworthiness contaminate,
Endowed it with all luxury divine,
And bade it intimate and spend the gift
With all its neighbours localised around ;
Then out of this same spirit and desire
To disappoint the Spring of all its fruit
We will henceforth disturb in harmony

The visible plan by Fortune laid at first,
And in discordant union of all ills
A forced and fanciful construction raise
That in the plenitude of a novel cup
Shall pour ingredients of all happiness,
Shall disappointment re-invigorate
Till it become a pride and joy to say
This vine has flourished where the thorn had grown
If each and everyone had sought his own,
In combination from the seed of Hate
By charity and good will regenerate.
Then, men of Parma ! join yourselves to us
As symbols of an old similitude.
O love Canossa !   She, its Princess, leagues
Herself with those who would enliven Rome
Beyond the innocent expectancy Romulus had,
For he foresaw not in Time's misty glass
What deadly passions nurtured tragic feuds,
What great designs are cut up by the root,
Or bit by the asp that disappoints all Hope,
Till their presumptuous arrogance lies low
Or vegetates in mockery of Time.
Then let me count on your allegiance,
Not to King Henry, for he is Rome's foe,
But to Matilda of Canossa, one
Born of a more than meritorious race,
Herself its essence, stay, and ornament,
That lives but to give the universe its due
By schemes more solid than mere union

Of creed and custom on concession based ; `
But in devotion's tried and tempered trust
In truths, if worthy, worthy hold we must.

———————

SCENE IV.—*Hall in Nuremburg.*

Soldiers—Barons.

Enter party of Soldiers.

FIRST CAPTAIN.

With one accord swear all upon this sword
Absolutely to this document !

SOLDIERS.

We swear !

FIRST CAPTAIN.

Then the fourth Henry loses Germany,
Supported in the symbols of lost power
By the forthcoming Destiny of Rome.
Only for him, had he but known of it,
Once this adjustment of our several Fates
For the resumption of imperial rule

Distinctly and deliberately fixed.
I wish that I were he upon the base
Of such a warrant for unusual deeds—
How I would make my home a paradise !
How I would reconcile conflicting points,
And each discordant string attune afresh
Till every heart on either side the Alps
Re-echoed to the melody that speaks
Of local to all distant happiness !
But it is gone, that opportunity,
And now his hopes that joined old Italy
To the dark Danube and beyond its waves,
A circle of ecstatic rhapsodies
To this despondent and reluctant clime,
At once we disavow and desecrate
Into a monument of his misdeeds.

SOLDIER.

Shall we cross swords with Henry Emperor,
And seal by deed of war this deed of words ?
Else how establish on such basis frail
Your novel and presumptuous edifice ?

SECOND CAPTAIN.

Know you that his son Conrad will unfold
His rebel banner simultaneously
With our remoter stroke for principle ?

FIRST CAPTAIN.

His infancy is incapacity,
His years are just an overture to Fame
To which he may make us the mounting stone.
Then like ourselves he may first hesitate
To plunge into the whirlpool of a war
That, while it dissipates the glance of Fate,
And warps the due line of prosperity,
The warm attachment valuable to all
May stultify, surprise, and confiscate.

SECOND CAPTAIN.

The tomb of Reason is treacherous alike
To either party and to every one.
Would you prefer to fortify the Alps
And garrison that natural barrier
Then, at the probable hazard of good faith,
And so on half repudiation live?

Enter Barons.

FIRST CAPTAIN.

My lords ! in deference to your requisition
I have assembled here to do your will
And answer your intent all in command,
Directing and maintaining in the field
Wherever questioned our Teutonic rights,

Whether dark Scandinavian legions pour
With ardour fretted in their frigid hearts
Which hold, like ice, just enough latent heat
That, fanned into a flame by discontent
Which coins true heroism from sheer despair,
Will force them through a multitude of ills,
Devoted energies on our central lines,
And place their banner on the Rock of Fame.
Or the false, fanciful, visionary South,
With humours that disturb satiety,
Built upon gratification with a careless head
Till satisfaction cannot satisfy,
And all their feelings crumble into void,
Wherein the loathsome monster Hate is bred,
And rushes in a sudden moment forth,
Clad in the panoply of chivalry,
To roll into contagion all our hopes.

FIRST BARON.

Be satisfied! your speech and your appearance
Will German independence guarantee.
It is not yet the moment to advance
In the broad basis of irregular,
Improbable, and inconsiderate acts,
Grounded on infidelity to all
And honesty to none.   A challenge sent
To hearts and homes no doubt united close,
And to themselves all that we could desire ;

And never sacrificed to infamy,
Not bound beneath improper tyranny,
Must have a policy exterior
Fixed on the point of all this nicety,
And to their opportune and necessary
And positive advantage influenced.
Now there is only danger from without,
By faithless arts and criminal intents
They hover round German prosperity
As round the Dove the Eagle in proud flights
To crush its excellence and balk device
Intended to expand authority
Not ours until a just authority,
Without dissemblance and devoid of strain,
Not quite to overthrow the parent stock
Or its prolonged encouragement outlive.
Shall I develop to your hardy thoughts
Excesses that steep Italy's renowned
Allurement for arts and arms into a base
And retrograde condition? knowing more
Than civilisation has to it bequeathed,
And doing less than civilisation loves?
So that their valour that destroyed the Alps
And reassured us with its worthiness
Cannot and shall not verify its aim
To build upon our territorial breadth
A basis for a kingdom that should shake
Not only Europe, but adjacencies
Whose name, breathed in a whisper, chills the heart!

For sanctioned might creates unsanctioned rule,
And wild dominion flows in conquest tide
Against the power that its stock disposed.
Has German independence hence no faith
On Fame?　Let it fall back on Fortitude
And not divine twofold indemnity
Against repudiation and reproof.
A while, and Henry, our lost Emperor,
Shall German counsels influence no more !
No more can thrall Teutonic hearts and blades
Whom all domestic constancy upbraids !
No more assemble with dissembled hopes
That round the altar of our rectitude
Play perfidy to promised vassalage,
And by austerity unnatural win,
Through a subservience habitual,
Our provinces' dependance and support ! .
But in conformity to wider views
A clearer insight into Right and Wrong
That perspicuity the Time demands,
Else all its value slips into the void
Springs the Teutonic tribe to its defence,
Defiance to the robber and the wrong,
Whose guilty nature might contaminate
His once conciliated German hearts
Whose vices might inoculate with shame
A race as yet irreprehensible,
Unstained by Sin and its associate Crime.

SECOND CAPTAIN.

Shall we renounce, then, Henry's confidence,
Or live out of his reach under his rule?

SECOND BARON.

Should he at this preliminary manifestation
Of rights our own and liberties decreed
Be moved again in quick and hasty mood
More rigidly to pass us under the yoke
Or set his foot upon the German neck,
Or treat us as we treat our forest curs,
Be ready at an instant summons then
Our project to advance by stroke of war
From those resources that have yielded good
To all Creation in their silent way,
And unperceived have gently urged upon
Triumphant Monarchs in their warlike path
So many precepts of philosophy
That meritless audacity they recant,
Eschewing Ruin deeply sown into
The fruitful soil of rash expectancy,
And hazard not on the mere cast of a die
All fortunes, all doubtful experiences.
Then we shall so adjust the balances
Uneasy Fortune blindly has disposed
That nothing more than this shall stand between
Proper presumption and its right result.
That Germany may rear on kindred soil

A banner that her sons may rally round
When future centuries shall have ratified
Civilisation with security,
And prove their title to indemnity
By impost and exaction, tax and toll,
Which exercised in bondage by the Sword
Had placed our Consciences in jeopardy,
Their trust annihilated by bad faith
Which a belief in virtuous majesty,
In heavenly obedience, had nursed up
Our noble, proud, and so far prosperous race
Without a sorrow kindred to suppression
Of that responsibility which elevates
Dignity and indignity alike,
Till the dark Danube's wave, that hopefully
Returned an echo to the shout of joy
That in a sombre link united families
Close akin soon to old patrician Rome,
Will altogether cease its cordial strain,
Engulfed within the tomb wrought by dishonour,
By incapability, and indifference,
And apathy to all that stirs within
Sensitive spirits to accomplishment
Of those designs that manhood reconciles
To his obscure and complicated lot.

FIRST CAPTAIN.

Let us revenge for some one else the loss
Of virtue that has summoned obloquy,

And all despondent spirits reassure
Before the crisis of sad circumstance,
Betrayed by lofty schemes to error's path,
Upon our heads devoted culminate.

SECOND BARON.

Let us first satisfy our principles
By prompt repudiation of the oath
We took supporting Henry Emperor,
Then in exuberance of former state
Believing in his sanctity and might,
And doubting not that degradation dull
Has all heroic patriotism effaced,
And buried us beneath the avalanche
Of despotism, whereof old custom warns,
Should Henry forcibly re-cross the Alps
And by compulsion vice disseminate,
To arms at once! and so return the blow
Intended honour to assassinate.
Meanwhile a proclamation shall be placed
On every cross and gate in every town
Announcing that a council shall be held
To further and establish all free choice,
Thereby ensuring all that we may lose,
That in the independent resolution
Which we united have together made,
Depending henceforth on integrity,
We may by our internal policy
By truth all regulations qualify,

With our dark origin be familiar,
Gaze on the future with a fatherly eye,
Seek in the ore of our good qualities,
By methods of refinement both acquired
From others and our own experience,
Metal more precious than he circulates
Whose mint for coinage is impurely base,
And spatters Cæsar's emblem with a stain
That all his famous points cannot wash out,
Preserve in our devotion to one aim
The elevation of all thought beyond
More necessary and more immediate cares
An obligation to the wondrous spell
That everything repairs and ordinates,
That breathes additional life to those long dead,
The grandeur of the future that evokes,
And for all hidden and material substance .
Their application sound and stimulate
Till we become in essence spiritual,
And in remote embodiment an indistinct
Reflection of the great unseen Divine.
In this avowal with all confidence
Wait the Examen of the Diet at Worms

SOLDIERS.

We will !

SCENE V.—*Market Place at Nuremburg.*

Citizens in eager conversation.　　Party of Senators.

FIRST SENATOR.

Such is our Constitution !　Then declare
Your recognition or refusal.　So
We then shall be enabled to decide
What course we think to take most requisite
For general safety to our novel cause.
There is success therein to those who know
Both how and when their suit to press thereto,
Capacious as it captivates mankind,
And servile as it serves such to the end.
With means and measures duly implicate,
With fond desires and fashionable airs,
So that the end is sometimes lost in those
Which should be oftener sacrificed to the end.
In future it will not object that friends
In all apology and with defence
Replace you on the right of sympathy
If Law offended sent you on the left.
Should any nicety of sense be touched
Scandal shall reap no beneficial thrift.
Your wives, and sons and daughters shall be saved
Sinister deed or cold provoking taunt.

Uneven treaties shall be justly weighed
Whether for gain or balanced chance of gain.
Transfer and purchase shall be registered,
Attested, and approved by surety sound.
Incoming and outgoing properties
Arranged and valued for the State expense,
That we, and you, and all of us may raise
A monument and guardian to our Land,
A warning to all rivalry beyond,
A beacon to prosperity within,
That all we worthily dislike may fail,
And all we love may live more happily,
From endless liability more free.
Then those who serve the State serve only you
Who in industrious skill, professional art,
All energy of science in its aim
The rugged path of Nature to undo,
And place hitherto undiscovered gifts
Within the reach of your ambitious grasp.
Consolidate the State. Consolidated more
By large unfolding of your model art,
Which watching you may then replenish this
By inferences drawn from the amount
Which in wide speculations has that range
To be a book of parallel similitudes,
Wherein all danger is most deeply shown,
And difficulty beggared by reflex
As in a mirror of improvidence
Wherein its multiplying hideous forms

Compel it to recover its original
Secure and more premeditated ways.

FIRST CITIZEN.

How if our treaty stretch its arm around
To emulate Polydamas, and grasp
In wild excess that which we lack without,
And blessed in this, dissatisfied in that,
As Nature is mercurial at will
And bound by no particular discipline
We penetrate beyond the stated bounds
And render our integrity a risk?

SECOND CITIZEN.

I have betrothed myself to one beyond
The fatherly and patronising Alps,
And vowed when Roman fortune stood my friend,
And my friends here had dropped off one by one,
Guided by no disparity of years
And no opinionative difference '
To bind her to me by the nuptial bond,
For general good indissoluble worth.

BURGOMASTER.

Unless Henry our Emperor promises
In providence and wisdom, as he should,
Neither by Hate nor Error re-assured,
Measures more suitable than those in use

We shall prohibit, mostly by a tax
Which shall not wit estranged reanimate,
Italian luxuries, so with wealth attained
By trading else with every other power,
The Turk, the Spaniard, or the Anglican,
Thereby asserting that our Faith with them
Has not been broken, howso different,
We then may purchase these forbidden things
And they our valuables so withheld.
To you to whom anticipation has been slow
In warning you of this our severance
In many a case from civilised success,
That is if civilisation means excess
Of care ostensible for secret sores
In many a case from all contrastive ills
To measure our own benefits otherwise, those,
Now theirs, by such deficiencies our own,
I would resent our wronged condition thus,
The present object of your love renounce,
Nor jeopardize your conscience by the suit.
An honest man and true to his own kind
May indirectly, and directly too,
Advise and rectify upon exigence
In this new State so likely to occur
In course and character the State itself.
What if a humour steps between yourself
And every prospect we encourage thus?
A humour born of ill-attempered thoughts
Which rounds its credulous clients with a net,

Then draws them into infamy and shame,
And leaves them blank on Immortality's shore,
No longer flourishing in immortality's Light
The emblems of its majesty and might !
Look to the goal of happier demands,
The satisfying meritorious wreath
That crowns his head and gilds his monument,
That rescues both his country and his hopes,
All expectations gratified by him,
The solace and the safeguard of his race.
Therefore good citizen your vows renounce,
Their double warmth already frozen thrice
By Italy's indifference to our lot,
And seal repudiation of the bond.

FIRST CITIZEN.

What are our frontiers and new boundaries?

SECOND CITIZEN.

Define this project of new liberties !

THIRD CITIZEN.

Determine our relationships all round.

BURGOMASTER.

Beware of Southern brides and Northern swords !
Both Pharamond and Amurath possessed
And have engrafted on an ancient stock
Prerogatives more positive than ours

That will reply to every utterance
Not fathered on the spirit of that age,
And have created a new element
That floats about and fathoms our designs.
We urge in our assurance we are free
With a conviction that is not yet ours,
And from the Heart that nourishes the Head
Wish to create new structures like our own
Of individual enterprises thus built up
Upon a greatness other than our own
Has nourished or can nourish for one end,
A constitutional excellence throughout
Which, if sage counsels influence within
And circumstance substantiate without,
Enables us better to regulate
In modification of their management
By reference, admonition, or advice,
Foreign and independent States adverse,
And dressed as rivals for sound decency.
We have sound hearts and swords as well as they,
But are we therefore capable of all
That offers as a guerdon to our greed
In composition to Life's bitter cup
Gratified to our voluminous desires?
That in the mere enjoyment of the good
We may be uncontaminate of ill?
That in the grasp of actual happiness
Contrastive wretchedness we may stamp out?
That in possession of the secret spring

Whereat sublimest coffers open out
Their undetected store to us at length
We shall acknowledge by discriminate
Discerning and indisputable skill
The application of that large amount
Whereof an earlier possession might
Have raised us to a level with those realms,
And not half humble, half vainglorious,
Half independent speculators thus?

FIRST CITIZEN.

What is the Constitution now of Britain,
Which Edward has to Harold just bequeathed?
Does it not illustrate our plightful State
Significant of no delusive dreams
Which you say have so long imperilled us,
And leave us yet a victim of dismay,
Lest in the wantonness of our demand
We may our false security o'erreach,   .
And not recovering but by your advice
And I do hope assistance as sincere
Our new-born independence jeopardise,
The scorn and laughter of the age become,
And with the sickle of inadequate zeal
Reap but a crop of corresponding tares.

BURGOMASTER.   .

Britain so many a change has undergone
That no reliance can be placed in our

Predominance in her many-coloured halls.
The spirit of sage Britomart revives,
And counterbalances good Saxon laws
Which, characterised by Continental sway,
Emancipated solely for herself
Breathes to the secret knowledge of this fact
Of our control the very principle.
And we have furnished this with ready arms,
Which sharpened by a little natural wit
Harold and his supporters may displace,
Return them beggars to their native homes,
Yea ! claim that very home as their domain.

SECOND CITIZEN.

Let us amalgamate with Britain then !
Unite our separate aims and ends in one,
And in one broad and comprehensive plan
So sift the applicable from the frail,
And hopefulness from mystery evolve,
That your fond points may be detached and saved,
And we may rival Italy and Gaul.

BURGOMASTER.

We are in spirit so with them allied,
Nor do they need the succour you advise.
We can assert as wide an enterprise,
And though we concentrate within a round
The gradual approach to the more pure
And elevated principle not ours,

It is a test but of a different kind
Of qualities thus opening in the bud,
That may in centuries of growth acquire,
Nourished by wisdom, worth, and industry,
The coveted wand of universal rule.
We cannot conquer but we have achieved
That victory o'er ourselves which I predict
To further conquest ultimately guides.
Untutored in such art Man is a child,
For whom a learned man can regulate
Its conduct and career.   So in a State,
Its industry and enterprise are warped
Into the coffers of another State.
Then Britain's polity is uncertified,
And the whole land is under doubtful rule.
We may establish here the Fatherland,
And ordinate under one common head
The insular and Continental sway,
One hand grasping our near inheritance,
The other seeking in remoter space
Some market for more produce than we need,
And win from them more luxuries than we know.

THIRD CITIZEN.

Sardinia, Sicily, and Corsica
Will yield us, if we hold with Italy,
This offspring of a too presumptuous eye.
And all that Eastern Asia can add
To that our own in envied happiness

Will be more easily thereby attained.
And if we treat with Africa equally
On terms as easy and as mutual,
With the same spirit we shall be supplied
That gave to Pharaoh grandeur and renown.

FIRST CITIZEN.

Carthage, though dying out, is still a key
To hidden stores of plentiful support
For ever lost if we renounce Rome thus.
There is a river flows on sands of gold,
Through endless groves which furnish luscious fruit,
Without harsh labour and corroding care,
And with the hazard of an untameable race
Of brutes that render residence dangerous
Are rare and strange productions we have not,
All injuries that heal and cure disease.

BURGOMASTER.

Prosperity with all its promises
Stands on itself and not your prodigies.
Productive of completion in design,
Creative of entirety alone,
All spirits renovating with its air
The aspirant and apathetic both,
The eager and tumultuous, the close
Absorbed, reclusive, selfish egotist,
This caught by the fire of his own eloquence,
Till its rabidities leave naught to glean,

Grasping at Fortune seen but at a glance,
And wreathing it into a Tyranny
That binds the world with chains of useless gold.
Or that that would absorb into his lair
Unseen, but not unknown, all competence,
And mingling daily with his kindred blood,
To praise and blame, to pomp and power averse,
Awakens Heaven to slumber with himself,
To the mean, the massive, the methodical
Changing, or in a uniform routine
Accommodating or accomplishing
With part fulfilment not to lose the whole
By abject servitude to giddy views,
Semblances of possession of a Truth
That we ourselves have never yet renounced.
These proofs of acquisition yet untried,
Prefer where their assurance cannot blight,
And with their prodigality annoy
The painted East and consequential South,
Rich but mellifluously meritless.
The Saxon claims not Britain for himself
To place his feet upon a pedestal
The object of derision of an age,
But to step through a frightful mystery
Wherewith Creation shrouds its worthiness
Lest it should be ingloriously acquired
Into a grave solution of a doubt.
We should not temper Life until its end
By the employment of all artifice,

All industry, all versatility,
Upon a territory thus surmised,
Itself athirst as we for other things,
Possessing secrets otherwise than ours,
Responding to our arrogance renown,
Based upon more profound or simple views,
Fulfilling duties of as grave a tone,
Uninstigated by the meaner springs
That hitherto has punished us with this :
A solitary spirit half unblessed,
Mature, but measured out and meted forth,
Half-fortunate direction of a wish
To place ourselves before our Age.   Resuscitate
The lifeless fragments of departing worth :
A wiser but more pliant Age forestall :
And with an almost boundless amplitude
Of far resources with our own wound up,
Create a centre of this present sphere
That will enable each one to direct
This Age and that, this spot and all beyond.

THIRD CITIZEN.

The scholars tell us of a Monarchy
Whose line already dimly seems to rise
Refulgent with a rare magnificence,
And girt with every symbol of success,
Before which old Assyria recoils
A wounded serpent from an eagle's beak,
At which the Ptolemies rise from the pyramids,

As if enchantment had their rest disturbed,
And Scipio and Alexander shrink
From urgent fire and pertinacious zeal,
Compared with such to heroism less true,
Into plain types of brawling infancy,
And Rome, whose valued embers you denounce
When in the rage of transient eminence
Viewed in the parallel eye's impartial glance,
Though in its arrogant and impetuous mood
The embodiment of greatness and its snare,
Before this institution shall invert
The glass of its career, and modestly
Its incorrect pre-eminence forego.

SENATOR.

You speak of the fifth monarchy, but these times
Hardly suffice yet for the justified
And ratified assertion of a Truth
Of which I know fulfilment is assured
To those who, by the first unsatisfied,
Conjure the wish, added to keen desire
To see and share also in the ultimate
And apt fulfilment of a rapt decree
That, guided by solicitude, invites
Ambitious, vain, but disconcerted man
To reap the harvest of a seed self-sown
By some successful oracle ensured.
Should you secure points already enjoined
Elsewhere when all our nobles have discussed,

Pronounced upon, and subsequently enforced
A virtual and valid constitutional change,
Formally embodied and faithfully worked out,
Complete and acceptable as our creed,
You may and can in a more distant age
Lay claim to this fair title of Repute,
Renown immortal, cynosure of applause,
And paragon of skill political.
In view of deeds ofttimes so surely blessed,
Attemper and attune your spirits then,
But do not let the hopeful prophecy,
Supported by each dark significance,
Deter you from proficiency at once,
From duties and accomplishments which shall
A more immediate happiness bestow,
More instant and more transient, available
Now, but the morrow leads on to its decay,
And raises up a crop we cannot reap.
In all the separate accompaniments of thought
That must surround us in a definitely new
Individual and general responsibility
It matters much what beacon light we have.
Some have carved out their course and fixed their hopes
Unwilling to believe the credible,
But deeming that Deception lay between
Their object and the industry of Life,
With stedfast gaze on some material end,
Not satisfying immediate demands,
But promising what we here cannot attain—

High consolation for the ardent soul.
In this they seek a home to realise,
But speedily forget the home they have.
We cannot thus create at will the end,
But let the end be subject to our will.
This to acknowledge in redemption sure
The daily occupation of our lives ;
Not that ourselves are herein dearly sold
To the grand object others would attain,
For that is hidden as delusion vain,
An apparition full of emptiness,
Foisted on foolishness by vanity,
But by incipient steps slowly led on,
Advancing and increasing gradually
By subtle art and sedulous adhesion
We may change irksome deeds and tedious
To practices heroically light.
A future age this age may certify
To have accomplished in analysis
Of this its own and our prosperity.
Then, other usurpation so let free,
Some stipulated point to have attained,.
Outstripping every other and our date,
The crisis of this world in arms and art,
The sum and summit of ideal joys,
In satisfaction of untimely griefs
Which industry and hope had buried low,
Recalling all with meritorious glance
Instances of success comparative,

Which, in the eye of all futurity,
Will centre admiration and applause,
Unite their veneration and esteem,
Compel their subjugation to our views,
And in the shrewd connection with each cause
That we and those our rivals have upheld,
Graced with a discrimination as divine,
A judgment as profound, but not a wit
As sharp, a zeal for good as close and keen,
They will their difficulties thus adjust,
Their differences decide, and regulate
All doubtful points, insoluble paradoxes,
All intricate and measureless prodigies
Which Hate and cold infirmity supply
Equally to irregular demand,
According to our wisdom in excess
Of other oracles and other paragons,
By our success immortally stamped out,
Outdone and fixed for ever in the shade
Of that immortal gloom we should deserve
Did we not emulate and verify
In our approaching and receding back
Struggles for political competency,
Their moderate and our superior worth,
Their gradual and our continued gain,
Their cherished but our chosen consequence,
Until disease and danger all put out,
Distress alleviated, mitigated woe,
Our lot no more is sufferance and shame,

Rebellious else against invited wrongs,
And rounded by a dissolution just,
We may achieve and others may maintain
In after years, when, the probation o'er,
We rest upon the laurels we have gained,
That Rock amid the universal wave
The refuge and salvation of our trust.
In all discomfiture thus well reposed
All Fate and Circumstance reposed in us,
We may ourselves deliver in the result
Triumphant, yet without exuberance,
Weakness betraying, or a favoured fault :
Bestowing, yet retaining as our own,
Those gifts that to us Providence first gave,
And multiplying on the wheel of Time
Advantages outbidding all our years,
Accumulated to their own dismay,
In overwhelming dignity o'erwhelmed,
Not in the downfall they had threatened us,
So to remind us no more of our date,
For this our date is every date at once,
But of the combination of all circumstance,
The contradiction of the ebb and flow
Of meanness and magnificence in turn,
Till when, philosophic principle disarmed
In vain solution of continued fall
And interchange continual of alarm,
All consolation falling incomplete,
And its existence harshly terminate,

We shall attain the centre of all years
The final and irrevocable style
And school of subsequent and former Times,
In that our principle infallible
That prompter and promoter of all views,
Suggester and supporter of all deeds,
Counsellor and controller of all schemes,
Of speculation the security,
The moderator of refined excess
In just excess of moderation mild,
That with unbounded wisdom all its own
With Wisdom's scythe shall reap whatever sown.

Enter HERALD.

BURGOMASTER.

Hold! stay thy course!　Art thou from Italy?

HERALD.

From Wurzburg, on State business.

BURGOMASTER.

　　　　　　　　　　Know'st thou this
That we are now an independent State,
And I chief magistrate in this strong city?

HERALD.

I bear this message to all Germany:
'Vexed with the alienation of your tribes

A Diet the Emperor has at Worms convened
Of separate State rulers and chief powers,
In solemn council there to justify
His claim upon your future vassalage.'

FIRST CITIZEN.

We have renounced our fealty, and are free !

BURGOMASTER.

Have all agreed, Princes and Potentates,
The object of this meeting to support,
To agitate afresh the settlement
Of differences which Time cannot cure
Only the present deed of separation?

HERALD.
All !
They meet at once at Worms.   Choose delegates,
That your opinion may be made as free
As you suppose your persons and your State.
Is your cause fair, 'twill have a chance as fair :
If an assumption, place it in the van,
As caught deserters to be soonest slain.

BURGOMASTER.

Then, Citizens, betake you to your spheres.
I will accommodate and rectify,
On this announcement of a reference

To a tribunal worthy of our cause,
All difficulties that delay and doubt
Have cast on this new feature of our Life.
We have protested against tyranny,
Domestic harshness, parental cruelty,
Seeds procreating future public wrong :
And if in prosecution of a deed
Supported not by scrupulous jealousy,
Upheld alone by deference to good
And not subservient to unrighteous rule,
Our race has ventured rashly to divide
Upon this point of national union
In bond for nobler objects fast allied
To those agreeing as involving all,
Let all account it misdirected zeal.
A general Diet now convened at Worms
In critical inquiry into rights,
Father of a declaration half-expressed,
Will, if it our capacity disprove,
Or royal provocation disavow,
Establish on some recent principle,
By moderate men like us not understood,
A fresh convention.

SCENE VI.—*The Brenner Pass.   Summit.   Rocks.*
A Lake.

ELDERLY LADY (*in walking dress*).

Here is the spot.   Let us delay an hour,
And in the loneliness of the retreat
Measure the singular particulars
Of Carl's addresses to you.   Was it not
His own unfettered wish as soon as Time
Had sealed the close, indissoluble bond
Without which all it offers is untrue,
In the meanwhile acquiring those nice arts
That realise in Life eternity
On your part, and on his you making friends
To gild with gold the circling hoop of Love,
To meet you on the smallest barrier between
Hope and the broad fulfilment of its dream?

YOUNG DAMSEL (*in walking dress*).

I recollect the hour and the day
When he predicted the accomplishment
Of this design.   Since that the winter snows
To our betrothal that have sponsors stood
Make way for truth and happiness, and depart.
Here we will stay our giddy enterprise

Upon the verge of its uncertainty,
Lest we o'erleap the incident in worth
And forfeit expectation's just result.
   [*They spread out shawls, and rest on a rock.*

ELDERLY LADY.

Innspruck and Saltzburg are not far from hence,
And Chemnitz has familiar friends in both.
If we delay upon this mountain ridge
Some passing traveller whom Chance directs
Our anxious thoughts will fortify with facts.
   [*A Chamois bounds across the stage.*
Stands there concealed upon the furthest ridge
A huntsman, while his eye pursues the game.
He may, should he descend into the pass,
Acquaint us with some resting place below,
More hospitable shelter for your youth,
More generous in its sympathy for years,
And in the social glass which it presents
We may behold the future of our Life,
All present speculations underlying,
Wherewith it doth embarrassment entice
With simpler trusts and twinings of deceit.
To-morrow raves of us, but in its fits
At lucid intervals illustrates our hopes.
To these we cling, and register to-day
As one day nearer our attainable home.
Grasped by the dangling light of incident

We close our thought in all that thought reveals.
Our present state irradiated thus
Uncertain, unadorned, is not forlorn,
Nor useless as an unrepaid attempt
Life's sacrifice to alter and improve,
For in the strange vicissitude of things
Which round the prospect actions agitate,
And bury in confusion contrary winds
Till they support our bark and urge it on,
We reap a magical philosophy,
Itself the fruit of nobler circumstance,
No other than the passport necessary
To enter on the distant outer world
To which we travel by the word of Time,
That doth control our prudence and direct.

YOUNG DAMSEL.

Success doth banish Time, and drive it out ;
Its sacred moments are twelve thousand years,
Or else the abrogation of Man's race
As some grim phantom of another date
Unrecognisable, inadmissible, denied.

Enter HUNTSMAN *and party.*

HUNTSMAN.

Hold ! Let us stand awhile upon the pass.
The dogs are close upon the heels of the hind ;

It will return, hoping to find another path
Unto the summit of the crested edge,
Divided by a torrent from the cliff
Behind us.

SECOND HUNTSMAN (*addressing the ladies*).

            I give you cheer, most noble friends !
Whether you linger here or hasten on.
There is a castle upon the rising ground
A league beyond upon the road to Trent
Will shelter you and offer that support
Those need who venture over the proud Alp.
And as for safety, let us be your guides.

YOUNG DAMSEL.

We are for Innspruck bound, and linger here
An hour or two.   The water on the spot
Possesses qualities that renovate
Departing health and vigour ; Brenner thus
Achieves a reputation socially
Void by its height above the sounding sea.
Having thus renovated our lost strength
We shall descend.

HUNTSMAN.

            Descend !   Impossible
Let us entreat you with civilities
Stronger by far than stoutest arguments.

It is a tedious road to Innspruck hence
Over the steep unfathomable abyss,
Which, while you wonder at the rugged scene,
Big toppling crags will wonder at yourselves,
As if they knew, and mocked at your applause.
Then stay and dine with us.   Marcian ! a fire !
Heap wood upon that rock !   Cut up the stag
We overtook and captured this day week
In the Sole Valley, where it opens out
And unto Cles and Malè favours us.

ELDER LADY.

Whence and what art thou, then, that we may know
To whom this hospitality we owe ?

HUNTSMAN.

To trust your life and fortune on the Alp
Without my recognition would be death.
Within the dull routine of life below
Where sleep the energies which I proclaim,
Ultimately peradventure to my cost,   .
Nay more, among the guides across the rock,
And the banditti that it has defied,
No name is breathed with such an undertone
Of mingled admiration and respectful
Honour as that of Ludwig Vandelstein.
Warned by the limits of low destinies
Early in life I left my father's house,

A practised shot, with every faculty
To cope with and defeat these difficulties.
Between that hour and this we have supplied,
I and my comrades, all the neighbouring towns
With that which oftenest graces royal feasts,
And furs which full-dressed dignitaries adorn,
A Judge's or a Cardinal's decree
Pointing with power and authority beyond
The fulsome arrogance of lettered wrath ;
And life we have delivered from the grave
That over curiosity has yawned
To engulf its peeping, careless, idleness ;
And Science aided in its reckless search
For secrets that its genius has aroused
To study for the profitable ore
That lurks within the lofty, caverned halls,
The huntsman's palace and perpetual home.
Spread out the cloth ! arrange yourselves all round !
For we would show yon strangers that in faith
We never are reluctant to stand forth
Alike in social as in hazardous turns.
Eat of our stock and store to-day with them
So that their kind acquaintances and friends
Stand us support when we the mart frequent,
Remunerate us largely for our skins
And all the game that we no longer need,
And from pursuits and pastimes all their own
May cast a thought or holy wish for us.

       [They all sit round a prepared collation.

ELDERLY DAME.

Brave Vandelstein ! it is an anxious hour !
Fortune has placed circumstance in the scale
With an event foreseen by circumstance.
Young people will be rash and venturous.
I have been young and know Life's elements
Are in the outbreak treacherous and wild,
It may be to secure a prize which, lost,
Entails an age of ruin and remorse.
Theresa had a childish passion when
Years that fit out a maid for womanhood
Halt, as if all creation is at fault,
And leaves a vacancy we cannot fill,
But with the conjuration of some spell
That the conflicting atoms reconcile.
Which done it moves, and we ourselves again ·
Reanimated spring to second Life.
Her Lover was a young Italian Count,
And the suit prospered. Rumour whispered round,
However, that he was already engaged
To a patrician girl of Saxon birth.
In the commercial business which took place
Arezzo then between and Nuremburg,
A German lapidary introduced himself,
Carl Chemnitz.   Jewellers' business hesitates
Without a spark of sentimentality,
And Carl and my Theresa often met.
It was not love, but friendliness alone,

And in the casualties of friendly intercourse
A tale of a betrothal animated'
The lazy pace of unsubstantiated
Securities for much invested gold.
The pedigree of Hofenstaufen's house
Is represented by a gentle girl,
So, when a young Italian Count makes love,
So far, so good.   What is his name? is asked.
His name is Rinaldini.   What a scene
A mother in her garden then beheld,
Summoned by the loud shriek of broken faith:
Theresa senseless lay in Chemnitz' arms,
Who watched to stay Life from pursuing Love
That yet the love of death bravely outsped.

HUNTSMAN (*filling the glasses*).
Confusion drink all round to the false Count!
                    ·[*They drink.*

ELDERLY DAME.
Slowly our daughter vanquished the hard stroke
That all her Lover's treachery revealed;
And when the time arrived when the two met
To sanctify by ceremony the bond,
And consecrate successful overtures,
And no impediment survived between
As far as the Count's improvident ideas,
Which always marked a diplomatic wit,
Could see on an exuberance of Chance
The hope of happiness and joy itself,

With feigned sincerity he made those vows
Which bind a tender maiden to accept
And justify a sanguine Lover's suit.
She listened not, she heard not, but pronounced
A positive injunction to depart
Then and for ever from her Father's house.
The Count was thunderstruck, and loudly cursed
The hour of his inheritance and birth,
And registered an oath to be revenged
On all and each that lived upon the spot,
Within the door and those without the door,
And all that treated with us, and agreed
To season their life with our seasoning,
And all that ventured to uphold our cause,
As base, unloyal, misdirected souls
Who cancelled worth as they defeated want.

HUNTSMAN.

And where was Chemnitz? Did he not appear
Rinaldini's retribution to divert
Upon himself, the prompting impetus
Of passion of which he was not the dupe?
He surely should have hurried to the spot
Of rivalry, in discountenancing wrong,
And shared the difficulties of that hour !

ELDERLY DAME.

Relying on Theresa's carefulness,
And furthermore desirous to apprise,

As soon as circumstance permitted it,
The family of Hofenstaufen of
The critical position they were in,
To Saltzburg he had gone the day before.
Thrifty, careful, and calculating, he
Has expectations of a fortunate
And favourable end to many schemes,
Encouraged by the prevalent desire
Of Germany to have the very best
And choicest gifts that Nature can produce.
So he seeks to employ in that his art
Perfection in remotest foreign skill,
Till he can dazzle when he cannot win.

    [*Second Huntsman enters into conversation with
      her.*

HUNTSMAN (*to Young Damsel*).

May I inquire with no curious view,
But with the thought to aid you on your way,
What you will do should things not all turn out
As you seem naturally willing to expect
When you arrive at Innspruck?

YOUNGER DAMSEL.

                There are those
Who at the mention of Carl's confidence
Would, if he has deserted Innspruck, or
For fame or money ventured to Stamboul,
Yield us support and succour to our need.

HUNTSMAN.

Then you propose to stay in Germany
Awaiting his return, and will not cross
This year again the snows of Brenner's Pass?
We seldom leave our mountain fastnesses,
And should you venture into social life
Among the salemen or the storekeepers
Of Innspruck or of Saltzburg, intimate
Our calling, its great object and intent,
Supplying officials with the symbols grave
Of potency and pride predominant,
Impressing policy and extending rule
Upon the soft and pliant hearts of those
Who doubly bow beneath their single yoke
That they may some day elevate themselves
Into the very chair which they pretend
Is too far off, and wholly out of reach.
Make goodly mention of bold Vandelstein.
You need not add that this our liberty
And all that it includes within its wide
And unsophisticated latitude
Is a career with a consoling thread
To guide its followers to a better home :
Which knowing, they too consolation find,
By shadowless decoys long unallured ;
But say how much we owe to them and theirs
In perfecting this effort of our Life
To realise enough wherewith to cheer

The vacillating humours of old age,
And gratify its too fastidious taste
With less excitement yet more genial warmth :
All which they have, but we must waste our years
In simple admiration of the fact,
Till we acquire what they have never lost,
And measure our attainment by their rule.

YOUNG DAMSEL.

For this your timely aid in this strange place,
And worthy honour of my mother's years,
Whose great experience cannot quite foresee
What difficulties edge the path of Life,
Leaving you on our arrival in the town
That fortifies the entrance of the pass,
Your prowess and your pains I will announce,
So that if any feeling they possess
Who dwell at Innspruck, and gain more thereby
Than they deserve, not only those, like you,
Who venture all for risk in the result,
But those as of a less elastic mood,
Who from alleviation win encouragement,
Yet constancy and industry ignore.
In variable mood they shall bestow
The substance which I offer but in name,
And with appreciation of your worth,
Considerations of a cordial kind
Which fire the eye and fructify the heart.

HUNTSMAN.

Should you return again, or any of your friends,
And from the abyss the precipice ascend,
The mountain robber, with his unprincipled hate
Of everyone that ever lives or loves,
Will vanish at the utterance of my name
Though I myself may hover leagues away:
More eager and more common in pursuit,
More versatile and not so prescient
Of difficulties he himself has made,
And therefore not so doubtful of myself
As having broke no universal bond.

> [*A shriek is heard.*

YOUNGER DAMSEL.

Now Heaven have mercy on our hapless race!
Some spasm has my mother overwhelmed.

> [*Rushes to catch her falling mother.*

SECOND HUNTSMAN.

'Tis true!   Yea! every word of it!   I'll swear.

YOUNG DAMSEL.

Vandelstein! fetch some water from yon spring,
It is a fainting fit, and that is all.

ELDERLY DAME (*recovering*).

Theresa ! once again, and now more dear
In that we must once more together dwell,
Each other's arms the only fond embrace,
Each other's friendship all our ecstasy,
Since nothing better will this world support
In all the variable ways of Life
That can be conjured for its sustenance
My frail and faltering clasp with your fond hand !

YOUNGER DAMSEL.

What strange catastrophe in this world's round
Of possible and improbable designs
Has pointed such a tongue with such a curse?
Tell me not that Carl Chemnitz is no more !
I will become a ghost myself at once,
And wed the spirit of his hopeless corpse,
And we will wander on together thus
Through endless time united, endless space.

ELDERLY DAME.

Place thou a barrier upon final grief,
Which is a grief that thou canst never cure,
But these harsh rocks that rudely round us frown
Are so many corporeal witnesses
That the two powers that they so divide,

Compelled by the gradual rupture of good faith
Which formerly every difference smoothed away,
Every bond have revoked. Yes ! Your Love-
    Bond.

YOUNG DAMSEL.

A nation's bonds are not the bonds of Love !
These will survive when nations separate
On formal stately circumstantial terms,
And cast around a spiritual charm,
That while acknowledging the difference,
And wholly not abjuring such decrees,
Resembles Heaven's light that shines on all,
To be appropriated with a holy will.

ELDERLY DAME.

But Nature is not Man, at variance
Who dwells with things his metaphor and type,
And contradicts with seeming interest
Half that they designate or intimate.
The cord has snapped between the rival States
Whose passionate interests we now divide
And sadder symptoms easily discerned
Foretell a solemn grave renunciation
Of every interchange of fellowship
That long time has existed. War will be next,
And to prevent all doubt upon the point
The German barons have exhorted all

Loyal and faithful patriots within'
The range and limitation of their name,
General and personal intercourse to renounce,
Whatever be its purport and intent,
With Italy.

YOUNG DAMSEL

You knew then we were attached,
Chemnitz and I.   A moment's happiness,
Prophetic of a union as sincere ;
So full of promises made to be ratified
At every risk within a single year.

HUNTSMAN.

The lapidary then succeeded to the Count !
And so you were to meet in Germany ?

ELDERLY DAME.

Business has strange digressions.   If in love
Carl Chemnitz sought my daughter I knew not,
But she requested me to cross the Alps,
And I have many friends in Germany.

HUNTSMAN.

'Tis plain why he the interview forsook,
Whereon the first attachment was annulled.

YOUNGER DAMSEL.

Of course I need not say when Carl returned,
He pressed me to his heart, and called me his.
Mother, let us descend ! forgetting all :
Only remembering this unhappy spot.

   [*Vandelstein turns to his troop, and changes his
       dress.   The ladies prepare to depart. Van-
       delstein returns as Carl Chemnitz.   The
       ladies advance. Younger Damsel shrieks
       and falls.*

CHEMNITZ.

I did not mean to startle timid nerves
Into mute disavowal of my claim !
Look up, Theresa !   Look on one who loves
With all sincerity !

[*Younger Damsel recovers.*

YOUNGER DAMSEL.

Theresa, me !
It is Carl Chemnitz that I now behold !
I thought that we were never more to meet,
And now we meet, oh ! let it be for aye !
I ventured in fulfilment of that vow
Both made in Florence just a year ago
To seek you thus, and succour memory

Dim with oblivion of such bright resolve ;
And then should circumstance support the truth,
To manage the completion of our plan,
Or to defer it if impossible,
And meet the tardy wish of all around.

CHEMNITZ.

Theresa ! step a single yard this way
And I will welcome you !

THERESA (*advancing a pace or two*).

      'Tis as you wish.

CHEMNITZ.

Now, you are safe at length on German soil !
Oh ! that this soil you honour were your own
As it is mine, to my indifference
To all that it can prosper or produce,
To all that it can honour or support,
To all who claim its consequential aid,
If fettered like myself by ruinous laws
That every real affection compromise,
And for the sake of the united whole
In discipline to preserve its honour intact,
That sever emblematic union !
As if a monarch lost a precious stone,
Polished and cut to suit a foreign crown,
If he bid more than the first monarch gave !
Oh ! Pride and Prejudice in things so high,

How can you lay our private pride so low !
With one austere and stern solicitude
Thus blight the secret solace of the heart !

THERESA.

O Italy ! O Germany ! O Earth !
And thou celestial universe around,
How art thou fashioned out in quarrelsome parts,
Each so deceptive to itself that thou
Mayst glitter in fecundity replete !
If so, what happiness is laid in store
For integral Italy and Germany ?
No elements conducing to the whole,
But of a refreshed and simple composition
That to the whole proclaims it has no friend,
No living rival either in arts or arms
To be confederate with or associate to.
If so, what a mere chance shot at a venture,
Unworthy our approval or applause !

CHEMNITZ.

But let it labour on.   Our bark upset
By too much cargo will throw out its guns,
And in despair will seek a foreign port.
The crew may quarrel with the captain, and
A new and liberal constitution forge.
In the first stroke of this our enterprise
To be a separately noble State
It may seem at the outset creditable

To be too pertinacious and severe,
Too positive, too scrupulous, and particular,
And Germany being the more immediate cause
Of all determination, and resolve
Either to become distinct upon such different
Creed, language, impulse, motive, aim, and wish,
Or to dislodge its joint unhealthy heads,
Might seize a moment to achieve a point.
So this seemed then to crude Teutonic minds
Wrought into action by the fairest thoughts
That always takes position from the best.
Then let us hope this also at the last
Will in its time assume predominance.
And when this Germany has fledged its wings
It will betake it to a nobler flight,
And hold its nest already thus secured
Universal toleration's oracle.
Or else all trade will utterly decrease,
For no one is sufficient in himself,
Devil or God, Sinner or Saint be he,
To say I am, and all I see is mine,
But in conciliation he may find
A multitude of homes instead of one.

ELDERLY DAME.

This is indeed a sad and stern decree !
We live but for ourselves we always know,
But in the arrangement for the common good

We must repose our fortunes and our views
That all our worthiness may not be found
To be unworthy of the larger use
And more abundant offspring of the gift.
Let us no more our vanished plans deplore !
As soon as War is officially pronounced,
And the entire and positive estrangement
Of different races absolutely certified,
Such crisis, and such only, justifies
The separation of your union
If War is not deduced, diplomacy
Will seal within its sheath the impending sword
That would have turned your wished-for wedding
     dress
Into a worthless cloak of tattered rags.
Supposing the two countries are combined
Renewal of old fealties will succeed,
And each will thereby reap prosperity
From correspondents that will buy its wares,
And in the prompted natural intercourse
Of dealer and recipient once again,
You two, in spite of casual difference,
Shall ban all meritless authority,
Which knowing knows not, loving loves not us,
Nor aught that naturally may be frail,
For Nature says that they are natural,
Shall your projected union complete,
Shall prove your faith superior to itself
As in more moderate circumstance revealed,

And in decrying early consummation
Of views faith graver cannot disavow
Contribute to State policy far more
Than those who pay a single deference.

CHEMNITZ.

Theresa, then remain as I am true :
A mournful yet most genuine patriot !
Fond of my country though it breaks my heart,
And by dissolving laws turns it to stone.
I serve it by myself.   What buttress poor
For civilisation's falling tenement !
Its countless luxuries ever hoarded up
Till everyone is choked with his own worth,
And different minds by different motives fanned,
The same mistakes must foster and parade,
The very errors that they might have cured,
By regular comparison disproved
Become an insupportable disease
Till social crime or civic discontent
Imperil or corrupt all politic ends !
On this day year, if all be settled, then
I will resume my trade with Italy.
Afford not Rinaldini any chance
Of filling up that odious gap of Time
With Southern blandishments of perfidy.
He would be also insincere to you,
Bestow his promises but not his heart,

Make much of this Italian difficulty,
And he, the cause of our discomfiture,
Reap the whole harvest I myself have sown.
Should the Italian laws be less severe,
Or they forget their duty to themselves,
The Count may venture into Germany
And wed the Countess Hofenstaufen, but
This to accomplish he must run all risks,
Conceal his birth and nationality,
Assume the airs, and character, and dress
Of a disciple of the Teuton Creed
Only that he might lose such love as yours !
When I reach Saltzburg I shall ascertain
Upon what footing stands his overture.
But be assured, Theresa ! he must wed,
Or else mankind reduplicate not in me :
For he has ventured where men will who wish
To weigh their merits in your gentle scales.
Till then a sad farewell !

THERESA.

Carl Chemnitz, stay !
I will, further addresses to avoid,
Enter a convent and live secret there,
Free from a world which, in rejecting yours,
Has neutralised my love of earthly joys.
If you do not return within a year,
I shall assume the irrevocable veil,

Devoted to true piety the more
That in relieving all beneath my care
· I know and feel their own, and once my share.

ELDERLY DAME.

My child Theresa ! he will surely come :
Chemnitz his second promise will fulfil.
State animosity is no disease,
'Tis but a temporary distemperature
That tries our consolation to the base,
Then leaves it in its former healthy state.
A year will break the hateful barrier,
A year of animation in suspense,
Germany's jewels then again be set
In our enhancing high-wrought minerals,
And wealth with twofold vigour shall destroy
This narrow-minded creed impolitic,
Homes that have severed, yea, more kindred hearts

CHEMNITZ.

Then true to me, Theresa, you will be !
I as the star, and you the dutiful sea,
Each linked to each by their infinity.
And·let your conduct be as the diamond pure,
Your character as the ornamental gold
That all admire but only Lovers wear.
I leave you and descend to Germany,

You leave me and return to Italy,
With visions of joint happiness more sure
Decreed by the delay we must endure.
> [*Theresa and Chemnitz embrace and separate. The
> two ladies descend one way, Chemnitz and
> the Huntsmen another.*

ACT II.

Scene I.—*The Palace at Turin.*

EMPEROR (*walking up and down an apartment alone*).

This is the upshot then of my appeal :
Before the convocation of all Europe
I stand a heretic ecclesiastical,
And most unworthy of my own domains !
Is there no valorous voice, no sword undrawn
On either side of the inveterate Alps
That will not then its wonted force exert
And free my name from infidelity's stain ?
In what a man relies they know not of
Who perjure conscience with such foul abuse.
Is Germany oblivious of its origin ?
Has it no faith in liabilities
Which crowd around its spirit and enthral
With unforeseen and irreconcilable threats
The regular, accustomed, and complete
Fulfilment of a certain Destiny ?

What of the Diet? it was overruled
By one ambitious and unconciliatory
Close-bound and close aspiring arbiter
Of spiritual and effeminate concerns
That to a class but not to the whole world
Pours in a balm to cure their fanciful wounds,
That care discovers that they never felt!
A monk to rule the world that he has fled,
To be the head of what he was the heel!
Who cares then for his prelate prophecies?
His pomp is neither royal skill nor address.
Has he no exigence to probe and find
Religion has its mockeries, as well
His predecessor Alexander knew?
Surrounded by a myriad of foes
Henry of Germany all the aid required
That the Tiara could accommodate,
But Gregory, ascetically false
To all the causes of redundant Life,
Is jealous of all power that counteracts
Hostility to human happiness,
And so pronounces me incompetent
To be a close supporter of the Faith.
To rule a wife and have a wife I urge
Is the enjoyment of a house and home;
And though the Germans know the wholesome law
They do not feel the worth of it, and call
A tyrant, capable of all alarm,
One who has held them in true vassalage

Because they were not fitted to be free.
Life immature is in dependency,
And Time cannot mature their crudities.
I do not underrate the Teuton horde,
But it has but endurances of ill,
Ills that have crushed his Northern rival down.
Further beyond an ace and but a space
Severs philosophy from all our grace.
Its claim acknowledgment of Paradise,
Perpetual fruitfulness and endless day.
Prudent austerity disclaims us both.
It is not wise this early disavowal
Of Races under Nature's patronage.
It stands then thus logically straight and close
Germany has more front than Italy,
Or that it, knowing how little this has to lose,
Would rather lose it all than this should win·
This game of civilisation to itself.
Passion, one's guide, is more within control
Than prejudice, the others, is with them.
A wrong part in perfection then is best,
Perfection not completing what was right.

Enter a COURTIER.

COURTIER.

May it please your Majesty one waits without
Demanding urgently an interview.

KING.

A German or Italian?

COURTIER.

                He is a Count
Of noble race and fortune.

KING.

                   Show him in.

Enter COUNT RINALDINI.

KING.

Advance, good Rinaldini!   Here is cause
For much consideration in our cares.
While Italy is not all that it should,
Germany is all it should not be.
It has declined allegiance, and declared
Principles hostile to sound unity.
Have you heard this?   Do you know Matilda,
Daughter of Bonifacio of Canossa?
She is in league against me with the Pope,
Who, once a monk, has so outrun his cause,
As to approach ambition's last effect,
For he announces that when our joint States
Have chosen and agreed upon their rulers,
Unless with that choice he is satisfied,
The so-called dynasty which we ourselves

Are proud to centralise into repute,
Carrying it to the utmost point of power
That subjugated vassals will permit,
And venturing to assert predominance
Where only its authoritative frown
Would crush good metal from the ore of Life,
Becomes annulled, and they must choose afresh.

RINALDINI.

A vain assertion !   'Tis to make the Church
Beyond his rule as dictatorial as
The Church within and our lay subjects are.
The former are not numerous, nor brave,
They could not force such interference home.
I cannot think Matilda of Canossa
Means more at present by a union
With such a bold and independent man,
But yet without a sphere, as Hildebrand
Than her refractory duchies to disarm,
And regulate affairs in Lombardy.

EMPEROR.

Count, you are yet unmarried, nevertheless
I heard of a betrothal yesterday
Between you and the Countess Hofenstaufen,
A daughter of a rich and ancient race.
Remember, Germans in domestic life
Borrow of conquest the volcanic flame

That spreads and verifies the flame of Love
With promise of explosive rivalry
That with a shock the earth shall agitate
Till it return to Love in violence
All that it hazarded as presumptuous gain.
Yet all our State attachments end in loss.

RINALDINI.

Encouraged by the unity between
Roman diplomacy and German arms,
And glad to authorise it with a seal,
I have a suitable alliance sought
With a high race of Saxon origin,
But I have just received a messenger
With tidings that a meeting was convened
At Wurzburg yesterday, and an idea prevailed
Affecting the position of the States
You rule, relatively, north and south of the Alps.

EMPEROR.

It is most true, unfortunately so,
But at the Diet I myself will summon
My good friends of a tried fidelity
And quickly re-establish my control
Where faults can never justify reverse.
The Bavarian palatinate is mine,
Therein whatever spirit animates

The untaught energy of cunning man
Only by my high deeds is re-assured,
And by a lofty tone of enterprise
That does not waste itself in savage creeds,
That in fulfilment never lead to aught
But some extolled prurient variety
An early chosen civilisation's son,
Decent accomplisher of those designs
Some day shall rival Normandy's result,
And this last enterprise so imitate
That the wide world is fain to look on both
With a discerning and impartial glance
Before it quite perceives the difference
Between the real and artificial gem.
The rest are of a cold dogmatic kind,
Saving a principle which always seeks out
Their natural infirmity how to conceal,
Not that they have sound principles like us,
But give their excellence a broader base.
Yet virtue never lies in option's loss
Whether you shall or not be virtuous,
But to be bound like Ixion to the wheel
That circles wisdom's true circumference
Is but a lazy Phantom's rash pursuit.
Better never to value nor condemn,
If we make war on such, 'twill fan the flame,
If they make war on us the end is ours,
And with superior discipline and arms,
Divesting us of all our sophistries,

I will admonish and chastise a spirit
That came to learn its worth and worthlessness
By straight admonishment and chastisement.
Meanwhile continue, Count, to prosecute
Your suit with her of Hofenstaufen's race.
The jealousy of a brute will not be theirs
Where animosities are not general
But personal to all of every Creed
Social, political, and religious too.
And should Teutonic boldness die in its birth,
You then can have no reason for alarm
If the alliance be your honest aim ;
And should Teutonic boldness grow apace
And thrive on common hope, to them held out
With more than with a justifiable grace,
And with renunciation not content,
Adopt for me a hostile attitude.
Adjourn fulfilment to a later date
Which shall ensure and realise all hopes.

RINALDINI.

To persevere at once is dangerous.

EMPEROR.

Impossible ! What have you heard beyond the aim
Of some wild tale-bearer so gratified ?
[Enter a MESSENGER.
Whence art thou ?

MESSENGER.

         I from Wurzburg straightly come,
Behold a letter from the Prince of Tours.

[Delivers letter.

EMPEROR (*reads*).

' Herein I do inform your Majesty
That in the conclave held just now at Wurzburg
The Pope has promulgated the sacred ban
Of excommunication on our Emperor.
A large proportion of the nobility
Seduced by this, and aided by the rash,
Have seized the moment and renounced your rule.
Stand still some faithful spirits like myself
That will, if you take measures speedily,
Aid and assist your joint authority.'

EMPEROR.

Herein is treason more than treachery,
Because it strikes first at our sacredness
Then at our safety.   Gregory, thou fiend !
Whom to have died a monk, not lived a Pope
Had blessed and prospered unblest Italy
What would I not have bid for thy repulse ?
But I will summon the elect at Worms
And test the validness of a support
In which alone I can at length rely
The vacillation of the North to turn

Into allegiance to their Emperor.
Rinaldini, now is the right opportunity
To prove the value of your love of me,
The use of all your love for Germany.
Repair to Worms.   Straight, summon all the heads
Of all the principalities around,
Imply that I have forfeited my rule
Unless redeemed by all assurances
Uttered by fate, by reason, and themselves.
Call on the Prince of Thuringia to aid
A cause too young to be so soon renounced,
And all whom Life and Luxury has nerved,
And answers to all prayers on such behalf,
Or leave to Ruin their half broken vows
And future hopes, as Civilisation's egg
Buried in accident and wanton sand.

RINALDINI.

With all alacrity I will accept
This diplomatic passport to a wedding.

EMPEROR.

                        Go !
Fulfil both wishes.   One is for yourself,
The other for my Country and my Crown.

SCENE II.—*The Diet of Worms.   Hall in Castle.*

Assemblage of Princes.

DUKE OF CARINTHIA.

My Lords and Nobles ! hither are we met
To overlook all minor differences
And pledge ourselves to ascertain how far,
In the right regulation of affairs,
Henry the Emperor till now has gone.
Acknowledged by all Germany as one
Whose spirit can control and guide an age :
Alluring to prosperity unknown,
And without envy emulating well
Only those who have taken Fortune's near
But narrow, difficult, and hazardous road
To that success Humanity approves.
That if that tortuous way be overspread
In deviation's imminent temptation,
By clouds of their own virtue misapplied,
It doth become us in significance
Of that high moral tone, nor this alone,
That true parental love of kith and kin
Which long has cheered our solitary way,
Ceasing to exercise its wonted sway
(Beguiled by some security to us
Who revel not in luxury unknown),

Upon the mind of our good Emperor
Henry the Fourth thenceforth to venture from
In duty that to principle only sworn
To advocates can never be seduced
That do not this one principle sustain.
I do not quarrel with the monarchy
That has administered providentially
And to our errors with a due concern
Such requisitions as we chose to make
To rear a constitution immature.
I viewed it safe, a hazard immature,
When views could neither flatter nor beguile,
Quite undiscovered in the lap of Time.
Now shall we set aside our infancy,
And grasp at shadowy responsibility
As if we could that prize at once attain ?
Is it an overture too long delayed,
Or shall we wait until events have proved
Its abject but too late necessity?

PRINCE OF THURINGIA.

Conrad, the Son of Henry, is our friend.
But he but puts his name into our hearts
With the pretension of a nobler soul
To follow out the same unworthy ends.
Can Germany be Germany alone?
Is there no vital spark of inborn worth
Our course exterior to animate
Into an integral and healthy state?

Another Emperor to head our cause
Would summon allies from remotest Space,
Conciliate vacillation, aid the brave,
Determine inclination in the bad
In search of some profession to his taste,
Absorb all skill into the royal ranks,
Neither to foreign spheres diversified,
Nor for their gain irregularly transposed.
The Dane is not more staggered than the Greek,
A Southern climate is not warmth of Heart,
Actions that spring from passion are not sound,
Well to establish that which they extol.
A feeble mind on lengthened lassitude
Qualities early bestowed may supersede,
And all the capital of speculants
Assured to them will be invested here.
Let us the Rhine and Danube fortify.
Wurzburg is capable of strong defence,
Pforzheim, and Heidelberg, and Halberstadt,
And Rastadt, Kaufburen, and Ludwigsburg.
The seed of this detachment from old rule
Must yet with a prudential hand be sown,
Else it were vain to dictate terms around,
And then to teach our vassals not to yield,
And undermine our own authority.
Let us precede it by a substitute,
Establishing among us by our free consent
Another for the Monarchy renounced,
Substantially sound but not intolerant.

DUKE OF SUABIA.

Who would support the kingdom if 'twere made ?
It is not for a moment to be thought
That Italy would tacitly observe
Treaties made with it by a State part of its own ;
And if we plunge for independent rule
Into a war with Italy alone,
It would be well firstly to calculate
Defeat resulting as the end of war.
Could Germany consist as well as now,
I would its freedom were as well assured
As is its welfare deep within my heart !
I would it stood alone a paragon
That other States might wonder and admire !
It has within it work, and wit, and wealth,
But wants a principle to guide them all.
Then if you will erect a monarchy
Out of confused and rough ingredients,
You cannot find a man who would resign
Of Life in temperate security,
Of all its requisitions and demands,
His present weal for unexpected woe.
Granted that he fulfilled all our demands
And placed us in our new integrity
On a fair footing with our neighbours round,
Would you secure it to his son and heir,
Or any relative he might select?
Taxes would not repay his diligence,

H

Taxation must be his inheritance.
For the redemption of our State from debt
Not satisfying all posterity
But only now, and therefore truly all,
He must not mortgage future energies
For gain but for one day his own, and ours,
Unsordid, and unselfish, and yet true,
Because the Truth is a continuance,
And Falsity a temporary grace
That Time and the Event learns to efface.
There is the bond of brotherhood so strong
That on its virtue in the hour of proof
We can depend upon its sanctity.
Yet tried by the fire of more vicissitude
Untempered for the troubles not yet ours,
It may reject the remedies for ills
That follow upon rash experiment.
We are not of the mould of other folks,
But built on failures that the fruit of Time
Fate points must be redeemed by everyone.
Then those who played so carelessly their stakes
Have lost the Truth, nor venture to deny
To them that lost may not be saved for us.

KING OF BAVARIA.

To emblems not our own if answerable,
We are not answerable to our own.
The type of our success is hid in depth
Below the close inspection of the Sage.

A secret spirit and obscured so far
Asks in development a longer time,
Therefore, to separate from Italy,
And into a new State ourselves resolve
Already and immediately at once,
As from the brain of Jupiter complete,
Wrapped in War's panoply, Minerva sprang
Would contradict the secret of success.
To capture or to captivate all round
Is not the Destiny of Germany.
Of its own merits yet incognisant,
Jealous of faults opportunity descried
Which earnest application can retrieve.
Unwilling then to play a second part,
When these atoned for and her tone improved,
I should be anxious for her happiness
That this our Land should so be twice our own,
Governed and ruled by one of us alone,
Internally a model of enforced
And yet subscribed to regularity,
In all its close machinery of post,
Affording all an opportunity
That can shake off our strong, besetting sloth
To order, criticise, and characterise
This field of Fortune and its devotees.
A dread to rivalry externally,
Which now out of proportion in the South
Will animate the Spirits of the North
As soon as our integrity proclaimed

To breathe exasperation from a fire
Kindled from some unseen but certain torch,
Against another bolder tyranny
Than that which they are learning to despise.
All this, if this were all, attainable.
But in the sudden burst of enmity
Fanned by the priesthood to infirmity,
And therefore the more easily led away
To Pride and empty Superciliousness,
Curing its own while blaming other faults,
No ground is found for that security
Which we all know must foster farther threats.
Is there no remedy for tyranny
Than its own weapons turned against itself?
The many natural qualities we have,
Good in themselves and capable of more
As they grow slowly to maturity,
Should they be moved to a progressive action,
And take the lead when they should follow on
The acquisition of the Fatherland
To many an unborn and ambitious man
Of rights in preference to those we have
Impulses may create, but not safe steps,
To deeds of inborn and external weal
Beyond that which we have not but we know,
Which may be turned at last to our disgrace ;
So in the dispossession of a claim
Dishonoured in the breath that it is made
We must the crisis of our risk forego

That feeds on recognition later on,
And our secreted treasure multiply
With patience and forbearance into wealth
Beyond the standard pitch as now it stands
That national independence has decreed.
Therefore I, full of generous designs,
Full of all honesty to every soul,
Do urgently a fresh rule recommend,
Less likely to redound to our distress,
As certain to discover fresh designs
More probable to end in happiness.
Choose a fresh sovereign for Germany
And these dependencies otherwise our own,
Better our own when we are more ourselves
Will learn by fresh decrees from a virtuous head
To eat the good and leave the bitter fruit
Which circumstance has proffered to our taste
With cautious preparation definite,
And with a circumspection virtuous,
Their independence from too much control
In system to correct and moderate,
Its proneness rectify and regulate,
And treaties propagate with all around,
Thereby replenishing the edifice
With strength that renovates antiquity.
Another Emperor would please the Pope,
And reconcile all now dissentient States,
And we rejoicing in the remedy,
And adding to its value by support,

This contradictory knot may easily solve.
Then when our Northern neighbours are more shrewd,
And mellowness has tinged the Southern race,
Emerging from obscurity, begirt
With more of civilisation's ample idea,
Without offence to this side or to that,
Nor stirring provocation by an act
Of cold renunciation unprovoked
Of critical and venomous prejudice
By some unnatural readiness impelled,
Seizing we may appropriate what we grasp.
Not leaving all to Time's uncertain step
Fed and brought up by avarice and lust
Affected into the insatiable,
Because to stop would open up a wound
Which Time could have prevented earlier.

DUKE OF CARINTHIA.

But Germany is but a blossom late,
And bears the finer fruit on that account.

DUKE OF SUABIA.

We who have conquered Britain to be thus
Compelled to stoop to time-worn usages?

PRINCE OF THURINGIA.

Usage is but a name and we its echo,
Guided to loftier destinies beyond.

Enter RINALDINI.

RINALDINI.

Princes and Nobles !   I, the Emperor's friend,
Avail myself of a kind moment when,
Without offence to all your dignities,
I may his solemn protest interpose
Between the rash expression of these views
And the fulfilment of their consequence.
Should Philip of Capet join my master's cause,
Halstein of Sweden, or the Norseman Olaf,
Sancho of Spain, or Portuguese Alfonso,
Or Michael the great Eastern Emperor,
Your bold attempt would be a great mistake
Not to be compromised so easily,
Because, your independence once assured,
This side the Alps has no acknowledgment
Unless agreed to universally.
The oath of your allegiance sworn to him,
If broken in an outcry of alarm,
May probably in a short campaign be checked,
Your homes dismantled, your bright hearth-fires
     quenched,
And all your option to coercion trained.

KING OF BAVARIA.

Have you the Emperor Henry's seal to this ?

RINALDINI.

I bear his passport, and this document
Will hasten his intentions to express.

[*Unfolds a scroll.*

COUNT HOFENSTAUFEN.

He is a noble of accredited fame,
And in negotiations trustworthy.

KING OF BAVARIA.

Then his wild master has a willing slave.
(*To Rinaldini.*)   Has the Emperor seen the Pope's decree
For certain irregularities placing him
Outside the pale of Christianity?

RINALDINI.

His Majesty the Emperor of Germany
Believes no prohibition of the Pope
Will temporal differences justify.

DUKE OF SUABIA.

But none of us more than the Pope himself
Wish to continue Henry's feudatories,
We are too similar peradventure in our origin,
Our lives and fortunes now become our own.
Civilisation's wand has animated us
For separate interests to strike a blow,

That separate privileges we may have
Unpoisoned by the vicious element
Of discord in the reigning family,
And unembittered by the old resolve
That bound us to an unnatural Sovereign,
As if his eye were moral light indeed,
Or his good will the heart's best sympathies,
Which, while they prate of that which he has not,
Announces the success of that we have.

KING OF SAXONY.

Besides, we have a realm beyond the sea,
England with its advantages is ours.
We must, so false to our prosperity,
The credit of this enterprise renounce,
Forego the grandeur of enlarged domains,
Relinquish subjugation in its pride
Of a vast tribe of rugged Islanders
Who should not share the cup of luxury
With one who shall not drain it to the dregs.

RINALDINI.

Not far from hence the Imperial family
Dwell and abide till you have stated how
And in what way you will be reconciled.
If you are guided by the Pope of Rome,
And excommunication deem correct,
Steps will be taken to appease the Pope.

DUKE OF CARINTHIA.

Then why have they already passed the Alps,
Knowing at Wurzburg what was registered?
Should he not be royally exercising
In Italy all his left authority,
From every State exacting homage due?
He cannot hope that we should fear him here
Who have an optional fealty to designs
That mock our natural humanity
And change our loyalty to settled Hate.

PRINCE OF THURINGIA.

The wisest and the best plan would be change
An integral Germany is best of all,
If not a new Imperial dynasty
Uniting fresh under a different head
Conflicting antagonistic influences
That rush, with civilisation in their rear,
To the high goal of all the human race,
A consolation, satisfaction none,
For sacrifices we are called to make
In exigencies nurtured by ourselves.

KING OF BAVARIA.

Depart, Count Rinaldini! hence convey,
Welcome or otherwise as that may be,
After investigation due and sifted views

The Diet's just decision and decree.
Tell the Fourth Henry, sometime Emperor,
In stern renunciation of his rule,
To guide and guard two different destinies
Through contradictions to contrasted good,
And lead the issue to acknowledgment
Of the round world's obeisance and applause,
A rule unnatural yet once necessary
Since Nature should be crossed, not we ourselves,
Nevertheless, our honour pledged to such,
Serving ourselves afresh and Nature more,
Lest we should be significantly sealed
With self-destruction in a simple course,
Looking at him and his, and us and ours,
On these with jealousy, these with respect,
In reference to the last with proper trust,
The former with repudiation, now
Holding suspended further exercise
Henceforth of rights unlawfully enjoyed,
And not conducive to the public good,
We will another Sovereign elect.

SCENE III.—*A Drawing Room in Castle Hofenstaufen.*

COUNT HOFENSTAUFEN.

Come, Rinaldini ! speak out your design.
Ethelga wonders at your apathy !
Does some suspicion labour in your heart
Its worthiest advices to o'erthrow?

COUNT RINALDINI.

When first I left my halls in Italy,
Full of devotion to my proffered love,
And actuated by no other tone
Than jealous suitors have at their command,
I could have ventured to assert no stroke
Of Fortune could have made impediment
To the fulfilment of such natural views.
Heaven smiled above, and all around success
This meeting shadowed on my vivid heart,
Full of contentment, happiness, and hope.
And we are here ! But who is here ? Are you
To carry out the project still prepared?
Had I but made a bargain for the Emperor,
My union with Ethelga had been fixed ;
But all your States are in a hostile mood,
Your Princes echo but the popular voice.

HOFENSTAUFEN.

And where is Henry our sage Emperor?
Has he no more reliance than yourself
On Germany with its heroic thoughts?
Surely he does not think his cause undone
By the first sign of immature revolt?

RINALDINI.

He has resolved to stay at Oppenheim,
And there to watch the current of events.
Should you assure me of support beyond
The bounds of these unconciliatory States,
Philip, the King of France, should he decide
To join his arms with ours in confidence,
Matilda of Canossa and the Pope,
As yet against us in a formal league,
Would yield to their united influence.

HOFENSTAUFEN.

Then Germany would be Italian,
And German maidens soon Italian wives.

RINALDINI.

And what more likely, what more probable?
Italian girls are full of treachery,
The fire within their eyes is nought to that
Which lurks within their deep volcanic breast.
They love you, and they love you not, nor he
Is ever safe with them until betrothed.

HOFENSTAUFEN.

I did support you at the Council board :
Whatever turn events may henceforth take,
The obligation lieth at your door.

Enter COUNTESS HOFENSTAUFEN.

COUNTESS HOFENSTAUFEN.

Ha! Count Rinaldini!   Welcome to Germany :
I thought we should not see you for a year :
Time passes quickly, or events beat Time :
There is much in the marvel of our hearts
That action instigates in spite of both.

Enter ETHELGA HOFENSTAUFEN.

RINALDINI.

My mission is of Love.   [*Bows to Ethelga.*
                    Not only Love,
The Emperor Henry has entrusted me
With some State business, so I ventured on
Beyond the discipline of skilful minds,
All eager to control each other's fates,
Our intercourse so pleasant to resume.

COUNTESS HOFENSTAUFEN.

It is but candid and sincere of you
Thus to avow all friendliness.   There is much
That has been said and listened to of late

That I should like to mention.   First of all,
A messenger from Florence has arrived
Declaring that if not already wed
You are to marry an Italian girl !
Perhaps the Emperor Henry knows of this?

RINALDINI.

He knows that to your daughter I have pledged
Preliminaries to matrimonial bonds,
And he, wishing the State to re-assure,
Considers our alliance should be sealed.
But what if ruptures of a higher range
Counteract inferior domestic fates
And separate us?

ETHELGA HOFENSTAUFEN.

Never !   You have said
That with the formal elements you are agreed,
And I have sealed vows closely to my faith.
Move now the institution of a rule
Sworn at betrothal to be certified.

HOFENSTAUFEN.

Am I to understand then that unless peace
Is signed before the Congress to be held
At Wurzburg, immediately you are to be released
From the fulfilment of a solemn pledge?
And we from all advances are absolved
That strengthen and confirm the married state?

RINALDINI.

Not if the rupture do not lead to war,
Which might be deadly or interminable.
I must secure my lands to those I love,
And they must be about me, eloquent
Of practices that cannot be disturbed.

COUNTESS HOFENSTAUFEN.

Then we are just to await the ultimate
And positive decision of the States,
And then conjoin or separate by such?
Your love can only be attachment's ghost,
By politic disparity exorcised,
Or laid by the adjuration of a priest !

ETHELGA.

Should war break out I will desert my land
Of birth, as in its mood my mood discharged
And exiled from the heart for evermore.

RINALDINI.

My mission to the States convened to sound
The impulses by which their views are fanned,
To action leaves me no opportunity
Such contradictory counsels to direct.
Give way not yet, Ethelga !   I renew
My firm determination you to wed.
Let obstacles offend me as they may,

There is a term to opposition such
That will pronounce our union solemnised.

HOFENSTAUFEN (*to Countess H.*)

And who is this Italian damsel then
With whom you say that you have been informed
The Count here has been playing fast and loose;
Is she of Royal or of noble birth?

COUNTESS HOFENSTAUFEN.

Of lowly origin I am coldly told,
But whom by unremitting industry
Her father, dealing in precious stones and gold,
And ornamental work and bronze device,
And decorative carvings and designs,
Has with a marvellously large dower endowed,
And she is to redeem his lands when lost
At play, or to a Jew for money pawned.

RINALDINI (*to Ethelga H.*)

The Sword I say is lord of all, not Love.

ETHELGA HOFENSTAUFEN.

Should Love be lord of all, what is the Sword?

RINALDINI.

Then why such false attachment from your sheep?
Their want of faith has conjured up that sword,
That all our fondness would have laid to sleep!

Ethelga ! had their blood been good as mine,
Imbued with all that Romulus admired,
Inflated by our Cæsar's victories,
Refined by age on age to something pure
As the impartial oracle of Life,
Then would there hence be no occasion here
To paralyse confusion not our own !

HOFENSTAUFEN.

It may not be this grave comparison
Of States with single individuals.
There is perhaps a vague analogy,
But that is better to be thrown aside.
Within ourselves our hearts are all our own.
If war succeed to ruinous designs
Upon the wholesale wide development
Of nations with each other satisfied,
We might adjourn to neutral territory
And previous engagements there adjust.
Then, when the war is over nought is lost
In Time, or to attachment lost for Time,
And Hearts united then will be more free
To exercise the object of their bond.
Then, if their union were on this or that
Favoured approval of our changeful choice,
To-day 'tis Gaul, to-morrow Germany,
Changed by the fateful doctrine of the stars
To the far West or yet still further South,
When shall start up some aspirant unknown,

Caught by the past and future under veil
And make historic facts reel round again
To fit into his own performances,
We may consolidate what they have lost
Or mutually enjoy what they have found.
But Chance which changes them may bury us,
Then, Rinaldini, make your choice at once !
Why linger on so frail an element
As indecision in its vaunted home,
When none of which will have you for an hour?
Our union will do more to satisfy
Uneasy regions than your Diet ours.
Henry will thank you for the sacrifice,
Because it is a harbinger of good,
A staid suggestion of the general wish
Which advocates a widespread harmony,
The whole a healthy constitution sound,
Not a sad thing decrepit and diseased,
Wearing around its neck strange amulets
To warn or to affright impending ill,
Each kingdom separately a different charm.
If marriage is a lottery where we draw
A prize or blank, it surely matters more
The speculation to accommodate
Than all your treaties with the Diet serve,
And in your Emperor all prosperity,
Either to rectify the Pope's disclaim
Or overrule Bavaria's advice,
Or paralyse the game of Normandy.

RINALDINI.

You said that I was otherwise engaged.
This is an accusation, I assert.
My claim hence on your hospitality
Is but to farther the affairs of State,
Not to absolve me from betrothal vows.

ETHELGA.

Which thou canst never do ! or oaths are vain !
Your own and national honour all a boast !

RINALDINI (*to Count H.*)

I would in me your confidence renew
As an approved appointed emissary,
In business ripe and ready as yourself,
As conscious of its present gravity,
Upon the point of Honour positive,
Proud to uphold Henry the Fourth Emperor
And Monarch of the tribes of Germany.
I do not mean to say that if this fails,
Then to redeem my promise sealed by oath
To wed your only daughter I shall fail.

COUNTESS HOFENSTAUFEN.

Because her champion, then, will challenge you !
And satisfy lost Honour with spilt blood.
Shame ! thus to mock at our credulity.

RINALDINI.

But as my efforts are but to cement
Imperial links so loudly thus disjoined
All this would be a pastime rash and vain.
I should be wise to calculate before
Entering upon so grave an enterprise
As union with a strange and alien soil
With the frail phantom of a marriage bond.
Therefore I say let it stand over now,
More distant, but as certain as before.

ETHELGA.

Remember that the day is fixed by me,
Who do not choose an hour to delay
Beyond the time agreed upon when first
You preyed upon the passions of this heart,
When wagering on the matrimonial state,
And picturing your life in Italy,
And estimating providential claims
Upon its soft luxurious residents
To be fulfilled by our encouragement.
You wrung a sad and gradual consent
To terms you now so willingly renounce.
Rinaldini !   Then if you decide——

RINALDINI.

To change the day
To a remoter date is all I wish ;
By that time international differences——

COUNTESS HOFENSTAUFEN.

Will sanction your Italian union
With one below both your rank and our own.
I will not have this mettlesome dispute
Between two rival too susceptible tribes
Create a barrier to nobler hopes.
If war succeed to their disunion
It will be of a transitory kind,
Either establishing geographic realms
Or sacrificing limits natural.
During that period to adjourn our home
To Paris or Vienna I propose.
If you are true and faithful to your vows,
Accomplish the fulfilment of them there.

RINALDINI.

I love Ethelga, but mine Honour too,
And this includes my native country Rome.
If Germany be Rome, then she is mine,
But if these complications end in war
What terms of amity can then exist
Where enmity is thickly sown between?
I came to thank the Count for his support,
I go to tell the Emperor the result
Of this assemblage of the hostile States
Wherein was played the great political stake
With more than your domestic prejudice.

COUNT HOFENSTAUFEN.

Your gratitude would be shown truest in this match
Which will a current feeling intimate
To dislocate proposed disunion.

RINALDINI.

If Henry were to learn that I had sought
My individual interest more than his,
I could not introduce my wife to him,
Nor he, to look further in the maze of years,
Stand sponsor to my offspring.   Let it rest,
Time has more sorrow to heal up than this,
And circumstance more weakness to conceal.
Farewell, Ethelga !   Every hour between
The wished-for consummation and this day
A tedious century will seem to me.
Countess, remember Italy in your prayers,
And in my heart your hospitality
Will, Hofenstaufen, live immortally.

SCENE IV.—*A Room in the Castle of Canossa.*

MATILDA.

My forces then have conquered !   It is time
To save Canossa in the scale of States,
Henry the Fourth shall tremble on his throne,

I will no longer humour his designs
To carry out Teutonic arms and arts
Through Italy, our devoted ultimate,
And so employ creations not his own
For his own personal private purposes.

Enter a MESSENGER.

MESSENGER.

For this intrusion I implore your grace :
I bring despatches from the Holy Court.
  [*Matilda opens a letter from the Pope and reads.*
'Greeting and high consideration to you.
This is to acquaint you that the Infidel
Styled Henry the Fourth, Emperor of Germany,
For heartfelt injuries and iniquities
Lies separated from his German States.
They have denied him, and have broken out,
And, as a tyrant, have renounced his rule.
I, as the guardian of morality,
In virtue of the power I possess,
Have banned and barred him from all sacred
  rites.
Accept yourself the blessing he has lost.'

BUONVICINO.

Possess also one kingdom he has lost.
If once the German nobles have lent ear
To this grave malediction of the Pope

Henry the Fourth will cease to govern them,
And soon will vanish his dominion south.
The popular beacon lit by this fire-brand
Will blaze on every hill in Germany;
The precept of rebellion kindled thus
Will deeply dwell within their thinking hearts
Until their crude opinions, reassured,
Shall centre on some prince that they admire,
Till they become irreparably fixed
Upon some being they will consecrate
And Gregory will also sanctify :
An image fond of their devotion deep,
Until a rival nurturing the result
Of Henry's mean and miserable ways
Springs like a panther on inferior life
And sacrifices all to glut his maw.
Let us adopt the only course in view—·
Canossa to exalt, and help the Pope.

MATILDA.

I would at Tribur first present myself,
And at the Diet certify my claims ;
I am not quite content with Lombardy:
Tuscany, with pretentions unjustifiable,
Should in a larger territory be absorbed
Where growing confidence might build a throne,
And so a monarchy stablish and create
Less liable to encroachment and attack
Than this disjointed principality.

BUONVICINO.

By leaguing with the States of Germany,
Where the stability of Henry fails,
Though with some potentates on better terms,
We might divide at once his southern realm
And free ourselves from one great obstacle
To the enlargement of your present rule.
You are the firmest friend of Gregory ;
To Tribur you should accompany him at once.
Your introduction to the Princes there
Whatever change to Henry might result
Would make us more secure in Italy,
Less liable to prone conspiracy,
Plot, and rebellion, and discountenance
Oppression, and restriction, and restraint.
Then the succession to Canossa stirs
Everyone's inquiry into the beyond.

MATILDA.

I will unfold to you the Book of Fate,
And save your calculations instantly,
And it will also further your design.
The reigning Duke of Bavaria has a son,
Should Henry fail to manage Germany,
This Prince, called Guelfo d'Este, I will wed,
And so demolishing the Alpine chain
I will these rival destinies twice unite,
And the succession will be guaranteed.

BUONVICINO.

On this first ask the blessing of the Pope,
Who, as he reins in Henry in his rule,
Might feel displeased at your expanding power ;
His temporal sway, not now so wide as yours,
Will then be more inferior in that scale
Wherein earth's votaries weigh everything.

MATILDA.

Be satisfied, he shall accompany me ;
And more, I will bequeath him when I die
Some favoured portion of my patrimonial state.
My son will yet be a great Potentate,
Than Henry an example nobler far
Of Southern jealousy and Northern wrath.
Unbound from prejudice by latitude,
In thought and action far more unrestrained,
With not a shade upon his honour cast
Of love dishonoured or of bridled sense.

BUONVICINO.

Have you informed Bavaria of this ?
The Duke may have no predilection, but dislike
For any loose acquaintance with our race ;
And trusting in his German consequence,
He thinks he can elect in Henry's stead
The Duke of Suabia as Emperor,
So that another Teuton autocrat

Will break the Alps and the two lands unite,
Strengthening the Pope and stretching Italy
Into the midst of Europe and its heart,
With doctrines and with dogmas not his own.
Again and then for ever will be tinged
A territory roundly Catholic
With views creating universal Rome
Of our agreement void, and confidence,
Supported by collateral resource
Of every hue and character but ours,
Our best decrees an echo to their laws,
Our nation but a bud of promise crushed,
Just vaunted at the moment of its birth,
Then pledged an ornament to a victor's train,
The triumph of a conqueror to deck,
Then fade into insignificance !
Matilda, know Germans hate female rule !
What if your Guelfo d'Este Italy hates?

MATILDA.

But then our children will be free of all
Deadly incumbrance to prosperity.
Our hearts are not our only Empire, thus,
Large realms with its affections governing.
Looking beyond my son will have real sway.
What if allegiance false injure his pride,
He will unite the bondsman and the free,
Distributing advantages to each
With a reluctant haste and measured tone

That true contentment gives to natural hope.
The land which now dissembles to rejoice
Beneath encouragement it cannot love
Under his sage and pointed management
Will lift itself to Rome's high parallel.
The people turbid, gloomy, or morose,
With efforts undirected, insincere,
Will claim new judgment from rights recognised,
As one to whom all principles are none.
Bavaria should have thought of this before !
He seconded the Pope in his resolve,
And stirred the Emperor's discomfiture.

BUONVICINO.

He must have watched the future : what of that ?
Bavaria's Prince has other views of Life
Than simply to annihilate the Alps.
The German race increase and multiply,
They do not centralise but emigrate,
From east to west they claim all that they see.
'Tis true they have no friend beyond the sea
That separates them from the Polar sphere,
But should they form with these a common bond,
Customs and usages amalgamate,
And join to mineral wealth wide forestry
Upon a soil luxuriant as ours,
With uninterrupted, unimpeded joy,
With thought and feeling evermore sustained,
What care can have Bavaria's Prince for you ?

MATILDA.

We are civilisation's firstfruits yet
That has fulfilled the promise of earth's spring,
On us dependent Earth may flourish till
Emancipation form crude properties
The acceptance you propose has justified.
Beyond the southern sea may be a land
In different productions rich as ours,
Our own in preference to Germany
With all their tendency to emigrate.
Are we not then the enviable State,
Observing which and honouring which all round
Must calculate on speculating yet?
Or here or there further for unripe ends
To bury seed in for all future hopes,
To join with us in prayer for the result,
And with our present hearts and winsome grace
Engage with certainty in the hazardous game,
To which the anticipated Future comes
Almost a speculator wild as we ! '
Buonvicino, war will regulate
This century the whole affairs of man,
And Europe be the theatre of alarms
Which have not shaken it for many a day,
Since Fontarabia and Roncesvalles
Burnt out those passions which Time has renewed
Into a conflagration quite as fierce,
And leaving in its ashes precious gifts

For those whose steady judgment guided them
Above and far beyond mercenary decoys,
Or the mere love of self from servile ends,
And it will then produce for other hearts
The social satisfaction of a day
Wherein all satisfaction is withheld,
As one fulfilment of a long decree
To live in the economy of years
On thrift in their enjoyment of a day.
Then I will wed a race who will secure,
Firm in the belief of all I say,
To the next age and ages long in store,
That satisfaction we dare not expect :
Willing to go to war for his own rights,
For mine if different or divisible,
But thinking that an union of parts
Into a whole not heterogeneous,
Not therefore pointing each another way
But of an opposite balanced tendency
Will subsequently turn war to account
In that day when all principles are proved
To be the origin in sound experience
Of general gain in every exigence,
Safe to us all ! true, trustworthy to each !

BUONVICINO.

I do not blame your wish to be engaged
While life's blood runs so quick and hopes are high
But at the Diet to your station look,

Its aims, its wants, and its embarrassments,
In every other skilful guise so poised
As not to appear against the Emperor,
Of doubtful crimes witness and willing proof.
Should he displease the principalities,
And with an undue confidence in themselves
To elect another Emperor they proceed,
You will not have suggested in exchange
The Duke of Bavaria, who doubtlessly
Accepting and appreciating the bait,
A vassal our fair Italy will treat,
And hold in subjugation such a race,
That were its merits known would throw him off
And with its allies in the Tyrrhene sea
An independent monarchy create.
Now as it is should he ascend the throne,
Then his son Guelfo d'Este, recollect,
Proud of authority assured his own,
Would seek a wife more suitable than you.
Regarding your domains already his
By natural superiority of place,
Let Hildebrand pronounce the ban of the Church.
You cannot gain by Henry's overthrow.
The ban pronounced, request attention then
To the arrangements this side of the Alps,
And seek and sift opinion everywhere.
Milan, Verona, Venice, and Ravenna
Are cities we might easily annex ;
They neither have a system in themselves,

And each with each at war continually,
Not only check and thwart and warp their own,
But others' satisfaction and success.
With these amalgamation would be just.
The Adriatic leads Rome to the East,
Just as Livorno to the West invites,
To Piedmont adding ports, and Lombardy
Would lend us wings to Turkey as to Spain.
Interests reciprocal would lead to terms
Of aid in difficulty and acknowledgment
Of our importance and prosperity.
So thus being ruled ostensibly we should,
Possessing some authority of rule
In future ages, when ripe time arrives,
And we from thraldom shall emancipate
A race whose passions and whose personal
    hate
Stand only in the way of their success,
That independent integrality assume
With language, faith, and customs all our own,
That will turn arts that we alone possess
To our own good, advantage, and renown,
Not theirs, whose common contumacious word
Has falsified too natural esteem,
And veiled us in a shadow of regret.

MATILDA.

Part of my plan, its origin in fact,
To give it all the value of effect

The Diet now convoked in visiting,
Was to make matrimonial union
A step not only Henry the Emperor,
From ill-used rights and confidence abused
No more a favourite in Italy,
From joint co-operation to depose,
But to be the link on this side, he on that,
Guelfo d'Este, the Duke of Bavaria's son,
Whom if proposed the States could not refuse
In elevation to the Imperial Crown.
But I will first confer with Gregory :
He may divide the princes to command
Confusion to subjection to this side
And rule the world with art as well as arms.
If otherwise I shall attain my end
It may be mine soon to perpetuate
A name Otho's successor has despised,
Or if in recognition he assumed
A friendly aspect, curtailed it behind
With cross designs and purposes insincere.
This marriage speaks of future weal and woe,
That which predominates will come the last ;
It is a brave experiment at least
To tempt Fortune to do its best or worst.
We long have lingered in the shade of renown,
The star of Glory I will thus invite,
Which, if it shine again, will never sleep.
Then if it sleeps, tell us what luminary
Will there be time enough for earth to evoke ?

BUONVICINO.

A Power discerned, but hardly recognised,
'Will then provide for that emergency !

[*Prepares to depart.*

ACT III.

Scene I.—Rouen.   Hotel de Ville.   Trial Court.

JUDGE.

Bring out the prisoner !   Who is his accuser?

CLERK.

Bonnières the goldsmith claims a crown of gold,
The fashioning of which he gave to him ;
And in return, dressed with inferior art,
A set of coloured crystals has received.

JUDGE (*to Prisoner*).

What is your name, abode, and avocation ?

CHEMNITZ.

I am a lapidary from the Tyrol.
My name is Carl Johann Chemnitz, I reside
Chiefly at Innspruck, on the Sill and Inn.

JUDGE (*to Bonnières*).

What is this accusation you prefer?

BONNIÈRES.

My Lord, one night, when all my work was done,
And I was putting everything aside,
I heard a gentle tapping at my door.
On opening it a cavalier well armed
Entered and charged me straight to make a crown,
A crown of gold set round with precious stones.
For pattern he referred me to one worn
Three hundred years ago by Charlemagne.
I undertook the business, and was paid
At once one thousand marks; in one month's time
He said he would demand the crown or gold.
Knowing the taste of foreign workmanship
The metal work I ordered from Sasselli,
A jeweller of Florence on the Arno,
The finding and the cutting of the stones
From Carl Johann Chemnitz here, the lapidary.
In one week I expect the cavalier,
And for the work which I should furnish then
Of rare fine gold set round with genuine stone,
I have but this unpresentable toy,
Crystal for gems, the metal an alloy.

CHEMNITZ.

My Lord, I do intreat you of this charge
Sasselli and myself are innocent !
The fashion and the metal work are good,

The work is of the choicest Florentine make,
The jewels are as true as the mid-day sun,
No cloud to harbour their significance
Till more convenient or more praiseworthy ;
No mist their glowing metaphor to hide
That dubitating pyx-tests oft invoke
Some incomplete industrial arts to mark,
But stood straight out, a beacon for the world
To gaze upon, admire, and idolise.

JUDGE.

Are lapidaries and assayers here ?
Produce the crown and ascertain its worth.
Bonnières, who do you say that it was for ?

BONNIÈRES.

My Lord, I am not free to mention that.
The interview with him that ordered it
And tendered me forthwith one thousand marks
Happened when light was at its darkest pitch,
But by my lamp I saw a noble face
Where War and Thought had writ expressive lines,
A brief chronology of his whole life,
But yet his name and rank I cannot guess.

       [Produces the crown, which is examined.

ASSAYER.

My Lord, this is amalgam, not pure gold.

LAPIDARY.

These gems are only crystals, often placed
On maces, crosiers, and church furniture.

BONNIÈRES.

One hundred marks I first to Chemnitz sent,
And added by a friend three hundred more.
Surely he thought that all the world were Jews,
Too glad of an exchange to care much what
They purchased of a man, or what they gave,
As all their safety lies in intercourse :
Or thought that Madness prompted the conceit,
And Folly would be pleased with anything ;
Or kings and councillors had only brains
For battles, treaties, marriages, and laws,
And added only one accomplishment—
Artifice to prevent the assassin's blow.
I could not to the cavalier who ordered this
A substitute so equivocal present.
And then he will demand his moneys else
Which I had sent to Chemnitz in great part
To hasten and facilitate the work.

CHEMNITZ.

The money sent was honestly applied.
What cause was there to doubt my honesty ?
I used my greatest skill.   Sasselli's touch,
Experienced in Italian artifice,

Supplied all that was wanting to complete
The gorgeous proof of potency and pride.
Putting the crown within a massive chest,
I sent it by a trusty messenger
At once to Rouen.   He returned again,
Saying he had to Bonnières delivered
So skilful an advertisement of art.
Before I could require acknowledgment
That all was well two gaolers forced their way
Into my house at Innspruck ! Damning proof
That Bonnières had played me false, unless
Some villain had waylaid my messenger.
These swore that imitation stones and gold
Had been by me composed into a crown,
And I must pay them down four hundred marks,
Or straight accompany them into this place.

JUDGE.

What did the Duke of Bavaria say to this?
It being his territory he could have resisted
Attempt made to transfer the case to Rouen.

CHEMNITZ.

Count Rinaldini, an Italian noble,
Saying Sasselli would be compromised,
And of the base deception guilty found
If I were innocent of the offence,
The Duke persuaded to renounce for once

The integral purity of his domain,
And with this strange, unheard-of sacrifice
All honourable principle disown.
So I was seized, and chained, and brought to Rouen,
A martyr to those principles of trade
That seek to prove in reciprocity lies
The secret of the world's prosperity.

JUDGE.

Where is your messenger?   Let him stand forth at once.

MESSENGER.

My Lord, I did but rest one night on the way,
So anxious was I to fulfil my trust ;
Macon the place, the province Burgundy.

JUDGE.

Did you observe, reposing there the night,
Any particular stranger in the town
Avoiding observation, looking round
With careful mien and ceremonial air
As if he thought of no one but himself?

MESSENGER.

I noted one who in a careless tone
Asked how I slept, and if it mattered much
If I would sup with him.   I gave consent,
But chose the room, and during supper-time

From off the chest I hardly took my eyes,
But saw the stranger never noticed this,
But eat and drank in merry, lightsome mood.
He entered into conversation oft,
Much of the Saracens and Arabia,
Conspiracies of the Empire of the East.
To Arggropulus how the poison cup
Zöe his wife deliberately filled up,
And to the Paphlagonian Michael gave
The sceptre of an unexhausted rule.
How Calaphates on his death was raised
By the same magic charm to sovereignty :
Short-sighted mortal, whose much envied sight
The keen-eyed Zöe suddenly stole away,
Then disenchanted him of the imperial robe
And with Monomachus tying the nuptial bond
Created him the Emperor of the East.
He paid the bill and I retired to rest,
Fell suddenly to sleep, and woke to find
Phœbus driving his team already apace.
My host assured me everything was right,
And I proceeded then for Rouen straight.

JUDGE.

Could you identify this man again ?
Describe his look, behaviour, and address.

MESSENGER.

He wore a velvet mantle trimmed with fur.

His face was twice on this side, once on that,
Dark with a rigid diplomatic smile
That ever said, *I'll credit thee this time
But not the next.*   His voice 'scaped from the guttural
Occasionally to a purer tone,
As if the former were his natural taste,
The latter an acquired accomplishment.
His speech was in the Suabian dialect,
With now and then a soft Italian phrase.

JUDGE.

Had he no written notes or documents
Indicative of his professional walk,
If grade he had of any sort or kind?

MESSENGER.

One of his letters had the Royal arms
Of Italy embossed upon the seal.

CHEMNITZ.

It was Gangarelli, the Emperor's minister!

JUDGE.

But he could not transfer your chest away
Without replacing it with one as good.
Do you remember any crack or knot,
Or twisted vein in any of its sides?

CHEMNITZ.

There was a small round knot upon one side
Just down below the fixing of the lid.

JUDGE.

                    [*Judge inspects the chest.*
There is no mark whatever of this kind.

CHEMNITZ.

Then it is clear the stranger has exchanged
The crown of mine and good Sasselli's art
For this vile imitation that is here.
Grant me a warrant to search through Italy,
The nest of all diplomacy and crime,
And I will venture in a single week
Before suspicious Bonnières' time is up
The guilty perpetrator of this deed
Before your sight and senses to produce.

JUDGE.

But how could he have made another crown
Fashioned with all the skill and artifice
You say you and the Florentine employed?

CHEMNITZ.

Alas !   Strange devious ways occur to wealth
When they have to accomplish secret acts
Without disturbing outside holiness.

Sasselli, in an interview one day
With Gangarelli on imperial gems,
Presented me to Henry's minister,
And after some short pleasant intercourse,
Thinking he might discover on whose brow
Our workmanship was destined to extend
Symbolic proofs of lawful potency,
Or lawless, oversetting principle,
Proposed to show it the Italian Count.
Well, not to quarrel with the Florentine,
Having considerable respect for him,
To this concession of a secret ours,—
Oh ! had it been for ever only ours !—
Erratically I ventured to agree.
Of course with an Italian's worthless wiles,
That long have trimmed and tossed about the world,
He had it copied in inferior art.

JUDGE.

What purpose had the Count for the deceit?

CHEMNITZ.

Differences have arisen in the Imperial Court,
From these fresh difficulties have inclined to rule
That Henry can no more be Emperor.
A Diet has at Wurzburg been convened,
The German States, resolving to elect
Another monarch, signify dislike

Of this their present sovereign, and theirs
At present is the turn of Destiny.
But Henry is resolved to go to war,
And with a renovated plenitude,
Relieved of their endeavours to be free,
To re-establish that Imperial state
Which moderate measures could not renovate.
Believing in success success creates,
And Gangarelli, thinking to ensure
Henry the Fourth's triumphant victory
Over the dissonant Teutonic tribes,
Obtained by this false villainous artifice,
At a slight risk and no expenditure,
A copy of the crown of Charlemagne,
Which with either at Worms or Nuremburg
By an Imperial ceremony to seal
Newly revived authority and power.

JUDGE.

This matter must be sifted carefully.
Much hangs upon the issue here and there.
It will not do an odious crime to attach
To anyone at hazard for the sake
Of gratifying clamour or demand,
Nor yet all private ends to satisfy
With a solution breathed by petulance
Into credulity's attentive ear,
Whose conscience fear has drawn into a net,
Whence we are quickly called to take it out.

Now to the money, Bonnières ; you claim
The sum from Chemnitz of four hundred marks.
But tell the name of the negotiator
For the first copy of the crown of Charlemagne.

BONNIÈRES.

His name I know not, nor his rank, nor state.
Within a week he will be at my door
And I must have the money or the crown.

JUDGE.

If you determine to prevaricate
I must commit you for contempt of court.
Upon his word hangs your indemnity.

BONNIÈRES.

This is no matter of identity.
I tell you he left good security.
If a man's oath is better than his word,
His gold is better than his dignity.
My sphere is not political intrigue.
In vain for such as us States oscillate,
Exchange to balance in the scale of power
A province, or a castle, or a town,
Quarrel about their boundaries or define,
Break this established treaty, that support,
Though Reason its withdrawal might decree.
You trust the preservation of this earth

And all the planetary orbs around,
In its more venturous principles abstruse,
To the Astronomer's philosophy.
Time has no reason for its instances
On this point or on that of incidents
Which base-born slaves perceptibly amaze.
Events and great catastrophes that appal
And bring to ruin better hearts than heads
Astrologers have ventured to detect
And from obscurity their fiat exact,
Predict their sway and their result disclose,
Deaths, births, wars, marriages, poniards, and fire.
But are we therefore all astrologers?
Plying the whip and spur in the race for wealth
We place all honour, dictatorial patronage,
Control, direction, guidance, management
Of public and of social destinies,
Adjustment of taxation, and of dues
Beyond inquiry and solicitude.
We labour on to our vocation true,
And as dissentients others recognise,
Persuasive or reluctant in acknowledgment
As fortitude or frailty fashion them.
So Man to us is but gold's register.
His name and his identity are good,
And profitable if he have no wealth.
My customer had this.   I sought no name
But I shall know him personally enough.
His name will then be current everywhere.

JUDGE.

Then he will claim the money or the crown,
And you have neither to appease him with.

BONNIÈRES.

I will a valuation straight obtain
Of Chemnitz's premises and stock in trade.
Those of Sasselli's too, the Florentine,
And sell the value of four hundred marks.

CHEMNITZ.

The intervening week should be employed
In searching through the towns of Italy
For some diplomatist who serves that State.
I think I could identify the man.

JUDGE.

But should all your endeavours be in vain,
The money must be paid within the week
Or you must go to prison for the debt.
(*To Bonnières.*) He who commissioned you their crown
      to make
Will application make to me at once
For restitution of the funds supplied.
Since you refuse to give his name, and thus
To my negotiation on the point with him

Unhesitatingly close all avenue,
I must commit you now to custody.
Gaoler, remove the applicant at once.
        [Bonnières is taken out of court.
(*To Chemnitz.*) This question is reduced to two nice
  points.
There is no evidence to certify
And no sufficient proof is to be found
Whether you and Sasselli made this crown,
And foisted on the messenger the cheat,
Or while he slept at Mâcon in the inn
The diplomatic stranger interchanged
A crown he had had made for this I see.
I will direct the Norman emissary
In Italy for this principality
Transacting business quickly to inquire
For someone of the kind elicited,
Whom current circumstance induces me
To think he was the chief conspirator.
The money yet is due on this day week,
You cannot pay it and have spent it too.
I do not choose your goods to confiscate,
For this would be an arbitrary act
And quite unworthy of this generous age ;
I will make all inquiry and due search,
Without explaining my direct intent,
For the unknown knight who at the midnight hour
Of all this difficulty sowed the seed.
You shall appear in person this day week

With your too trusting messenger in court.
By that time proper news shall be procured,
Relieving you and Bonnières of suspense.
You and the messenger now must go to gaol.
The crown both missing, and the money paid,
Demand precautions of a serious kind,
Since equity must rule, though kings preside.

        [Chemnitz and Messenger are removed.

SCENE II.—*Vercelli.   A Room in the Hotel.*

CONRAD.

I have dissembled long enough with all,
Mostly Buonvicino with yourself.
Germany reels under mismanagement,
The man who sets it right must be myself.
This is no time for moderate device
When all my father's views and ill designs
Breathe only harshness and impiety,
The settled lines of action overturn,
And mock at regular consistency
Which would have sanctified his worthless home,
Which would have clasped his friends in his embrace,
Which would have conquered or conciliated
Adjacent rivals never now his friends,
Which would have summoned both sides of the Alps

To do all homage to his government
Beneath whose star all devotees grew glad.
Now who so sad as they ! so wild as they !
Before their temper culminates therefore
From alienation to hostility,
Pointing out where the difficulty lies,
It seems to me the best and wisest plan,
Before so grave a crisis has arrived,
To raise myself to the Imperial throne.

BUONVICINO.

The army may support you or desert !
Better to raise an army for yourself,
Then fortify the position that you hold.

ODONE OF SAVOY.

Every true lance and sword of mine is yours
And all that virtue adds to fidelity,
Attempered to the love of your renown
From vales that call the sun under the Alps
To turn their creamy snows to crimson wine,
The wine to blood that boils at the indignity
So long endured by Bertha and yourself.
To penetrate the Emperor's degenerate camp
Will suit their mountain-taught hostility.
So every impulse Honour can incite,
Seconded by every pious principle,
Shall be in numbers or devotion yours.

EPPONE OF ZEITZ.

Before the Emperor moves we must decide
In measures to co-operate at once
And rectify this error of all time
By remedies I know are within grasp.
The Diet's bid may you, our stake, outbid,
But if war's hammer falls when raised by you
In an immediate vociferous claim
The promised land it covets will be yours.
And yet all will be gained by Germany
That does not wish to break imperial bonds,
But hesitates to shield imperial crimes.
So if you stablish straight a better rule
In which the best affections are esteemed,
If you forswear secret and hidden perfidies
Not sown at will but those will cull who sow,
If you will season all infirmities
With an impression of ability
That marks a staid career with all renown,
And not perplex with all proficiency
Into whatever channel work be called
With those obstructions to its course undue,
That to perfection offer no security
But mere confusion add to confidence,
And instigate no windings to one end
Lest they mature and end your own career,
I will forthwith and with all worthy aim
Support your claim to be our Emperor.

There may be zeal for your success in this
Beyond what northern rivals else might feel.
We are of cold and calculating mood,
In energy and enterprise often lax,
But of an obstinate, unflinching will,
Irregularly following our desire
Apparently as if not loving it.
It may be imperfection, or a wand
Experience exercises in its path
Before enthusiasm mortal joys
Wraps in a certain fixity of purport,
Seasoned with, but without all its fire,
The glad expression unimportunate
That Nature paints on all the South accords.
Howbeit we use sound sincerity !
Consistency, as far as moody souls,
From crude tenacity could aught attain :
And a simplicity, not of ignorance,
But of a slow engendered manliness
That dubiously broods within itself
Until a glorious gleam is uttered forth,
Dispelling rapidly all moral night
And doubling the redundancy of light.

Enter MATILDA OF CANOSSA.

MATILDA.

I hail you, Conrad ! as the rising star
That glows all difficulties to disperse !

Is your rebellion ripe as Time is ripe?
Like twins they will grow up together well,
And illustrate the page of History
With all the candour of frank union.
Bertha, your mother, I remember well,
For in the early guilelessness of youth   .
Her intrepidity instructed me
In independent arts of royal rule
That rendered irresistible my claims,
That furthered readily my noblest views,
To fortitude that lent philosophy,
And vanity sequestered from success.
What benefits therefore must accrue to you,
Inheritor of talents such as those !
Then let us join in close confederacy
This tyrant Henry straight to overthrow
With measures far superior to his now
Who has invoked desertion on his House :
Sure pomp and glory are not so ensured
Within the trap of his intelligence
That they are actually out of reach,
And Rescue and Recovery are at fault?
That arms cannot obey a second law ..
Which leads them to attain what Conscience claims,
And what it dictates worthy to secure
From Imputation, Blame, and Calumny,
So us as to a fortune to ally
In rights which Honour never compromised?
Let us compute, ratify, and conclude

A solemn and irrevocable bond
Upon this spot and in this very house
To lend all ardour, warmth, and earnest zeal
To render the domestic home secure
From harsh severity and tyranny,
Which, like the ivy creeping round the oak,
At first appears a harmless parasite,
When Fortune smiles it ravages unseen,
Then lives the assassin of the monarch tree,
In tortuous encroachments blighting it
Till it falls victim to the close embrace,
And nothing but its skeleton remains
To guard our institutions from abuse
To which humiliation paved the way,
And taught charity to repudiate
The chords of sympathy no longer touched :
These, with due clemency to fallacies
Uneven Love or even Hate has forced
Into the current of inferior life
To rival Earth's ambitious candidates
For glorious acquisitions to be gained
By a more steadily progressive course,
Securing as decided advantages
All adjuncts to developing the rest,
Let us attain by close and sinewy touch
Those unknown quantities and qualities
Whereto Intrigue and arms and arts fall short
In mystified pursuit and aimless grasp,
Struggling for what all know, of which is nought,

Since palsied adaptation of good means
The ends of expectation never win
Till expectation dies of atrophy,
And earth becomes a wilderness of weeds.

CONRAD.

How my heart beats these insults to revenge !
Rather my conscience, for the heart is more :
It is an author that impels us on
The cravings of our lust to satisfy
Whereof the gain or loss is certified
Upon soft conscience as a register.
Ah ! my poor mother ! whose sad accents fall
In their dishevelled dissonance on the ear
Filled with affection not to be returned,
In restitution of thy injured rights
I now can only draw the sword in vain !
But for my own and the more venturous part
The world upturns all its resources rich:
Summoned at once by pity and contempt
Gifts of indignity to the outer world
To warn it of its grave predicament
And censure its luxurious idleness.
With these I will my Father's wish defraud
To render this his son subservient,
On whose original birth sated desire,
Saved in fulfilment of an oracle,
Presided and announced earth's part complete,
And prophesied as possible all resolves,

And guaranteed desirable all ends,
And counted on, not courted all success
That from my dreams I sought to realise.
Cloudless my horoscopic atmosphere
My days should be more numerous than my deeds,
These last outstripping those in brilliancy :
And renovating all as from a dream
Prolific in all contrasts of itself.
Summoning my allies then I will advance,
Chastise my father and his guilty friends,
And with war's triumph hallow victory
By my enthronement.

BUONVICINO.

               You deserve a crown
If crowns are won by intrepidity.
Pope Gregory is journeying with us,
Advancing slowly into Germany
As far as Tribur, where the Diet holds
A meeting to draw on us strange events.
Meanwhile, lest a fresh sovereign they elect,
You must announce and follow up your cause.
They might advance the Duke of Suabia.
Rudolph possesses much, but yet wants more.
You will lose more by far than he will gain.
Summon your Court at Monza, I will provide
Those decorations and insignia
Wherewith authority is first announced,
And speedily advance in urgency

Any financial aid you may require.
From Tribur I will send you word, ere long,
The course the States determine to pursue.
The council may break up without result.
From different sources men have different ends,
 And different means complete the difference.
Sound judgment is a plant of tardy growth,
And personal jealousies of integral fiefs
In unanimity may paralyse
Exertions which the exigency requires
Should be at once emphatic and precise,
Since your success will answer all demands.
Should news of this reach me at Augsburg, then
I will advise them to be reconciled
Once more to the deserted dynasty
Under whose star they have lived just so long
 As to be certain of a valid worth
Which other upstarts might exaggerate,
And break, which infidelity survive,
Those foreign treaties time has sanctified.

EPPONE OF ZEITZ.

But loyalty of feeling to a cause
And not a monarch animates Germany.
Its counsels like its views are moderate,
The latter not evoked by discontent
With matter or the manner of its mould
In every object we desire to gain,

The first impartial and unprejudiced.
Each separate measure sifting prudently
As it were poison or an antidote
On which threatened vitality depends.
To your claim to be Emperor giving my help
I feel I but reflect the Diet's choice.
Then prosecute with diligence your aim,
And your success, or partial, or complete,
The Diet in approval will endorse,
In richness of resource reanimate
Replete with every virtuous principle,
Renewed protection gilding with a sigh
For some perfection never yours nor ours.

ODONE OF SAVOY.

To love like yours for heaven-born purity
My own devotion is equivalent,
Impelled by no improper *impetus*
To reach the unattainable in Right,
For Moral right must sanction every Right ;
And now ambition's lurid flame for once
That long has dazzled and to ruin led us,
In bog and quagmire mischievously set
Where human step had never ventured but
To doubt or daring seemed untenable,
Will lead to glory in no perilous path.
Prompted by prudence, nor presumptuous thus,
The heart is dead that looks unnatural,

Otherwise in prosecution stands involved
And will the States' decision counteract
Should it not be provocative of good.
Gone is stability if-based on sand,
What sand so slippery as divided faith?
With their inheritance checked by principle
On undefined and undecided points
They will even principle readily eschew.
So falling from a height they could not reach
By methods of experimentalists
That never fail the simple to attract
In evidence to others not themselves,
Who, being as they think infallible,
No evidence would satisfy themselves,
They will present in their analysis
A ripe and ready road to happiness
That man may wonder at, but never choose.

MATILDA.

Separating then on this we will agree
First to overthrow Henry's paramount
Invidious elevation and unjust,
As one which Germany will precipitate
Into a false position with its friends,
Into a strange commotion with itself,
And forge a sad example to the world.
Then to support you, Conrad, in his stead,
A model of regenerated worth,
That having led us so far from ourselves

Will in you place us deep in other's hearts,
Just now to every point so sensitive
That all attachment is at once undone,
Tainted with the remotest calumny.
One spark of fire Normandy ignites,
Another stirs up Poland to a crime,
Caledonia's king a chief assassinates,
So Saxony may experience a reverse,
Therefore it will be requisite and wise
For Germany all measures to correct
In the correction of undue advance,
Already in the rear of its device.
No measure can more elevate them now
Than to reject social disunion,
Wherein all habits henceforth are forced out,
Encouraged by unhealthy laxity
The units of their origin beyond
To poison all political cabals,
And in the utterance of further rights
Accepted truths to complicate with wrong
With principles validly elicited
'Gainst mysteries beyond our cure or care
We shall a problem, questionable now,
And we ourselves only less formally so
For its solution to the timid world
Such, and yet not importunately such,
Present in valuation of its mood,
That they shall cry 'God save the Emperor'
Who whisper now 'Out upon tyranny.'

Hasten then, Conrad, to redeem both lands
From difficulties neither of us sought.
The southern sun is but too glad to melt
To sympathy in the north feelings paralysed
By no concession to their honesty,
No thought or wish for social happiness.
Armed with this principle, assure the world
That animated by a duteous call
To rescue industry and ability,
Disowned, degraded, disinherited,
Until threatened retaliation's curse
Should raise us from the Stygian lake dissolved,
 We shall forthwith obliterate all dislike
For practices inspiring noble ends,
And Italy's heads and suffering German hearts
The price of civilisation to obtain
Henceforth unite and guide in one career.

SCENE III.—*Lanslebourg.   The foot of Mont Cenis.*

HENRY THE FOURTH (*disguised as a traveller*).

What a dread scene perpetually surrounds
Ill Fortune to prevent another cast !
The icy thrall which now my soul appals
Is mirrored in the harsh relentless Alp.
So this would my redemption stroke prevent,

But I have foiled the Diet and its threats,
Mont Cenis therefore shall not interfere
And my control of Italy prevent.

Enter party of Shepherds.

FIRST SHEPHERD.

Your highness, it is difficult to-night
The fierceness of this winter to outlive.
　　　　[*Enters a hut.　Returns, bringing a fur cloak.*
Here is a garment worthy of a king !
It is the gift of one I aided once
When all was lost except the Star of Hope,
Which lit a ray that evermore survives
To rescue those in like predicament.

HENRY.

Winter is not the enemy I dread.
Could any of you point me out the road,
Concealed and intricate as I know it lies,
Begirt by boulder-stones and avalanches,
Beset by hasty wolves and hungry bears,
And with few spots of hospitality,
Where piety wishes to anoint itself
With royal liberality, but omits
Further to guarantee the help it gives,
Through which I might attain Italian plains
There in my home you shall be well received
And entertained with every gratitude.

FIRST SHEPHERD.

The passes seldom are available
Until the winds of March dislodge the snow
Which overhangs the way.   Each cross declares,
And there are many, counting up and down,
That, reckless and indifferent to Life,
'There have been who can never tell the tale
In mortal utterance to mortal ears
Who ventured in the midnight of the year
In Nature's palace thus to penetrate.
We who belong to it dare not do that.
Without an introduction, this we know,
The risk is heavy, win you what you may.

HENRY.

What is the Winter but a Tyrant's threat ?
Sure honest men like us fear none of these !
In a good cause with a good conscience too
Fortitude will support our energy
In such a sturdy conflict to o'ercome
Obstacles constituted but to try our worth
If it be superficial or more sound.
We are a party of rich travellers
Three brawny men, and women, these less stern
Of stuff, but of endurance capable
To encounter all ordained of Providence
This is an urgent opportunity

* M

And not to be derided by yourselves
Through hesitation to fulfil our lot.
Upon these waters let us cast our bread,
To be recovered after many days.
Born evidently to achieve the task,
Which mere improbability surrounds
Till skill the difficulty dissipates,
Increasing your renown and our surprise,
Then be the staff on which we can depend,
And name the value that you put upon
The requisite assistance that I claim.

FIRST SHEPHERD.

A hundred marks apiece for each of us :
And this but will induce us to accompany
Men like yourself of stout, athletic build.
If you desire to take the ladies too
It will attach considerable delay.
They can not overtop all barriers
With strength and cool discretion fortified.
The road is only intricate to us,
To them tedious as well as laborious,
And open to accidents they should avoid.

SECOND SHEPHERD.

I have a fresh and practicable plan,
Which will at once unite two ends in one,
Safety and expedition.   We will wrap

Prepared and well-tanned hides the ladies in,
And with new ropes attached to hurdles light,
Safe and preclusive of all accident,
A knot of us will draw them to the top,
Whence they can walk at leisure to the vales.

HENRY.

Well done !   So good though singular a design
All natural obstacles at once to crush
Decrees to you at once three hundred marks.
With all due speed and energy forthwith
This project to our liking carry out.
Reaching the top the money shall be paid.
Here is a modest sum for my good faith.

[Bestows a purse.

EMPRESS.

How can I be disposed of in this way ?
Invisible danger is the worst of all.
I deem it best to reconcile ourselves
Without reserve to Nature's cruelty.
These are no times to calculate our Life,
By moderate preservation best preserved,
If after all our enemy is man,
In his misguided but planned treachery,
His broken covenants for ostensible ends,
His self-abandonment in every cause
That in a grave dissemblance advocates Hope
And gives elastic wing to constancy.

M 2

When we descend to Italy 'tis there
The Foe exists for whom we should prepare.
The sinews of our natural friends unstrung,
Opponent hearts supporters will raise up.
Heads reeling round with thoughts of rivalry
With fiendish passions fostered by the Pope
For their recovery to his ultimate rule
Italian sympathies will so enlist
That we to cope with them with nerves relaxed
By every art that Science can avail
Will be a plain impossibility,
A strife not terminable in your reign.
Then let us boldly all ascend the pass
Quite unencumbered in our natural guise,
And take the edge off opposition's knife
By not avoiding easier barriers.
Reliance on ourselves is what we want,
Which will repay the untimely sacrifice
To ready wit of false preservatives
By that approval which experience gives.

HENRY.

These shepherds would not cross with us at all
If I were to accede to your request.
You surely will not rest upon the verge
Of difficulties we had skilfully surmounted
Had you adopted practices advised.
As we are now, transfixed, disorganised,

And deadened, we should morally become
Unequal to the burden better borne
According to the law which each directs.
You will when you descend if injured first
By simple struggles with a simple foe
Invoke at once dishonour and defeat.
Foreseeing this, whoever you consult
I will absolve myself from the result.

> [*Enter Guelfo d'Este, disguised as a Custom
> house officer.*

Good shepherds, who is this stiff martinet?

FIRST SHEPHERD.

I trow not! ask the question for yourself.

OFFICER (*addressing the traveller*).

I trust you are not going to attempt
 In face of all this penetrating snow,
 And with your convoy of fair merchandise,
 To venture o'er these pitiless straits to-night.

HENRY.

I do not count myself responsible
For anything that I attempt to do
To anyone.   Art thou a State official,
To whose too partial nod we tender coin
Upon the vague, indefinite excuse

Which differing nationalities assert
To fill their coffers by restricting trade?

OFFICER.

I may detain what I think contraband.
There is report of a crown lost on this road.
I have a note upon it made out thus :
' A certain noble in a merchant's dress
Has met a traveller on the road to Rouen,
Invited him to sup with him, and mixed
A strong narcotic in his wine, and when
This had produced a somnolent effect,
A jewelled crown which he was carrying
To Rouen for an order given there
Was secretly exchanged for one of brass.'
So I must see your goods and packages
And search your papers and your documents.

HENRY.

Where did this noble merchant play the thief?

OFFICER.

At Mâcon, a small town in Burgundy.

HENRY.

Passing Besançon I remained the night,
Travelling from Germany to Italy.

OFFICER.

He would return to Italy by the pass,
Which, if 'twere open, would protect the crime.

EMPRESS.

He had no lady with him.   I myself
Have travelled with this gentleman some time.

OFFICER.

Well, I will not detain you if 'tis so,
But merely all your packages unloose,
And satisfy myself that all is right.

HENRY.

If you consider our assertion true,
Which thus exonerates us from this charge,
Why seek to pry into our packages,
Arranged compactly for the difficult task
Of carriage over steep and pointed rocks?

EMPRESS.

It would be idle waste of time and strength,
And most unnecessary in every way
After dismissing value to the wind
To make our necessaries portable
Your simple curious eye to gratify,
And add a fresh example of good taste

In distribution of nice properties
Whose use we know can never those offend
Who have a tincture of prosperity
Mixed in the unpalatable Cup of Life.

OFFICER.

Our orders are implicit.   Private views
Once acted on becoming law at once
The sinews of the State would negative.
The Friends which we should make would be our foes.
In secret they would wonder why we took
Resplendency from lost ambition's goal,
And certain taints would ride upon the feat.
Assumed that we are never to attain
The point whose worth we labour to deny
Because we are not capable of all
That man may do, therefore not of a part,
If plain perfection constitute a part,
We suffer then with every grade of Life,
Give place to every object in our way,
Further our race dishonoured must decay
Deprived of all authority and claim.

HENRY.

Without exceptions no rule can exist.
National law is but an experiment
In all its operations, subjected
From versatile opinion to a change

In application of those principles
Which advocated may or may not procure
By straight administration of the cause
The value of a presupposed effect.
Adjustment, care, and adaptation of
So many contradictory ingredients,
Guided by measurement continually,
And fostered by a timely preference
For intermediate phases valuable
In their particular points as a result,
Would in the sphere of trial precarious,
And hardly offering opportunity
All to achieve, therefore, better a part,
Render more acceptable Life's great gift,
And, not debarring good laid up in store,
Enhance and prosper that we recognise.

OFFICER.

Then in a soldier's Life, seeing that Death
Surrounds his anxious gaze on every side,
Because that visible end hovers around,
You would advise the study of principle,
And rarer laws substantiating things,
And for their subsequent perpetuity
Establish a sufficient guarantee
To be revoked, rejected, and denied,
By the insufficient process of their lives,
Which henceforth would become an open sin.

EMPRESS.

To do or suffer is the lot of Man.
But we are told we need not suffer all.
Remote oblation is our sacrifice,
Therefore in principle, sound in parallel,
All that we can do we need not perform.
The spirit of Law is not its Letters read,
But offers to the eye of scrutiny
Mature interpretations subjected
In application to less diligence,
More option and more voluntary choice.
So with discretion due to exercise,
To each the separate law that he requires
Is the discernment which the Law fulfils,
And with its object properly agrees.

OFFICER.

I would that I could render to your taste
The task that while replenishing my purse
Too often is at variance with my views,
To serve the State and raise my family
To some agreeable grade by following
Directions State-necessity suggests.
In moderate trials there remains to me
Censure and blame actually to evade
By honourable change to something more
To conscientious thoughts congenial.

This, my irregular, not continual trade.
Pursuant of its laws I now fulfil
The duty, half vexatious, so imposed
Of searching all your packages and chests,
Inspecting papers, notes, and documents.
No articles should I discover contraband,
And should you not possess the missing crown,
Your papers, should they be loyal and affected
That they include no treasonable views,
Plots to dethrone, assassinate, or kill,
Capture, or harm subjects of any realm,
Or injure or wound anyone's life or limb
You then shall cross, with these good shepherds' aid,
All unresisted, the Mont Cenis pass to-night.

> *[Turning to his employés.*

Eustàche and Adolphe, loose these packages.

> *[These advance to the packages.*

HENRY.

I have the King of Saxony's signature
To pass me, trading under his name and seal,
Between all German and Italian towns,
The only impost being excess of weight.

OFFICER.

At present you are standing on French ground.
On certain points my rules are positive.
Besides, I may recover the lost crown,

Thefts of this kind our reputation stains.

  [*Reads the papers.　Adolphe and Eustàche open*
    a chest and produce the Imperial Crown.

Ha !　There it is !　Our character is retrieved
In accusation of austerity.
No longer mock us then, unjustified
In the commission of offences mild.

HENRY.

This is a curiosity, to me
Entrusted a repository to adorn
In Florence of old venerable rings,
Crosiers, Triptyches, and Crucifixes,
With ancient witnesses of heroic deeds,
And all that can authenticate new State.

OFFICER.

This is a modern production ordered in Rouen,
A copy of the Crown of Charlemagne
By some official of the Norman Court,
Of Bonnières, an eminent goldsmith there !
Secure the merchant,　Adolphe and Eustàche.

      [*Henry draws his sword.*

Frenchmen,　beware !　you　may　more　interest
  claim
Than I will pay on borrowed capital.
Shepherds, be true to me as I to you.

SHEPHERDS (*to Officer*).

Remember thou art not in Paris now
Surrounded by thy pampered sycophants !
            [*They seize him and bind him with cords.*
Thy accusation may be true or false,
These gentlefolks our courtesy have claimed,
And offered in return a liberal sum.
Therefore with all the packages they have brought
They shall the Mont Cenis pass ascend at once.
        [*They bind assistants, and place the three in a
        cave.*

HENRY.

Kind-hearted, noble friends ! and aspirants
To all that Honour offers Honesty,
Henry the Emperor of Germany claimed,
And by his well-timed liberality,
Your aid and help as mountaineers procured.
You are the seed of a nobility
Which future kings will rescue from dismay,
And their impoverished domains retrieve
As warriors from ruin and defeat.
That ornament the burg official found
Is the imperial crown I always wear
In the Cathedral, Court, or Citadel.
Your guiding star it shall be during Life ;
To him who wears it any time appeal,
And he will answer your demand forthwith.

Strange measures I am executing now
Which, like other proceedings of the age,
Creates or hazards all stability.
When these performed the future shall admire,
Say this was Henry the Fourth of Germany
Whose hazardous fortunes risked with us at last
On Mont Cenis our ancestors restored,
And rendered practicable a career
That otherwise ill-luck had blotted out.

EMPRESS.

I and my maidens joyfully attest
Our gratitude for this most welcome help,
And further we will, fearfully, alas!
But trusting in your energy and skill,
Permit you to enclose us in these hides,
Thus lightening your anxiety and care
For burdens that would else have been too great.

SHEPHERDS.

Never a whit!   Our labour will be joy
When you with such a grace our skill employ.
Our flocks demand attention on the hills,
Our sheaves require assistance in the vales.
Between surfeit and sterility we trust
To raise a healthy race for better hopes
When Earth shall be a stage more in advance.

HENRY (*bestowing a purse*).

Here are a hundred marks !   Let us ascend,
I wish to reach Turin within three days.
To Susa one of you shall come with me,
And on returning bring you gold enough
To add fresh land to lands already rich
In reputation for such character
As you this evening have exhibited,
The credit and the honour of this age,
Henceforth proverbial to the end of Time !
   [*Shepherds enclose the Empress in hides, and the
      party ascend Mont Cenis.*

SCENE IV.—*Vallombrosa, near Florence.*

COUNT RINALDINI.

I thought to meet her here ! but it is late.
The nightingale is due.   The skylark sleeps.
Delay not, Time, thy unmeritorious course.
My brain reels round with Love not to be cured
By careful glimpses of Philosophy,
Though if of this Love fails in its chance game,
Which it can never do if Love is Love,
What a deceptive flatterer withal !
Wreathing the heart round with rich promises

It never can fulfil.   A passion, yet a plague.
What will the Emperor think if he knows this ?
But if he lose his Crown what matter then ?
The impediment between our match withdrawn,
I then shall claim Theresa as my bride.
Bavaria and Canossa save my heart !
And Conrad be our new-born Emperor !
Remember, Gregory, thy politic ban
That criminates, then punishes royalty,
Till it becomes more virtuous and less royal,
What labours for thy thin encouragement.
This Love shall the same royalty direct
That will the simple patriot desert
If he be sound and true to kith and kin,
Protracted evermore with rare device
The oracle that continually directs
The duties of the altar and the hearth.
'Tis this Theresa that would make my bride :
My heart this medicine ; that the head prescribes
If Henry should once more be prosperous
More favourable but less fortunate
To have prosecuted the far bitterer course
A feigned attachment to a worthless claim
Of similar rights to emptier instances,
Collateral views to parallel urgencies,
Capabilities reflected in a glass
That must the same abilities produce,
Till I had stamped with youth on mellow age
The forged fact of a false heritage.

Now should the stream of Time disclaim its own,
Or an undercurrent of affection roll
All unobserved down to oblivion's sea
To perish totally unrecognised,
Not a vague symptom of the transient touch
That helps or waives away suggested realms
Will have qualifications disorganised
That long have these supported for one end,
Nor will the ultimate happiness of mankind
To the ruin or conservation of a lie,
For sophistry or logic to support
Too nicely measured, have been sacrificed.

     [Conceals himself behind a tree.

   Enter THERESA SASSELLI.

     THERESA.

What a forlorn and hopeless widowhood!
Chemnitz is taken, and I am alone.
What has he done, and who has perjured him?
The Age is rife with national jealousy,
But unsuspected individual crime
Should have proved too inferior a fruit
To grow just now upon the social tree.
My father's skill, taste, and ability,
Gone to adorn some wild immoderate head,
To let irregularity on lease
To anyone who gives him his support,
And but for my exertion furthermore,

       * N

And in integrity to save our name,
The busybody intermeddling world
Now careful that the model be not lost
Had stole away the bright original.

        [*Rinaldini emerges from his concealment.*

Ha!   Who walks here in this secluded place?

RINALDINI.

'Tis I, Theresa! business with the bank
Brought me to Florence; having finished that,
I wished to rid me of uneasy thoughts,
But could not find exchange in any heart.
These times are difficult to analyse,
Containing ruinous ingredients
Which balk solution and imperil brains,
But your fond form their equanimity
Replaces in the balance once again.

THERESA.

The Forest is more beautiful than me!
Its colours, lights, and shades more curative.
Only a modest maiden's moderate arts,
However loved, however slighted, can
Seldom the canker-worm of care remove.
I have not seen you lately, and I thought
War and the tumult of State rivalry
Had taken you beyond a woman's sphere,
Where acceptable talents and approved
Are soon endowed with Fortune's iron rod.

RINALDINI.

You know, Theresa, that when last we met
It was on terms of closest confidence.
We hoped the Future soon would welcome us
At Hymen's altar as true votaries.
Your father had not given his consent,
But you are old enough to do without
His guidance and direction obsolete.
The world is yours in gravity and years
That ruled you with its years and gravity.
I have not startled some rebellious tone
I trust in this avowal of your state
Against those obligations which you viewed
Only with pleasure later to fulfil?
With earnest of review and with good faith
You must have weighed them well within your heart.
You must have analysed a woman's lot.
You must have calculated how much good
In her behaviour or ill depends.
Let no ill-natured spirit jeopardise
My future happiness or your good name ;
No inadvertent unexpected light
Maturer judgment dazzle and confound,
Nor comprehension in its winding road,
Whose grasp wanton deliberation mocks,
Dally with Truth until it disappears
And leads Confusion to assume a mask
That cannot long deceive a man like me.

Known as a favourite of the Emperor
I have considerable opportunity
Of giving your class that encouragement
Which leads it to prosperity and wealth.
I do not mean by this to throw a shade
Of imputation on your father's name.
I know that he has no embarrassments.
With perfect insight into character
He fathoms easily treacherous designs,
And fraud and forgery detects and foils.
This proves his sound respectability,
Built upon regular and methodical
Adherence to precepts that not to antiquated
Nor yet to modern tastes antipodal
Lead all round to a liberal management
Who wealth amass, disperse, or thrive upon.
But looking to Old Age and altered Times,
When victimised to heedless circumstance
The inroad of Fatality appals,
And friends are no more to be made at sight,
In whom, Theresa, will you place your faith?
You cannot live alone when he is dead,
Then linger not with him when he is old.
I love you, and I only think of you :
For Life would link your fortune to my own :
Dissimilar enough as now they are,
Yet as extremes may meet therefore will they,
And in our joint co-operation now
The range of action so far circumscribed

Will to our sons in action be more free,
Making them brave in opinion, wide in deed,
Bold aspirants to all heroic points,
Heirs to sound principles from opposite,
And sires to present impossibilities.
I have a palace and a large estate,
The admiration of the poor around.
Share you my title with me, and when once
The choice companions that I shall select
Shall give to you the watchword of my class,
You will be able to adorn our sphere
With more accomplishments and rival arts,
And multiply, and vary, and protract
Pleasures that only we patricians know.

THERESA.

Your words are good as you yourself are noble.
Since you were with us last much has transpired
That has not reconciled me to what then
I willingly avowed in principle
To be the mood of my dependent life.
I have re-modelled all my early views.
They were those bright conceptions of a day
When all is gold that glitters, cancelling
Improvident sorrows by providing good
To hover round me.   But the day has fled,
At least its dawn—its zenith hid in clouds.
So I resolved to negative such first thoughts
And flee such fond impressions ill-advised.

My father prospered, and of that curious craft
For which Florence is famed became the head.
Now look to what such reputation leads.
One evening late a lapidary arrived ;
He bore with him a strong and massive chest.
Was it an imperial decoration then,
To mark plebeian industry and skill ?
No, but an emblem of imperial might,
A crown, the true one worn by Charlemagne,
Barren of produce lest if singular,
With orders to be executed swift
A copy in the finest gems and gold.

RINALDINI.

Did you not know the bearer of the crown ?

THERESA.

What if I knew him ? Would that I did not !
A lapidary ; 'tis a modest trade,
Or all the world would steal his vivid gems,
And they use secrecy in everything
Till they have done their work and won their pelf.
This stone-cutter returned in three weeks' time ;
My father had exhausted all his art,
And from the stately model had produced
Work that the gems around hardly set off,
With all the varied rays of the angular sun,
In wrought and burnished, chased and fretted
    gold.

It was enclosed at once in the massive chest,
A cheque was tendered on our Florence bank,
And with the crowns the lapidary vanished.
The bank of Florence on the morrow broke,
And to the honest only so proclaimed
That all our work and skill in art was lost.
My father, stunned, recovered from this shock
Only to find more obligations due,
And lacking friends to meet them in good time
Lies now a prisoner in the Florence gaol.

RINALDINI.

This very day, Theresa, I just lodged
At the new Bank, Tarchetti's, situate in
The Via Vinegia, six thousand marks.
As an Italian, and of southern birth,
Italian difficulties are always mine.
Your father then shall make this sum his own,
But ere I sign the cheque you must declare
As Countess Rinaldini you will stand
Betrothed from now, and in due course become
Next the patrician's bride, and then his wife.

THERESA.

What would not his own daughter do for one
So tried and injured as my Father is?
But now, Count Rinaldini, still they say
Those that have travelled into Germany,
And different social complications know

That only they know who look deep within
The core and heart of Time's untempting fruit,
And are not caught by externalities,
In furtherance of a report that once
Acting upon I bade you cease all hope
Ever to contemplate our union,
That you have there to feelings utterance given
Once more to one, and for another cause
Which here to-day again you exercise
For me, for Italy, and good Florentines.
The Heart is its own Record, and I feel
Desirous of enscrolling there the truth.
Still there survives in Germany one who
Precedence in your affections has attained.
The story runs that she is of your birth,
That there exists no possible obstacle
To the fulfilment of your union,
That even the Emperor himself consents.
Before I carry out in recognition views
Approved by both of us when first we me't,
Since Happiness is the first-born of the Heart,
Vacillating prosperity that of the simple Head,
Your positive assurance I must have
That in the eyes of all the world, between
Ourselves, and furthermore between you both,
Completely now, finally, and for aye
The marriage once contemplated between
Ethelga Hofenstaufen and yourself
Shall be disowned, renounced, and broken off.

RINALDINI.

Then an Italian noble is no more
Than an adventurer, setting up for aught
That may or may not meet the world's demand !
This is a grave assertion, and I feel
The insinuation wrongs my pride and dignity.

THERESA.

Words had not lent expression to the thought,
But busybodies quickly fill the gap
Which by their inattention idlers leave.
There is a wish in all Italian ranks
To match themselves with untried Germany.
Our arts united with their rugged strength
And wished-for independence, never theirs
Until it fall in civilisation's train,
Make up a home of contrarieties,
Therefore I quite forgive the thought
In the broad range of Earth's admeasurements
That forced you to attachments such as these.
But friends will some day come to my relief,
Anxiety is therefore not despair.
Unless you promise to break off this suit
Put up your cheque, and I shall leave the spot.

RINALDINI

Theresa, never doubt my constancy.
As fresh impressions last the longest, know

No rival to yourself shall fill your place.
The loss to me would be too keen a blow
To value pride of earthly circumstance
And all it could concede or verify.
Marriage without a bond of unity,
Stronger than circumstances similar,
Would prove a blight and curse upon the sphere
Which round a happy pair should concentrate,
And every combination would fall dead,
Albeit encouraged by the magic spell
Concord and international harmony,
And its intentions wholly neutralised.
Some slanderer for some unworthy end
Has ventured to amuse you with a tale
Which, had it a foundation, I will swear
From this a quarrel has disruptured it.
I here abjure all German artifice
Protracted and advanced by subtlety
That would acquire then poison sympathy.
Then save your father in emergency !
This crisis in your fortunes should supply
Discretion, prescience, and sacrifice.
Your wishes and your tastes if different
For one good object learn to set aside.
What if your father in imprisonment
A victim falls to his tumultuous thoughts?
I, your best friend, will be your husband too.
Seal the agreement, and I sign the cheque.
The spirit of your sensitiveness in this

Devotion to the natural shrine of worth,
Your Life will characterise with that of Saints
Who shed divine intentions on our will,
And raise us to a level more divine.
Send me not to a disappointed home !
Consign me not to sorrow and regret !
Disable not my patriotic zeal !
Condemn me not to social fleeting joys
Whose very essence once the love of thee
Foregone would be the mockery of woe !
Extend, enlarge, and vivify my scope
In life's exertions by your confidence.
And your own happiness and my own secure
From envy, from anxiety, and doubt,
To which so many souls estranged are lost.
So regulating feelings not distraught,
We shall fulfil a holy destiny,
Blessed in the trust of what we exercise,
By faith in good and charity thrice blessed,
Thrice welcome to the world whose selfishness,
That bane and curse it learns too late to fly,
And in a bond of virtuous unity,
The cause of crime and sin dispelled and broke,
Those less temptations we must live to meet
Joined we shall learn the secret to avoid.

THERESA.

Lived there within the spirit of this age,
When virgin purity, itself a host,

As an example was more valuable
Than all that might ensue from its escheat,
I would, in spite of one sad circumstance,
Virtuously this pressing overture refuse.
But you have added your sincerity,
Which I had questioned now for many a day,
And for its absence banned you from our door ;
And to enhance sincerity given proof,
In the renunciation of the suit
With Ethelga Hofenstaufen of Saxony,
Of truth in the fulfilment of those vows
You pledged to me in early bygone hours.
A man can only love once and for all,
His passion be an undivided whole,
Consistent and undeviating, blind
To everyone that welcomes him but one.
Then she would gild his company with charms
That would create an universe of joy.
If I then am your beacon star of light,
And I alone to guide from error's path
Mortality too frail to be alone,
I will replenish to Italian stores
More, far more, than she might have gained
By intercourse irregular beyond.
Better to know the worth of what we have
Than seek to know the value of too much.
It is in happy homes and cordial hearts
A nation starts for universal rule,
Whose careful web when insecurely knit

With the foul skeins of close diplomacy
Lets out the treasure that it seems to win,
And leaves to unsuspecting risk at last
For want of care continual and extreme
Instead of all remuneration due,
Poor consolation as its recompense.

RINALDINI (*taking her hand in his*).

Theresa, we are one for evermore !
Here is the cheque I cannot now refuse.
Tarchetti of the Via Vinegia on receipt
Of this will pay you down ten thousand marks.
One half of this your father will release.
Early to-morrow morning I will call
In Via Pietrapiana at your house.
There will be no impediment I trust
In the paternal confidence in me.
Then after coming to close settlements
With all financial claims of every kind,
Recovering good opinion where it fails,
And Fortune speeding wheresoe'er it halts,
We will place Florence on a footing with
All towns in Italy and Germany,
In skill and honest sympathy as well.
Adieu ! Theresa, from that happy hour
Futurity all happiness shall date,
That with a borrowed gift will animate
Welcome forebodings of its taxed estate.

               [*They embrace and part.*

ACT IV.

SCENE I.—*Room in a Castle in Turin.*

AZZO, DUKE OF BRUNSWICK.

These are strange times that vary in their course
Until perplexity is all their rule.
I do not know what cause we may define
To give the uncrowned crowns and crowns disturb.
Is Man then thus the fool of Circumstance?
Or is his Wisdom reaped from Exigence
That Circumstance had always called his own
If he had been in league with it for aye?
Time was when errors never were like these,
When each position was a metaphor
Ruled by itself, or never ruled at all,
By Law, Theory, or Criterion,
And vaunted not in vain its excellence,
That excellence encouraged in the bud
Might gain maturity beneath the sun;
But when the flower expanded into fruit

The tree was blighted by the hand that nursed
And promised to repay experiment.
Then came the satellite of popular will,
And watching slowly its pourtrayed career
I see it will transgress the Orb of Day,
The embodiment and principle of rule,
And the kind renovating blaze put out.

Enter ADELAIDE OF SUSA.

ADELAIDE.

Say !   Am I safe within these barriers ?
A moment and my stake of life is lost.
A fugitive and yet a queen am I,
If queen can be applied to one who finds
How small a charm reposes in that word !
Azzo, can I rely on your good faith
Not to betray a woman in her need ?
Not to divulge the cause of difficulty ?
Henry of Germany, to whom I am allied,
Has trampled on the duties of a king,
And broken also every altar bond
That could have blessed a now deserted home
His tyranny to his son, iniquity enough
To beggar all domestic policy,
Would have resulted in a civil war
If blood has kindred blood in human hearts.
Oh, then what God, if woman fail to please,
Can save her from destruction and a grave ?

AZZO.

The fact that you have stated is at once
Of all our alienation the true cause.
If it will raise and vivify your hopes
And satisfy the cravings of neglect
Know that at the Diet held at Wurzburg
Henry was excommunicated by the Pope,
And one half Germany renounced his sway.
In so far you must surely feel avenged.

ADELAIDE.

I thank you for this comfort.   Know you next
Where I can find a temporary home ?
Where, as a daughter of the King of Prussia,
I may do good in kindness and advice   .
To those who have not suffered like myself?

Enter the COUNT OF PIEDMONT.

COUNT OF PIEDMONT.

You know of all the troubles of this date,
You Germans are so quick in thought and mood
As were Italians in Earth's early days.
It is strange news I hear from Normandy :
The Duke, who hates the King, utters a wish
His fertile territory to expand
Beyond the limits the false sea has made.
His father penetrated to the East with arms
That shook our confidence in Southern steel,

The son desires Britain to invade,
And those rich slopes and verdant vales that teem
Now with the fruit of Saxon industry
To nourish with the sweat of Normandy.

AZZO.

'Tis better than to claim a conquest here.
Thank Heaven the world is wide enough for all.
The most fastidious now can glut his taste
And never quarrel with his jealous friends.
But Britain has no friends except itself.
Why does it not stretch out its wings and fly?
Is it a Dove that lets the Eagle pounce
Upon its measured and retarded plume
And guzzle up the covenant of Life?

ADELAIDE.

No Dove is England, but an Eaglet, Duke!
Not fashioned yet by sterile Nature's skill,
And armed with all the teguments of fight,
It will, when you have taught it all your arts,
Assert its own imperial Right of Way
O'er all the regions of this ransacked Earth;
Provide itself with all Life's requisites,
Support itself on the most fanciful food,
Replete itself with carnal luxury,
And nurse a bold and insubordinate troop
All order far and wide to violate.
Its present aspect now is but a mask

* O

Its future realisation to conceal.
We know not in our penury of thought
That versatility of action its device
To win and move the spirit of the Age
Its enterprise with Courage to endow,
Till as the fish that on its rocks abound
The Rulers of the Earth fall in its net,
Fat victims to a surfeit of the Land,
Whose points material venerably soft,
Well seasoned immateriality to resist,
Should have been hardened by vicissitude
Dipped in that Styx, beyond whose waves they live
Who Earth, Sea, Fire, and Air adorn the most.

COUNT OF PIEDMONT.

The Norman Duke has issued a decree
Inviting all to join his moving force.
I cannot say success is positive.
Once a defeat and the Islanders will turn
In hot resentment to his cruelty.
Surely they never will obey *his* laws.
Show of authority will be powerless
His banner unsupported but by the winds
Desirous all extravagance to inflate
Whether or not its symbols are disowned.
But Saxon chivalry an arena wants
To exercise its secret energies,
Those energies that would be best on the field
Where martial honour follows martial might.

Madame, were Henry your deserving friend
I would with satisfaction prophecy
Herein would be the furtherance of his rule.
Saxony defeated, Saxony will not be,
Which would a stubborn element remove
From the rebellious German vassalage.
Architects then from their dark forestry
Would renovate Italian palaces.
Your foresters would till volcanic land,
Nourishing to excess indulgences
Which I could almost wish common to all.
It is an untaught element to require
A savage tutor not a worthy one
If all his virtues from original ore
Must be by strange ferocity purged out
Before it can be blended with the mass
That in exchange compares and rates the world.
Adelaide, have you been publicly divorced
From Emperor Henry?

ADELAIDE.

                    Should I then be here
A stranger and a suppliant if I had?
I love Henry no longer!   Cruel he,
Submissive me, with a King's blood within?
Is any contradiction half so rash,
Acquaint me, prince, in all your breadth of walk?
Not with my presence thus to weary you
And tire you with the virtues of my sex,

What course can you advise me to adopt
So not to be a wanton sacrifice
To the base passions of a reckless age,
When I have cut the principle of crime,
Of outrage, and of brutish violence
Off by the root in its most favoured soil,
Whose sun and shade alternately were sick
Its poisonous indulgences to cement
With other fragments of exalted Life,
Till orgies fattened frail felicity,
And fanned the sails of an intemperate bark?

AZZO.

Summon the Church its edict to pronounce
Annulling that alliance. Once more free,
Selecting first some prosperous abode,
You can yourself maintain a separate Court.
Surround yourself with all the great and good,
Then, having closed the Sorrows of the past
Within the cavern of oblivion,
What opportunities they must afford
For a more fancied, faithful union.
Your youth and birth and majesty of mien
All potentates will soon conciliate :
State festivals will show up worth and wit :
At pointed intervals restrain the tide,
And exercise all diplomatic art
To wear the diadem that you have lost.
There are more crowns than that of Germany.

Across the Alps on this side and on that
Dominion raises less in tyranny
And more on competence of wide control,
And in bad hearts is many a virtue lost,
Till rescued by an Union of Love.
On such a chance hang worlds of Happiness
Massed into feverish impenitence
Of all creation by unsocial art,
Equivocal reserve, and false surmise,
Which your superior principles could despoil
And from those mysteries develop Hope.

ADELAIDE.

Too well is Earth enabled to unfold
The unravelled plan of restituted rights,
But these forbode much evil in my heart
United with this greed of Normandy.
Continual changes mean denied advance,
Not yet the recompense of all our toil,
And till we be by consequence assured
All circles will be gashed by perjured sin,
Vice and sedition creeping cautiously
Where Time upon his heritage has laid,
Encumbered with too much for space too small,
Unequal burdens for expanded heads
To prop their accumulated infirmities.
To enter once more into scenes like these,
With hopes already by experience crushed
The sphere, however good or affluent,

The range for good or ill however large,
With every kind accessory to aid,
And one ready to add encouragement
And join security to proffered aid,
Would be adventurously credulous
Of a stability by States renounced.
I therefore, Azzo, cannot register
Adherence to a vow I have foresworn.
And though one instance stands not good for all,
And all the samples of our simple life,
And all the evolutions we complete
Have no resemblance to the original plan,
Nor can the truth be attained by reference
To things already proved beyond a doubt,
I cannot move design with fortitude
Royal amenities to undertake,
Helped and even relieved by princely love,
Until events and circumstances hope,
Extol, reanimate, and justify,
And place me in their fitful patronage,
Without which Love is but a dream indeed.

       [Azzo prepares to depart.

But give me your protection for an hour,
Perhaps the only doubtful one of life,
And you will not regret this interview.

AZZO.

When first I saw Henry our Emperor's wife
I did not quite expect to find her thus.

Cruelty and harshness have demolished quite
The gift and ready tact of royal birth.
What can have roughened over-haughty tones
And made the edge of skill to counteract
And to repudiate in their first cause
The foolish gains of avaricious ill?
However, I have done!   I have pronounced
In saying what was easily explained,
Views not yet quite so easily explained,
Or willingly urged with so much willingness.
In my insinuations you discerned
That I should like the first place in your Court,
And with the intervention of the Pope,
All previous difficulties stamping out,
A new alliance had been sealed between
Our famous houses.   I shall not ask you to affirm
In plainer terms that this can never be.

> [*Turns to the Count of Piedmont.*

Piedmont, 'tis you that seems to take my place,
And burn in the affections of this dame!
It is your soil, and I perhaps your guest,
But I as a prince despise your hostile roof
And all its weight invoke upon your head.
Draw and defend yourself—I challenge you!

COUNT OF PIEDMONT.

Then stand your ground, your second Jealousy.
Mine free and independent Rectitude.

> [*They draw swords and fight.*

ADELAIDE.

Help ! Murder ! Fire ! within, without there, help !
           [*Enter the Guard, who separate them.*

COUNT OF PIEDMONT.

Treason ! stand off, the sword is Italian law.

AZZO.

An honourable quarrel stopped like this ;
This is your famous Southern chivalry !

ADELAIDE.

There is no regular cause for an affront !
I have decided not to hold a Court
Until the Pope has sanctioned my divorce.
Pending his resolution and decree
I shall directly from Turin depart,
And at Verona in the convent there
Map out the problem for my future life ;
There is therein less of futility
Since expectation is more moderate.
Brunswick, put up your sword, and Piedmont yours,
Preserve your courage for a better cause.
Your satisfaction will not bless this world
In these new troubles with prosperity.
Symptoms of further difference and strife
To early fatal difference succeeds.
Are you so ready for emergencies?

To which of your supporters and tried friends
Have you bequeathed your sense and bravery?
Be sure of this, or you have them betrayed
Into a maze of misery and woe.
Patience can organise resources zeal
And readiness to quarrel might disband.
First snatch the sword from the stern tyrant's clutch
And scatter all his menaces to the wind,
And so discordant errors rectify.
Then those conditions, binding as before,
Relieving thus the grief that you deplore,
You may more conscientiously restore.

SCENE II.—*Hotel de Ville, Milan.   Night.*
Room lit with lamps.

BUONVICINO.

It is the midnight hour, and I dread
With darkness some of the triumphs of the day ;
But now the triumphs of the day are staid
By the turned sand-glass of a mood abjured
These night administrations, never wise,
Never by sedulous Fortune re-assured
As to the grade of their Prosperity,
Which halts, and vaccillates, and hesitates,
A moment up, an hour discomforted,
How they their gain demolish, though foreseen

Foreshadowed in the mirror of dismay !
How cry all welcome such a period
Since that the pale rehearsal of great deeds
Is marred within the precincts of the night,
Wherein are sown the seeds of consequence,
That to the daily vision starting up
No secret of their origin betray,
But blazing to the eye in falsity
A lesson read to the admiring world,
That trembles round to the fallacious point,
Or wears un moved the Star of Victory?
However, Conrad has the lesson learned
Which we have come to teach and not to learn
I would herein the accuracy prove
Of this indisputable axiom,
Wherein mankind, labouring at its designs,
Henceforth desired certainty should reach,
Not in anticipation of the end,
Or in fulfilment too methodical,
Or feeling aught remotely covenanted,
But of our notions placing in the van
Reliance, faith, and cordiality,
Passato pericolo : gabbato santo !
In hospitable adoption of a result,
Precepts and principles having acquired
To all safe round us and to those our own,
There may be yet those more deserving found
This interference so to justify,
From family rivalry than could have sprang.

Henry hates him who excommunicates him,
And then sows tares among the imperial wheat.
My Lady of Canossa knows too well
Imperial policy is imperial need,
And as she gives her left hand to the Pope,
Will give her right to some new potentate,
Who, instigated by ambitious jealousy,
Dislikes Henry the Fourth of Germany.
I do not think that that same man is he
Who will serve her the best turn of the two,
Young Conrad holding in comparison.
She is infatuated, and decides
With the false judgment of mistaken zeal
Against attachments comprehensible,
Which carry with them, void of all conceit,
The will of the uneducated world
And the staid fervour of more moderate men.
She may enlarge the sphere of her designs,
But what is strength without solidity?
A wanton bubble of ephemeral life !

Enter CONRAD.

CONRAD.

Welcome to Milan, Buonvicino !   Here,
To-morrow, is my coronation day.
Thus far I have succeeded in my plot
Disastrous consequence to overturn
By consequence unsullied and unstained.

Congratulate me on this victory,
Obtained by methods by my friends approved,
And everyone whose conscience is not seared
By vice's too conciliatory smile
On unpaid work and imperfect villainy.
How novel views of Germany my own
Race unimpeded through my rapturous head !
How visions full of measureless design,
Accomplishments of sure and radiant scope,
With wandering intrigues of curious point
And matchless schemes of fulsome arrogance
Wrangle for the approval of my heart !
But know you, Buonvicino, where she is,
My step-mother, the ill-fated Adelaide ?
She seems to have deserted her new home
Without intentions for some unknown sphere,
And might, revenging insult and neglect
By some inferior measure of her own,
All my new-born authority neutralise.

BUONVICINO.

Her policy was not to negative
A step that, hesitating on success,
Her husband, the unnatural Emperor,
Externally as she internally disarmed.
But now you have established a fresh rule,
And all but in the name the old dismissed,
I will not add to your solicitude
By saying that she finally resolved,

By doctrine of resource some women find
To their emergencies or consciences suitable,
The practice and profession of a nun
In a convent at Verona to embrace.
But yet she ventured on that uncertain style
Of independence too dependently,
On theories magnificently poised,
Wherein such good is found, but evil more
For those whom no continual content,
Measured to their own measure large or small,
Providence has given, and enjoined therewith
Continuance universal and consent.
Nevertheless of Royal birth and hopes
The Princess of Canossa, loving much
Piety and compassionate Charity,
And Adelaide your relative therefore more,
Has offered her an honourable home.
There in Canossa she can rectify
From observation of her ventured dues
Omitted points of ceremonial rites,
And in the circle of Augustan friends
Enjoy a home as good as she has lost.
Such is the passive share a woman takes
In all the trials of her mortal lot,
Leaving the initiative stroke to man,
Who, more responsible, is more restless thus,
Intriguing seeks the current of affairs,
And in preserving regulates observed
The indications of the giddy shoal.

To-morrow is your coronation.   Beware
You do not press good Fortune on too far,
And be the victim of its absent fits.
You should be well assured that your reserve
Is strong enough to fortify defeat.
If this upon your banners should attend,
Your failure is the shadow of presumption
Betraying with reproach its every step.
Yet seeing your success is also ours,
I shall throughout aid and assist your claim
And every difficulty turn aside
That doubt and malice fling across your path.
With this intention fraught I have resolved
Your coronation shall be dignified
With all the grandeur that the element
Of high initiation into rule,
To previous instances superior,
Can be established by and sanctified,
With this conformity encouraging
I hesitate not to re-establish rule
From treason to fulfilment rectified,
And therein justify those who obey
As far more righteous than their forefathers.

[Rings a hand-bell.

Enter Heralds bearing a crown.

BUONVICINO.

Accept, Prince Conrad, emblematical
Of future sway and vindicated power,

In guise additionally redolent
Of virtues not remotely verified,
But boastfully, and more sensationally
As worthy the importance of the stake
This faint emblazoning of imperial rank !
In elevated rule and pride of place
Matilda of Canossa's guarantor
Of her fidelity in your support.
And as it potency confers on you
Now and for many future unrolled years,
May reputation you confer on it
As in the eyes of all to render it,
And all it signifies and simplifies,
Such venerated objects most revered,
As will from insult that have nigh outweighed
The symmetry of their joint union,
To recognition and recovery
Of that which constitutes successful realms
United Italy and Germany,
Now and to all posterity redeem.

Enter Friends of CONRAD.

CONRAD.

Behold, good friends ! this proof, and loud support
In social value of my righteous claim
To unpresumptuous prerogative !
Ah, Buonvicino ! neighbour kind and true I
Whose deeds well justify the fond expression
Man puts upon his earthly circumstance,

In his probation had my father had
A counsellor so sagacious at his side,
Reminding him of proper decencies,
And on that basis elevating him
To Transalpine and Cisalpine control,
Creating admiration and respect,
Diffusing joy and happiness around,
With consolation circumventing Death,
And building up a Future, colouring this
To such example with obedience blind,
Which should be to the pattern fulfilment true,
As is the fruit fulfilment of the flower,
He had not so resigned Imperial rank.
Welcome the aid Matilda of Canossa
This fortifies, divines, and promises.
In all I do henceforth her views and ours
My laws and proclamations shall direct,
So that they shall not say Conrad the Emperor
Has reassured rebellious Germany,
But the Co-operation of events
By conscientious Scruples multiplied
Has raised its spirit to the pinnacle
Which from false worship and devotion changed
Has changed ever to the right that principle
Which makes or ruins many loyal souls.
Had I the slightest kinship to false thoughts
This glorious type of responsibility
Would chase the base intrusion from my heart,
And as it all irradiates around

With the close semblance of immaterial Light
It will encourage false humility
To step beyond encumbrances enforced
That with too cheerless spirit alternates
Till virtuous resolution dissipates
The two extremes that animate mankind
That do not know the middle Course to choose.
How shall To-Morrow's dawn such minds relieve,
Encouraged long but not till now consoled.
In vanquished hopes and baulked expectancy
Full many now had sought a foreign home
Who filling up the gap that we had made
Had plucked up nationality by the root,
Whereas I only tear aside the branch
Burdened with all the fallacies of art
Which eaten by the eager would have paid
For them all debts that fallacy has incurred
In that their dissolution had occurred.
Questions like these the Diet should have raised,
And based the precept of reserved Control
Upon disorganisation of the whole
If not by arms not artfulness reassured,
Arms that do not with speculation sleep
Until the day fulfils their giddy dreams
But life and limb valorously cast in the scale,
A hazard for solicitude and care
To be returned in remedies renowned
For all existing and expected ills,

P

And the diffusion of advantages
Only the sword discloses and extends.

BUONVICINO.

In the Cathedral here at the hour of noon
The Princess of Canossa, I myself,
Azzo of Brunswick, and Eppone of Zeitz,
Ugo of Clugny, and Gregorio of Ravenna,
Gundolfo of Reggio, and Everardo of Parma,
Will meet you and your officers on staff
And the nobility who join your cause
And place this crown of gold upon your head
For purposes to which we all agree.
The Church will add their ceremonial rite
By popular acclamation registered,
Anointing you with an unctuous holy oil
As with the Sacred dew of Providence.
For the State guidance free from all alarms,
With all that can the visions of the heart
Attach to all the elements of Life
By intimation and significance.
Then shall the grandeur of your reign commence.
Then shall the rising Star of Germany
As yet concealed among unnatural clouds
Burst forth and all the world illuminate.
Till virtues, that dwelt now in Lands obscure,
And from perfection's meed wholly shut out,
Labouring to grope their way to Happiness
Withheld from them for purposes better ours,

And ventured thus, we know originally,
Or nearly so, accustoming ourselves
As liable to others for repute
In so possessing and preserving long
The secret of all true prosperity,
For our own good in timely exercise
So finally and generally so
Upholding and enriching this decree,
Continually amid many an angry shock
Convulsively demolishing its aim,
Vibrating to the very verge of Ruin
The strong foundation of its many hopes,
Brought to the front our font reanimate !
Then in sound principles that high bestride
And mock the traitorous precipitancy
Of sordid jealousy and grovelling hate
That buried in its emptiness, devises
Schemes flattered in the outset in their birth,
And by a mischievous expectation fed,
And nourished by disorder and remorse
Into a grisly giant well matured
With promises cheating the gaping multitude
That their performance waits but waits in vain,
We may enlarge the Legend of this date,
Increase and multiply its Instances,
Upon its opportunities acquire
New origin for examples good as new,
Then turn to break the barriers that prevent
Extension of the range of Genius

Beyond the difficult borders that surround
Its oft perverted and much-paralysed point,
Till in the waste of centuries foreseeing
Past the broad shadow of perfection, its light
Gleaming with cold uninterrupted ray,
Respect acquiring in this famous gift,
We shall varieties create of all beyond
And all between that wondrous light and us
In anticipation a full step beyond
The measured tread of popular approach,
And in the Culmination of our hopes
Swiftly or slowly solidly avert
Impending ruin born of giddiness
To whose attack hot fever supervenes,
All practice correspondent to like end,
Of all its hidden value redolent,
Complete in all its rectitude revealed
In illustration so pure and select
Of means accomplishing our destiny
That while the distant future is a sphere
We look to but we cannot verify
The Present will, in manifestation of all facts
Readily around acknowledge everywhere,
Triumphant in the Confluence of all Creeds,
A line complete of central policy
Converging from all ages on our own
And from all lands to rescued Germany.

CONRAD.

Supporters and Companions ! Friends in Arms !
With such assurances of my success
Assembled with me here on this great eve,
Parting we meet and meet to part no more
In the great duty of remodelling
And reconstructing this united realm.
Hail to the morn when freed from sorrow's sting,
The anguish of impenetrable shame
The dull dissemblance of a strength elsewhere
In all inheritance of our lost renown
On the staid Care of incapacity
Until instead of joy it feeds on grief,
The cold inhospitable frown of Fate,
In plans unvalued and designs disowned,
And all the unadaptable, unmeant,
And tantalising overtures unsought
Which reach discredited and unsound ears
Will vanish at the prevalence of a might
To-morrow consecrates into a rule,
The next all application witnesses
Of ends for ours, and for the general good
Which years and Centuries will ratify.
Let your exertions never faint again,
In all temptations that may hover round
And buy your courage and true countenance
With their soft flippant and persuasive tongue
Till our souls sink into despondency .

With the incurability of social ills
That I have found and know are to be cured.
In all our future efforts to be great,
And render to the present age its due
The temper of this day will fertilise
The crude but not ungenerous soil we claim.
Great in its promises if we hold true,
And bide fulfilment with all confidence.
Its overture is worth more than we know
Though each unconscious of our actual worth.
The East has offered to some valiant souls
Room to report a fast progressing skill.
The West is fraught with vigorous designs
All rapt ideas involving in their aim.
There is in every quarter of the territory,
Of which as we are not in origin
The secret of a now prolific birth
We must look all the more like its result,
A spirit of confusion and alarm,
Fostered and nurtured by facilities
Before itself but not so with itself
Which beggars in its fortuitous career
All that our methods so mechanical
Can prosper in comparative competition.
We will be wise and prudent in reserve
Of such audacious capabilities
Of prospering that they may not well achieve
So guardedly to fix culminating points
As not to drive our chariot wheels too close

And overset it at the winning post.
Therefore, Good Friends, I bid you now beware
Not of false principles, for I have none,
But of reaction in those práctices
Others may fall into, for example fixed
For you and for myself in this intent.
Precaution in advantages may lead
From superficial good to gain indeed.

***

SCENE III.—*Rouen.   The Market.*

PREFECT.

This is to promulgate to all who live
Within the cincture of the Norman Land,
Or all beyond attached to Normandy
And wishing it success and happiness :
Whereas William, the second Duke of Normandy,
Born of the House of Blois of old descent,
Provoked into hostility by tribes
Which dwell beyond the sea among the hills,
Their soil has now determined to subdue,
And their dominion add to his domains.
Whereas as yet an insufficient force
For the accomplishment of this great end
Possessing in the roll-call of his troops,
The Duke offers to each enlisting in
His service, so to prosecute this view,

A grant of land as soon as he achieves
Over the Saxon troops a victory.
Whereas the Duke decrees a pardon full
To every prisoner within his realms
Conditionally that he shall forthwith
To the invading force attach himself,
Signing his liability thereto
To all such grave necessity requires.

FIRST CITIZEN.

Is this invasion justifiable first?

SECOND CITIZEN.

Supposing you defeat the Saxon, then
We must make treaty with the British churls,
Or be cut off in numbers, one by one.

THIRD CITIZEN.

Roland the Poet, does he approve the stake?

PREFECT.

Hopefully! The army will be organised,
And with all possible requisites supplied,
Encouraged each by every State device.
Before it sails the Navy will be blessed,
And priests will shrive your individual souls.
Let each produce himself in an attire
Which will be circulated round to-night.
Arms for the infantry, accoutrements

For those who would prefer to join the horse.
There will be no deficiency in aught
That ingenuity hastens to assure
Reluctant and unwilling infirmity
To make a show of courage in advance
Of brave fulfilment bringing up the rear.
Those among you who have wives and homes,
And wish to add to provident designs
By making fresh provision, having much,
But not enough yet for their future sons,
Far nobler spurs to such prosperity
Than anything can offer that we know
In this great project will attain and wear.
Those who have quarrels make them up at once,
Or leave your enemies to till your land.
The vigilance you used to edge the share
Save to add sharpness to the sword and axe.
Then sheathed in iron with a wooden key
This coffer's mysteries we will unlock,
Inspect its treasures with a curious eye,
All that it has with all we want compare,
Refresh our hoary age with something more
Than these our native overtrodden gifts
That taint and tantalise our weary eyes
Till over-surfeited sufficiency
Relapse into mistaught appreciation
Of gifts another's or of these our own.
Then from the torture of restricted force
To joy will now the Norman soul expand.

FIRST CITIZEN.

We will relinquish all for this attempt
Our small domains and destinies to enlarge,
And answer with a shout your fair demand
To join and multiply the regular force.

PREFECT.

There is I know too much of good and ill
Mixed and consolidate in Normandy
To let the tide of circumstance go by
And not to sail to Fortune on its wave.

SECOND CITIZEN.

Supposing conquest the assured result
Of this descent upon the English coast,
In all affection will the Duke return,
Having reduced his foe to vassalage,
And make this city the joint capital ?

PREFECT.

The Duke talks of a castle on the Thames,
From their chief city twenty miles away,
High elevated on an acclivity
That overlooks rich cultivated vales :
This leads me to believe that he will change
Rouen for London as our capital.
It has an outlet good for the North Sea,

And will the Vikings help us to restrain,
The northern provinces who threaten now
Continued attack, perchance possession too.
It would impoverish our victory
To countenance that covert treachery
And not use conquest to consolidate
The Picts and Scots and lawless buccaneers
Into a Western Empire, and remote
And further territories lying west.

THIRD CITIZEN.

Ah ! I perceive the end of Normandy !
England will be his care, and our good Duke
Will jilt his subjects for a foreign throne.

Enter COUNT GEOFFROI DE FACUNBURGE *and* BARON
VALERIEN DE ST. CHEVEROLLE.

GEOFFROI.

Brave citizens ! lay down all implements
For husbandry ; let go domestic use ;
Relinquish all applied conveniences
For stewing you as surfeited French hogs ;
Abandon shops and stores, leave the exchange
To those who love their money and their hour
More than more capital and a longer life,
And join this expedition heart and soul.
This province wants a sound security
For all you have, and which we vainly boast

The fruit of all that Europe can produce
Till you to its distrust add some domains
In proof of our sincerity of power,
Of which all that we see around us now
Is but the emblem and significant type.
The world will here enclose a character
Which for its bold aggressive *impetus*
Could rule that world of which we offer part.
Perhaps that part may lead on to the whole,
And the close spirit now relentless pent,
Fire, animate, and appropriate lands afar
That otherwise had consecrated rule
Already adverse to the Norman name.
What are the Saxons but demonstrative
And feeble illustrations of a stock
That breathe vitality but never burn?
As if its spark had kindled, then gone out!
The English, cold, unchivalric, and base
In stoic obstinacy that borne out
Which as a spirit of celestial might
If with the light adroitness we possess
Had advocated covert principles,
Had realised a nucleus that had spread
Maritime views to earth's terrestrial end,
Have laid the Roman sword-play that they learned
Too long aside to be successful now.
Then let us teach them martial petulance,
First to be spent in jousts and tournaments,
Then when we have refreshed their zest for war

We will with discipline both ends unite
To seek with them the empire of the east
Release Jerusalem from the Saracen,
And succour purified the Fount of Faith.

FIRST CITIZEN.

Our hearts are centred here in Normandy.
Will the despondent English marry with us ?
This bond would not, others would slip with time
Into the abjuration of our race,
And we become their slaves as they first ours.

VALERIEN.

Duke William has four sons as brave as he.
Think you they will not save his dignity,
And so prepare the way for your success,
And dictate rules for such a progeny
That will caress them into matrimony?
So that spark will inoculate your sons
Which of an occidental origin
Will give to us a fire that has died out,
With a spirit of discovery and research,
Inquiry moral and metaphysical,
And investigation into secret worlds
We guess and dream of but yet cannot know.
Only this spirit has created us.
With it reanimated and refreshed
Its forethought and its vigour well repaid
By opportunity for more success

As we move on more nearly to the heart
By. diligent eagerness will enable us
Affairs more troublesome, less venturesome,
More mingled with unfolded injuries
That as they never see can never cure
To regulate in Europe and the East.
Abandon this and we abjure ourselves,
Ourselves the point of interest and care,
The point and acme of all chivalry.
We cannot nurture friends that nurtured us
Wrapt in the swaddling clothes of infancy
When in the stole of full maturity
The heart's pulsations echo to a note
Breathed only by progressive vehemence.
What we encounter cannot be ourselves,
But being therefore greater than ourselves,
We shall not only conquer those but more,
And in increasing rights reiterate
Faculties which will develop mightily
Occult and dormant seeds of happiness,
Felicity, joy, and prosperity,
Without which we are seaweeds on the shore
Of some huge, unappreciated continent,
Immeasurably grand in secret store :
Secret ! to most to us attainable !
Such shall conduct us to our bitter end
With far more satisfaction than we have,
With less expostulation, more firm hold
Upon denunciation hovering far

And near to blight our apathetic souls,
And weary with intimidation.   Hence
Determine, whatsoever the result,
Each and all sons of Normandy to-day
To step at once to the first rank in the van
Of civilisation's hopeful pilgrimage,
Sink doubt and disputation in the dust
And claim for victory glory's equipage.

Enter the GOVERNOR OF THE GAOL.

GOVERNOR.

My Lords, and honoured Prefect, at your will
The law's offenders are all mustered here,
Committed to my care for different crimes,
The catalogue of which is various,
And doth embody deeds of all intent.
But in the scale of justice you have placed
Two elements, one for attack, one for defence.
The latter plea we generally use,
Which for a hostage holds the guilty one
Until your enemies come more to terms.
You now assure me of another view :
Your enemies then are of another kind,
Yet not aggressive !   This had been good cause
For violating precepts usually
Both salutary and satisfactory.
But since the extent of land requires aid,
And since defence is asked for by offence,

Your cause must be indirectly justified,
Aided, and supported by those enemies
Which I was fain to hope were all you had.

PREFECT.

Prisoners ! stand forth !   Do all of you agree
Willingly for invasion to enlist ?
Enrol yourselves among the sons of Mars,
All military duties prosecute,
All regulations cheerfully fulfil,
Not only those in the articles of war,
But also by expediency supplied ?

PRISONERS.

Yes ! yes !   No ! no !

PREFECT.

Who is it that I hear responding No ?

CHEMNITZ.

Prefect, my name is Chemnitz, and I claim
Consideration as a foreigner.
I am a German, and Normans cannot aid
England to rescue from the Saxon rule.
I traded here with a jeweller in gold,
Supplying amethysts and diamonds
In metal work requiring ornament,

And am lost to a perilous mischance,
Defrauding many others with myself.

PREFECT.

You wish to deal with us in Time of Peace,
Knowing our requisites and what you want :
Yourself enriching possibly in the end,
And leaving us to flourish as we may :
And, thriving on our nationality,
You will not on that point exert yourself
On which hinges future prosperity.

CHEMNITZ.

In England long an outlet has appeared
For interchange accommodating all,
And I would urge you not to venture now
To jar its serious, modulated state
By any alteration of its rule.
The Superstition of the Druids' dead,
The Spirit of a nobler moral Light,
Has actuated every social grade
To choose and verify a loftier aim
Than Life to study for itself alone.
Dear to themselves, as they were taught at first,
They now consider such their fellow men,
Devote themselves to projects not their own,
Irrelevant advantages fortify,
Goad on the wheel of acquisition now

* Q

Not for their own but for the general gain,
And so for speculation leaving room,
Redouble their own chance and others' too.
Why then disturb for some impetuous' wish
To hamper civilisation with its crust,
This valuable feature of to-day
With no more object than ambition's pride?
So seeking that which we might earlier find
By Art, that from the Cradle to the Grave
Succours and saves not only what we have,
But signifies its worth, which we have not.

PREFECT.

Then as a German why did you disturb
A tribe by all hypocrisy undefiled?

CHEMNITZ.

When first the Saxon held in Britain sway,
The pagan native, savage and untaught,
By the dark fiend self-will alone impelled,
With all the harshness of uncertainty
Of Life in their inhuman bloody rites
Appeased all conscience by the sacrifice.
Rome heard of this, and delegated one,
The holy St. Augustine, from the See,
The absent Ark of Heaven who supplied,
And advocated the great truths of faith.
The spirit that the Saxon had evoked

The Papacy in triumph carried out.
A character the Britons have obtained
Hence, and hence only, of morality.
But early if you warp the pliant shoot
You soon will have a dwarfed and stunted tree
Which you may hang your swords and spurs upon,
But plenty and prosperity will hide
Their timid faces in the mountain caves,
Whence all your force can never fetch them out.
Therefore I say this venture is a crime,
To Trade and Commerce most injurious,
A contradiction to versed art and skill,
Of retrogressive impulse born and bred,
In all its aspects monstrous, hideous,
Measured in its profundity and width
By all capacity in such distrust !

PREFECT.

Your arguments are good !   Well, I have here
Nobles, Duke William's representatives,
Who, if the project is a ruffian stroke
For some half-estimated, coveted prize
Which we know how to win but not to wear,
As half-blind, wholly selfish profligates,
In his behalf and for Religion's sake,
Here in the assemblage of the Norman race
For conscience' sake would willingly denounce.
Baron Valerien and Count Geoffroi, say
Is this a sound and creditable plot,

In every point of view considered well,
In test and trial adverse opinion proof,
Free from disparagement's accusing voice,
Bound every honest vow to recognise,
All righteous requisitions to fulfil,
To guarantee not merely to ourselves,
Advantages to be more fully tried
But more than that, in civilised improvement
To carry out at this particular date
Views founded on imperishable hopes
That Providence would urge us to fulfil?

COUNT GEOFFROI.

Apart from every wilful prejudice,
By worthy resolution to be free
From dictates of a too presumptuous mood,
Duke William has determined to attack,
Invade, and by close military strategy
Capture the strongholds of this various foe ;
Including thus all native islanders
Who Harold's standard rally to support.
A cause we only judge of by our own,
Which, neither Oriental nor yet central,
Accepts no luxury, has no satellites,
Nor in suggestion deals to all around
The motives and the sphere for exercise
Of energies and appetites that lust
For something in authority in return.
So Britain cannot be content, and we,

In mixing up its fortunes with our own,
May simply curiosity satisfy
Unto its projects in maturer years,
A nurse intelligent to a fractious child,
Who thus may find by aid of artifice,
And interruption to its prattling play,
The tardy secret of control and rule,
The application of all natural gifts,
The care of wants we feel as well as they,
But being more sensitive early thus express
Tumultuous sorrows in each different mood
Which Time and complications shall assuage,
And consciousness of merit rectify,
Till visiting our misdeeds with our grief,
We shall, withdrawing from our patronage
All fallacies irregular, dissolve,
Unite, or separate, as best may seem ;
Should we join issue we will straight advance
And in the channel of fresh circumstance
Accomplish something far more dignified,
Ambitious, in remuneration more,
And in alleviation of all difficulties,
A bolder and more comprehensive plan
Which all shall wish success and none oppose.

CHEMNITZ.

If this denunciation is the last
Of Normandy, and is the Duke's decree,
It is their joint extinction sealed at once.

If I go with your force of soldiery,
And in their ruinous deeds accompany it,
Negotiations you cannot renew
With principals of houses in our trade
Such as I am, although a prisoner.
Should such impediments a barrier
Between their past and future thus erect,
If both of you are ruined blame not me.
Better to stimulate our industry
And leave us to increase our costly store,
So you can supplement your victory
With a display of continental wealth,
Sending us back those metals they possess.
Britain has copper, tin, iron, and lead,
And these of purity invaluable.
Of course they know not how to work them up,
But we are well accomplished in this art,
To perfect which have all conveniences,
Possessing secrets we shall not divulge,
And skill we only know how not to teach.
Therefore, most honoured Prefect, and my Lords,
Excuse me from enlisting in this cause.
Should you involve resources in the risk,
Or lose what it is difficult to find,
Credit for loans on small security,
Who will refit the vanished treasure house?
Should your troops falter and your courage fail,
And Saxon prowess prove invincible
Who will supply the claimed indemnity?

Should William, Duke of Normandy, become
A prisoner to the defending force
Who will advance the ransom to be paid
Unless I and my friends the jewellers
Remain uninjured by the feat of arms?
Who will to such adventurers restore
The sinews and the material of war.

PREFECT.

·There !   Since you prove the element of war,
In strength so frail, in point so hazardous,
That the attempt, however bold, admits
Hardly a possibility or probability
Of war's remunerative victory,
You argue the necessity so far
Of adding, in whatever way we like,
To organised battalions that we have.
Then if you stay and cannot find release
From chains that may or may not be deserved,
The hidden wealth you say that you possess,
Or can command the issue from the earth
Alike unavailable to you or us
Had better in Earth's bowels long remain.
I and these barons cannot set you free
Simply because you will not go to war.
Then should the Saxon or the Islander
Discover none of us to be men of wealth,
Attaining some advantage in the fight
They will make short work of our soldiery,

Despatch them with unheard-of cruelty,
Kill every prisoner immediately,
Spread consternation through the residue,
Drive back the uncontaminated rear
Into the heart and centre of the camp,
And we, martyrs to them, to you in turn
Become the victims of your avarice,
And place you in our debt eternally.
I am unable to admit your claim
Or lend my ear to such a soft appeal.
Serve Normandy and perish in the risk,
Or you will not return to Germany
To find your stores double their present worth,
When then you may a capitalist preside
In those negotiations for State loans
That seize the brains of kings and ministers.
I now enroll you with the volunteers,
A pressed man taken against his own consent,
Fulfilling not the enjoinments of the law
But able to exonerate himself,
To sail for Britain with the invading force.

Scene IV.—*Pforzheim.   A Prison.*

COUNT RINALDINI.

Seduction ! how it paints upon the air
Secrets impossibly otherwise transfused !
And they know least that lend a willing ear

As well to every scandalous report
That flatters but to poison social life.
Ill fares the age that warrants by ill fame
To rupture uncontaminated bonds,
Unstained, undesecrated, unalloyed,
Without the shadow of a severance,
Sanctioned and sealed with all oaths utterable,
Naturally and supernaturally safe,
For ever unconditionally sound !
Such as through many a changing day and year
Outlived between the Emperor and myself
Have bound us in all solemn grievances,
From mirth resounding on to mellow times,
For different ends indissolubly allied,
In apathetic or in boisterous scenes,
Or earth was full of jocund revelries
Or mourning lingered to resent the same,
Half-witted the one, the other satisfied,
That shaken with sublimity that shakes
All the world round it but such difficult men,
This tempered to malignity by woe
That disentangles and detaches all
The diplomatic cords that bind us up
Into conventionality of aim,
Or that which to our being gives indirect
A power to supplant Death's javelin,
And the right both for ourselves and all we know
To raise the burden of each other's cares,
And place them in the stubborn patient earth,

Then raise the spirit into ecstasy
That else had dallied with harsh misery,
And with the consummation of success
Endow the world that we arrived to bless.

Enter Jailer.

JAILER.

My lord, a high-born nobleman is here,
Who seeks to have an interview with you.

RINALDINI.

Where emperors are true nobles become false !
Inquire his name and proper references,
Also his national faith and prejudice.
In such a strange predicament as mine,
Friends may be foes, and enemies be friends.

> [*Exit Jaile*

Jailer *re-enters*.

JAILER.

Count Hofenstaufen is the visitor's name.
He says that you are old acquaintances,
And both your houses are a home to each.

RINALDINI.

Bid him come in at once, and then withdraw.

> [*Exit Jailer*
> [*Enter* Count Hofenstaufen.

Good morrow ! opportune and generous friend.
Here you perceive I am a prisoner,

On whom has fallen all the ills that wits
Originally prescribed for Fools and Knaves.

COUNT HOFENSTAUFEN.

This is an unheard of, unexpected, strange,
Unwarrantable, improbable event !
Anticipation could not have heralded
In all the liabilities of Life
To which we all stand differently risked
A shock so great to social harmony,
So deep a wound to sacred social health
As this profane reversal of the true
And equitable course of Circumstance.

RINALDINI.

Where monarchs to their subjects falter in
The prosecution of the same success
Which waits on both or foils not only one
I could have borne my sympathetic fall.
More so, that since the commencement of intrigues
Which have two rival factions occupied
And turned the brains of many an honest man,
The error has crept in to cry out upon
Imperial authority and myself.
Then I could have contented my frail spirit
With noble as imperial philosophy.
But not in the course of internecine war,
Or in the turbulent assault of words,
Between your native country and my own,

Has any noxious feature or base fact,
Diligently foreseeing its way to mar
The majesty and dignity of man,
The given line of rectitude reproached
With cowardice, flight, or incapacity,
With turpitude or two-faced falsity,
So that its even spirit thus repulsed
Or crushed beneath impending obstacles
Might sink a victim to incurred remorse.

HOFENSTAUFEN.

Then to what sinister or base origin
Some criminal intent enamoured of,
And its result in notoriety,
Has in performance of its fiendish view,
In contradiction of a high decree
As sacred as the altar of our faith,
Produced so grievous an emergency?

RINALDINI.

Your presence cheers me up, since you can feel,
Like me, mixed indignation and disgust.
But criminals have many friends as well
As those who are not guilty of misdeeds.
Their perjury that no one can confront
Of possibilities incontrovertible
Hover around virtuous credulity
Till it proves all though it convinces none,
So that I cannot filch from Innocence

The key to free me from the realms of Guilt.
Better resign myself to this my Fate,
And venture far beyond the haunts of Hope
Into where desolation finds some home
Where the fierce woes of the soul are hushed by plagues,
Gone joy, grief, recollection, everything !

HOFENSTAUFEN.

By which of the passes did you reach Italy?
And what direction varied your return?

RINALDINI.

Rudolf of Suabia was our mortal foe.
You heard at the Diet how he rated us ;
This was the symptom of hostility
Which ended in the field of Fladenheim.
I had the charge of the Italian troops.
Like to a game of chess which neither wins
It was a contest close in the result.
Pope Gregory was chosen referee,
And in the hostile spirit which impelled
His dealings with the luckless Emperor
Whenever called upon to interfere,
He to the Duke of Suabia gave the day.
I was a responsible hostage left
For the fulfilment of conditions signed
At once between the two belligerents,
And took up my abode in Hagenau.
Herein I had not tarried many days

A victim to a patriotic zeal
Which leads to evil though it points to good,
When I was suddenly set upon one night,
When I was meditating greater views
Than common mortals give me credit for,
Disarmed, secured, fast-bound, and carried off
By a detachment of the Suabian force,
And for the supposition of a crime
The incidents of which I never heard,
That is the theft felonious of a crown
Sent by a Florentine jeweller to Normandy
To grace some scheme improvident of the Duke,
Imprisoned in the fortress of Pforzheim.

HOFENSTAUFEN.

That the Duke had resolved, I was aware, ·
England to add to his dominions.
Of course he will be crowned the king of both
If he can reconcile the world to such
Attainment of an independent state,
The boundary of which we cannot guess.
Saxony, knowing this, the move will stop,
So Eastern potentates will look with scrutiny
Into a vortex of such turbulence
As will spring out of all this rivalry.
In Europe there is not a single State
That will not its existence agitate
With some fierce doubt that it will undergo,
Some strange unruly metamorphosis,

In this attempt to occupy the West
With choice but overrated chivalry.
William of Blois need not regret his crown !
The hand that might have won it will lay low,
Buried by some of the monks of Canterbury.

RINALDINI.

I thank your courtesy, it augurs well
For our external policy and theirs.
Though all within a house Love regulates
All those performances approved the best,
The world is open to exterior views
Which often burst with their own vanity.
I never grudged ambition friendliness,
But when the self-plagued passion seeks its own
Where it is never likely to be found
Down with ambition, and aggression too !

HOFENSTAUFEN.

Possess you no connection any way
With any of the agents in this case ?

RINALDINI.

Nobles have no concern with working men,
Why not enquire do I know William of Blois ?

HOFENSTAUFEN.

I merely wish to simplify affairs

Whose complication just creates a doubt
Not only as respects your innocence,
But to what party to attach the guilt.
There should be several witnesses to find,
And to your reputation testimonies.
You have a friend here in Bavaria,
Summon your banker, and some Florentines,
And place them with the accusers face to face.
Unless that they can prove you stole the crown,
The possibility that you did the deed
Improbability will at once destroy.

Enter JAILER.

JAILER.

My Lord, a certain person waits without—
Signor Tarchetti—who from Florence comes
Some private business to negotiate.

RINALDINI.

Caution him to be careful in his speech :
Then if prepared to be so, show him in.
[Exit Jailer.
[Enter TARCHETTI.
Welcome, Tarchetti ! breaking no good faith
With me or any good Italian friends,
Tell us if you have heard aught of this plot,
That, in involving me, stirs Italy
And every worthy son of southern soil
To work revenge on some mysterious foe.

TARCHETTI.

Without being compromised in any way
With the conspiracy on this side or on that,
I come to give you what support I could
In recognition of your rank and wealth,
Hearing you had been implicate therein.

HOFENSTAUFEN.

Has the Count Rinaldini no connection had
With any Florentine herein concerned?
                    [*Rinaldini signs silence to Tarchetti.*

TARCHETTI.

His business there is usually imperial work,
Transactions with the different state officers.

HOFENSTAUFEN.

Then I am to infer he is not known
Personally to one or other of them?

TARCHETTI.

Whatever be the social regulations
Which render Florence an agreeable resort,
Where feed at leisure on reflection those
Whose deeds elsewhere may not at her door lie,
They would not, I know, generally accord
That social freedom which you intimate
Might have associated participators
In a peculiar business of this kind

                                        * R

So as to break all barriers between
Hereditary rank and respectability.
This might not perhaps free him from the charge,
But just three days before the event occurred,
Alone in Florence to my office came
A military person of your build—
A soldier half, half a diplomatist—
And tendering the necessary cheque,
Demanded in return one hundred marks.
Finding it bore the honourable signature
Of Gangarelli, Minister of State,
I willingly advanced the sum required.
Hearing shortly of the theft of the crown
At Mâcon on the road through Burgundy,
Immediately after of your apprehension, then
To come to your assistance I resolved,
As a well-tried and honourable friend,
And give your reputation one good chance.

RINALDINI.

Tarchetti, worthy son of Romulus !
You have relieved my hitherto heavy heart
With a good antidote to poisonous grief.
Have you no farther knowledge to complete
This kind solution of so base a plot ?

TARCHETTI.

A due investigation must be held
Here, or in Wurzburg, or in Nuremburg.

'Twixt now and then I will abate no care
That can from secret circumstance unsolve
The person's name to whom I paid the gold,
And what his habits are and mode of life.

Enter JAILER.

JAILER.

My Lord, a soured enquirer waits without,
Who says he is the landlord of an inn
Wherein the theft of which you are accused
Was perpetrated in night's darkest hour ;
And having heard that now you are detained
Unworthily upon the criminal charge,
He thinks it would be better first repeating
The casual incidents rounding the event,
Some secret information to disclose
As to the characters of those concerned.

HOFENSTAUFEN.

This is indeed a welcome visitor !
This evidence must prove your innocence.

RINALDINI.

Admit the innkeeper at once, then leave.

[*Exit Jailer.*

Enter COUNT BUONVICINO *in disguise.*

INNKEEPER.

My Lord, I have remained in trouble long
As one whose implicated honour lies

Levelled in dust by this discomfiture.
If anything I can reveal would save
My reputation and your liberty,
You are as welcome as the sun to vines,
Which become harsh to intercepted rays.

HOFENSTAUFEN.

Repeat to us the incidents which bear
Closely upon this melancholy event,
Excusing not remote particulars.
My friend is most unjustly victimised.

INNKEEPER.

Your honour, I will unravel all mystery
That thus has vexed you with deceit's alarms,
And so I would unmask all criminals
That suck the credit out of honour's vat,
And with a reputation vaunted thus
Beguile the world, and beggar it of good.

RINALDINI.

Describe the parties at your inn that night,
Their gesture, mien, style, and behaviour.
In dress how were adorned and decorated,
The language and discourse that they employed,
Whence they arrived and whither they adjourned.

INNKEEPER.

A lapidary, Chemnitz of Bavaria,

Had sent a crown to Bonnières of Rouen.
The man who bore it was of address reserved,
Of dignity austere and mien upheld
In contradiction of all circumstance.
He spoke to all on different instances
Pleasantly, all direct questioning to avoid.
But one among my guests was otherwise.
To the insinuating serpent's glide
He joined the eagle's cold sagacious glare.
In not pretending much he uttered more,
And was most busy in encouragement
To solve the leading riddles of the day.
With him, as urgent lover crossed in a suit,
The agent of the Bavarian jeweller
In the most intimate terms was soon engaged.
I marked that lusty eye and frozen lip
As he unwound the tale of falsity
And wound attention on his rapid reel.

HOFENSTAUFEN.

Did any grade his style of dress disclose,
Device or any symbols national ?

INNKEEPER.

His costume was of leather, braided round
Of tasselled lace, as he loved the chase.
A crossbow, and a dagger, and a horn
Completed the exterior of one
As skilled in arts as in a hunter's arms,

Which arts with all audacity he used
And then abused with pointed recklessness.
That first I wondered, then my guests deplored
That such a man should have no regular mood,
But suffering much from vague perplexity
Could not their told perplexity assist.

HOFENSTAUFEN.

He was employed by Philip, King of France.
The House of Capet hates the House of Blois,
Whose vassalage into independence soon
Turning might turn the sword against themselves.

RINALDINI.

Of course the gallant hunter was the robber !
In what direction went he from your inn ?

INNKEEPER.

He took the German road, by the Jura ridge.

HOFENSTAUFEN.

When is the Court of Inquiry to assemble ?

INNKEEPER.

Six witnesses are ready to attest
Each the particulars that they observed,
And offer calculations on the point
Of individual identity,

Or leaning liability to crime,
On Thursday next at noon in Nuremburg.

HOFENSTAUFEN.

For this attention take this purse of gold.
                    [*Bestows a purse on Innkeeper.*

RINALDINI.

Can we not unravel now at once
A mystery that should not be so deep
As all our joint penetration to evade?
Has any papal spy on royal deeds
Forsaking indirect for direct principle
Foregone the reputation meritorious,
Which laymen have not but would emulate,
And England's would-be Conqueror thus vexed?

INNKEEPER.

I do not wish to injure innocence
Or bring the blameless into disrepute,
But not in a venture insight to let slip
On supposition's doubtful confidence
If proper circumspection blunts the edge.
A person I have met with twice of late
Is one whose qualities might have been employed
So wanton a misdeed to perpetrate.
Born an Italian, and of old descent,
He yet has aspirations of that sort
Which favours seek by secret services.
 Following early the profession of arms

He reached a high command and great success.
This gives him confidence in those concerns
Which do not to his calling appertain
But lead him in irresolute, daring strokes,
Betraying some reliance on a trick,
To interfere and dedicate afresh
A trophy for the means and not the end.
The Marquis Oberto is the officer's name.

RINALDINI.

I see then how the error has crept in !
The spirit of rivalry or fond support
Of one whose difficulties are our care
Has led Oberto to this perfidy.
Like me, he has a separate command ;
Like me, enjoys the king's full confidence,
Whose cause in the ascendency to advance
And place surrounding nations at his feet
Upon this point Oberto has deserted
Principles it was his duty to preserve,
And stirred the Norman invader to revenge
Upon my luckless head injuries
I never advocated nor provoked.
My host of the ' Rouge Dragon ' this surmise
Considerately and cautiously tendered, me
And my good friend the Count of Hofenstaufen
Who knows me better than suspicion likes
Forthwith from all anxiety relieves,
Myself as to the upshot of the doubt

And from a false position looses him.
By satisfying one you have served two,
The harmony of whose social unison
Discordantly and unsuspectingly so jarred,
Waiting until the trial and its verdict,
Irrevocably had been sacrificed.
When the inquiry opens at Nuremburg
Furnishing yourself beforetime with the facts
With those I have asserted bearing upon
The Marquis Oberto's private character,
Be ready to impeach him then and there.
My legal friend will serve him with a writ
To appear and answer to a felonious charge
At the instance of the Duke of Suabia,
Thus acting for the Duke of Normandy.
Here is a purse holding a hundred marks

                    [Gives Innkeeper a purse.

To pay yourself and other witnesses.
Spare neither gold nor trouble for a cause
Not sold for secret pride but a wide world's applause.

                    [Exit Buonvicino.

HOFENSTAUFEN.

Think you Oberto travelled with the King
When he left Germany for Italy?

RINALDINI.

No ! He never at first accompanied him
When he left Turin for the Diet at Worms,
But with the army stayed in Italy.

Affairs were not so tranquil for a time,
Disturbance and derangement everywhere
Demanded caution, and I should have thought
He hardly had the time for such a deed.
Then he could not have done it for himself,
You know the German temper thoroughly,
The Saxon monarch might have sought by this
To have insulted William of Normandy.

HOFENSTAUFEN.

Rudolf of Suabia, who desires our throne,
An agent might have paid to filch the crown.
He is a jealous and emulous adherent to
A meed of fortune the Stars smile upon.
But many men of conscience like myself
Think it is early yet for Germany
To choose a man of quick and ready wit.
We like a man who binds us each to each
By some unfelt, invisible, secret bond,
With a suspended curiosity
As to immediate gain or ultimate end,
Each one at liberty to choose his own
Aloof from every kind impediment,
Absorption or dispersion of emolument
Which else had been a risk ulterior
But has been saved by a conventionality
Which makes the universe's resources his,
To be disposed of not for common good
Or for his own peculiar benefit,

But that by process progress rectified
We may ourselves and others all the more,
For some great principle's healthy exercise
Our sordid faculties expanded out,
Accustom to a wider intercourse,
In which closer responsibilities
On a broad line of treatment so conceived,
Might, as less irksome and more generous,
Supply the envied good which we believe
Is ruined by too natural a support.
The liabilities of these avoiding
So to act partners in colossal schemes
For too great sensitiveness to good or ill
Which aim at everything and nought fulfil.
Men gradually, step by step, forewarned
Of difficulties that in destruction grow
And reappear from wrath's impassioned flames,
With the procrastination of the tortoise claim
The prize its faster rival sleeps to lose.

RINALDINI.

Then while your whole community loses thus,
Though for a time, which time must seem an age,
As novel faculties gradually arrive,
The uplifted flag of universal sway
Will dazzle you as us who led the world,
And may again after your transient reign,
On whom has fallen late a retributive curse,
Or else a worthless superstitious cloud

Portends the interruption of a wand
Which the happiness of the whole destroys in part,
And which the vague dissemblance of success
Suggests a sure proof of its fallacy,
That fallacy which after all Time might revoke
As played within the mystery of years
Which had upon pure vision thrown a cloud
Till it obscured its insight original
So true that the whole world bowed to its nod,
As conscious inferiority that troubled finds
No satisfaction but in acknowledgment
Of virtues that its haste had overlooked,
By everything rejected in its turn,
Who for one end rejected everything ;
So moderate mediocrity is all,
And furious zeal unjustifiable
Because it teaches arts no more its own,
In process careful, perfect in result,
And in this faith we triumph finally,
Fulfilled each item of our Destiny.

SCENE V.—*Room in a Palace, Florence.*

AZZO, DUKE OF BRUNSWICK.

Herein is now made manifestly clear
Without dissemblance that we must adjure
Fresh Fortune Heaven to carve out for all.
The Alps that separate so many friends

A newer bond of union would suggest
Than similarity of sympathies.
But let not therefore any venture to sow
That we in Hope may reap not but Despair
The harvest of so grave a speculation :
Productive seeds of further difference
Venturesome in the outset we may be,
But as the Cause and Consequence are viewed
And we emancipate from dark to light
It would be wiser not to risk our hopes
In constitutional integral effect :
But in a nursery of prodigal
Or thrifty scattered worth as it may be,
Within all time the bud so nurtured up
Would never ripen into fruit at all,
Or grow a harsh, unprofitable fruit,
The shadow vexed of business disavowed
Smouldering beneath ungenerous ignorance
As the pine watch fire that the snow puts out
And leaves the hazardous adventurer
To die of cold before the dawn of day.
The policy by rapturous Spirits shed
On National jealousy ruptures may Create
Which only made to tantalise the Sword
May trifle too much with prosperity.

MATILDA.

Which hangs upon the Sword being laid aside
Till it recover.

GUELFO D'ESTE.

There you are at fault
Man then too sick quarrels with man the more
Full of hot blood, and never knowing thwart.

AZZO

War may enrich, but never can impoverish.

GUELFO D'ESTE.

You look too far into futurity.
At present you can never hope to find
That satisfaction is a greed of the substantial.

ADELAIDE.

The priesthood will disseminate principles
That man will elevate from wanton bliss.

AZZO.

The priesthood never educate the heart.

ADELAIDE.

Because the Heart cannot be imposed upon
By direct rules and favourite examples.

AZZO.

Within it Conscience lies which never sears
But lives and blooms an everlasting test
As long as we live thus consulting it,

And while it thus invigorates the heart
This needs a strong support to hold it straight
To the true goal of all ambitious plots.

GUELFO D'ESTE.

Ambition has a clear and measured course,
Dictated by the gravity of the hour,
And never vaunting more than it can do
It therefore does more than it undertakes.

ADELAIDE.

It wants some regulator to its pace
That points at times to something more than truth
And something less.   It may consist of good,
If not an evil form in embodiment
Unnoticed by a sanguine temperament
It is a relaxation of desires
That unimpeded runs wrong in the End.

AZZO.

Which end is what?   Some occult principle
Denuded of ingenious disguise
And into operation brought to play
All unexpected on the Theatre
Of combinative evolution till
By one adroit stroke of the Magician
The dreams of Earth become substantial facts
And stern realities become a dream.

MATILDA.

Man is not even disappointed yet
If from the old materials turned out
And distribution of re-altered parts
He can from out the fresh entangled mass
Pluck thrice as much more as he hazarded.
Why then deter him from this proper End
With vain allurements he may not forsake?

GUELFO D'ESTE.

He would forsake them if he saw the End.
But if that End is unsatisfactory
Or doubtful, or too problematical
The other objects thrown across his path,
If not injurious in their effect
Or contrary to wisdom in pursuit,
Are better followed, whether he chooses them
Or accident waylay him with the Cheat.

AZZO.

Three feelings animate us here on Earth
And on the wings of impulses like these
Attempting first the one and then the other
We speed aloft in search of happiness.
Avarice the first, of expectation born
And nurtured by the risk of gain or loss,
Or the excitement of the clash of Swords.
The admiration as a secret thought

Of some particular element of Life
Which though a social atom is a Spring
To which carefully struck vibrates the Soul
And popularity, even infallibility,
Rises immediately with a sudden throb
From the unseen establishing success
In different points visible to the querulous world :
This is another motive of our whole.
There is one more which ably actuates
The urgent votary, 'tis the Spiritual Search
For the direct line of regular Cause and Effect.
Early in youth then having discovered it
Applying the secret at each different turn .
Of circumstance, till a glad opportunity
Lifts the possessor into a higher world
A wider sphere for the exercise of power.
Yet this is but a guide to something more,
Till with position he is satisfied,
When he leads public opinion with a glance.

ADELAIDE.

Are these the Ends of Life or Interludes ?

AZZO.

'The one selected and persisted in
This for the object chiefly held in view
Is the transporting principle of Life,
And turns all that it finds to Happiness.
The others must be as religious vows,

Which frequently obtrude upon the thought
To disappointment reconciling us,
By substituting something more ethereal
Than the fond substance that evades our grasp.

GUELFO D'ESTE.

If Love contains the solace easiest
And leaves the brain untrammelled and more free,
Provided that its object is attained
Without too many trials of the Heart
To trace out and pursue a different course
Resulting in an opposite Success,
So that the World can never quite discern
Which is the probable end you had in view,
Or is or will be at some juncture fresh,
I think I will adopt the Lover's part.

ADELAIDE.

If in sincerity your suit you urge
And your devotion dress with Constancy
So that the hidden Sword of Jealousy
Pierce not the Armour that protects your Love,
Nor in that object of your choice Distrust
From evident distraction of attachment
Most easily perceived but seldom shewn
Unanswered all your protestation leaves
And so another secretly prefers,
The impulse to be great you advocate
Endows a man with claims to a Career

Respondent to the wants of those around
With a more social and more generous turn
Than the Support of Arms, or rescued Gold.

AZZO.

In our attachment wheresoe'er we turn
The mystical embodiment of Love
Reveals a sort of hidden Intercourse
With other objects than those visible.
In this association to our taste
With many others or with only one
We canvass every point we prosecute,
Advise, or are admonished in return.
Difficulties that are positive amalgamate
With others as of partial difference,
And in return disinterested share
Others' sufficiencies or inefficiencies.
So far So good : But in detained Success
Either in the fulfilment of our plan
Or in the desirableness of the result
The instituted system we have joined
Accumulates its weight upon the head
Of such inapplicable appliances
That long before we can our steps retrace
Or substitute a different design,
The Heart grows cold to every Earthly Joy.
Therefore some passion should precede rather
Than follow in the urgent steps of Love.
Some possess Strength of Character enough

To vanquish this deficiency at once,
But most lament the want of its support.
Let impulses be less injurious
Or give them regular encouragement
Lest man become a terror to himself.
His vows rejected he becomes demure,
His overtures neglected or refused
A warning to adventurers dissolute.

MATILDA.

There is on either side much to deplore
Looking at it whatever way you will,
The Man possessing everything his own
Unless he wear the apparel of possessions
With all the talent he observes around
Or all the plausibility they have
Who seek possession under the garb of Love
Will his wife's sanction and the goodwill of the Worl
To mutual happiness never perhaps attain.
The World's opinion is an introduction
And goes no further, that which follows then
The test and trial of those different parts
Perfection or unworthiness in which
Alone the welfare of the future lies,
Between the opportunities which Circumstance
Usually confers on those who look for such
If all is well at first and true, to prove
The measure of our confidence : so far
The looked-for union is a happy one,

Putting all unforeseen events to flight
By opposite or joint philosophy
The point of the stroke traitorous that will turn
At once aside, or heal the surface wound.

AZZO.

But then if either party late discover
A slighted rival poisoning the Cup
Which all your plans have failed to Consecrate?

MATILDA.

Granted that personalities are dismissed
That only read with Confirmation doubt,
And shower validity on suppositions
Which in themselves are instances of Change
And interchange of obligations due,
Carry them howsoever far you will,
Elaborate the mysteries of Life
Into so many pleasurable episodes,
That though they cheat not Time with Circumstance
Preserve Life in a perfect harmony
And illustrate up to the very point
Of infallibility propounded theories
That stir the brain into a giddy whirl
Unceasing, unrelieved, unsatisfied,
Without some indication of results
Which partially soothe as finally attained
The vortex of a creed unjustified
The joint solution practically fails.

GUELFO D'ESTE.

If so the bond of Man and Wife are thus
The mask of falsehood, under whose disguise
Nor wholly or in part hardly revealing
At will the principles of happiness,
The truth, to others never shadowed forth,
Is strangely and unworthily known to both.

ADELAIDE.

That is if no attachment sanction that
The ostensible union of half-satisfied
But fully gratified experimental Love.
I mean in contrast or in similarity
Thoughts and opinions, tempers and ideas
Productive of substantial consequence
By joint co-operation generally.

AZZO.

Attachment is an optional idea.
To love is not so certain to be loved.
Mutual attachment solves the mystery,
Then this is liable to some reserve,
That which is strong in substance is not so
Compared to that which has no visible,
Clearly developed, definite result.
This furnishes all food for jealousy,
And matrimonial happiness undermines.
Then what is wanting in a union

Depending thus on antecedents which
Demolish matrimony by its axioms,
Supposing all correlative concerns
Rather produce agreement than defy,
Is what is never wanting from a king
In celebration of such festive rites,
This is a free and liberal pardon given
To those who have offended social law.
Such clemency will more widely dissipate
The seeds of sin and scatter them on the rock
Than that unfeigned hostility which provokes
More crime to render cruelty justifiable.
The enmity that sleeps awhile disarms.
Supposing virtue to have been the root
Of the unwelcome inauspicious fruit,
And rendering a conciliation firm
The basis of your superficial pact,
Consolidate on more than principle
For its own sake, not for another's good
Embodied in additional worthiness,
A lasting, sound, unquestioned purity,
Against suspicion and aspersion proof,
A bond indissoluble, not for ills
That might not be created, but for the spread
Mutably and beyond the dual claim
Of those advantages which while two assume
Hence an enlarged futurity can secure,
And for fresh bonds fresh races reassure.

    [*Exeunt Adelaide and Azzo, Duke of Brunswick.*

GUELFO D'ESTE.

Matilda of Canossa, views like these
Speak as with inspiration's sacred tongue
All baser principles to counteract
That round our palaces and castles long
Have hovered, hospitality transforming
Into a weeding out of differences
That by impartiality have crossed Laws
Irreconcilable, retaliatory point,
And taught reaction to be too severe.
We who have waited for philosophy
To turn our unexampled hearts aright,
And by good counsels to emancipate
Hereditary grief to future joy,
And animate a bronze feudality
That never can convince while it controls
To something more of immaterial worth
Than meaner fortunes have ascribed to it,
Should hasten severally first, and then,
When we have individually subscribed
In our respective spheres to illustrate
Doctrines already thus sufficiently
Enlarged for our attention without art,
And for adoption without sinister
Surmise of what due malice had been provocative
Of evil that described we know not of
Though possible in the range of likelihood,
We should apply to it the dual test.

MATILDA.

Excuse me, Guelfo d'Este ! this appeal
From theory to practice comes too soon.
Acknowledged in the utterance almost
The sage deductions of experience
Might in an application hastily
Attach us to a weight of enterprise
Without a symptom as to its event.
Disordered empire frowns on character,
Perfect in its acquittance as may be,
And drives it out only to laugh at its
Continual whirl of comprehensive cares
To evils that can only now exist.
Therefore with all approval of your glad
And quaint conversion to a discipline
Of thought and action, meritoriously
Enough advanced, I still must it defer
Our single, individual, separate good.
For in those spheres of application due
Of all this fine and fair philosophy
Which now the Alps divide I cannot find
Enough of correspondent symmetry
Which nicely adjusted might be wrought to fit
The confident expectations of the past,
The Future's admiration of its own
Fulfilment singularly antedated,
The requisition of the present time
In all its arbitrary wilfulness

Together won in this one union.
Let us examine cordially at first
The value of the lesson we have learned.
In all obedience to the right result,
If so we can discover this at last,
Our own immortal gifts we should apply
With single zeal to manifold success.
So adaptation of experiments
In the correction of our social wants
Will place more rapidly within our grasp
The missing ends we hope to circumvent
Than hasty vows of combinative aim.

GUELFO D'ESTE.

Thwarted and blighted in the bud of Spring
Such principles shall never turn to good.
Time trifled with reverses each decree,
Taken at sight which proves infallible.
Doubt and dissimulation, conjured by delay,
Wear out all honesty original,
And turn rejected purity to shame.

MATILDA.

Balance all honour on mine own henceforth
That will not cheat the age by Hate for Love,
Its great, absorbing, grave predicament
My tantalising methods ridicule.
The task of re-adjustment of staid rights
Recognised by yourself thus cautiously,

By many with a wild avidity,
Their ruin that involves in their career,
Making the blind fulfilment of their will
A stepping-stone to ruin or disgrace,
Your character will stablish and draw out.
Time hesitates and halts for such as us,
Then let us each now watch with eager gaze
The avenue which leads us to success
Valid and ultimately permanent
When that we know and feel our ground is sure,
And will not vanish from beneath our feet :
And individually and separately throw
Our stake in for a prize or its reverse.
Gifts that are silver now will turn to gold,
And all we have, and valuable view
In the frail estimation of a world
That has no test for worth but in result
That accident has placed within its reach,
Ripened and mellowed in the experiments
That others hazard in their forfeiture,
Instead of being repaid in fleeting joys
Will be secured, and to us so returned
As to be recognised available,
Not in the moderate expectation that
Common satisfaction duly creates,
But, to the admiration of the world
For purposes once their own now wholly ours,
We then shall have for their advantage, so,
Also for our enjoyment of all good,

The scale and satisfaction I deny
Proceedings imminently rash supply.

GUELFO D'ESTE.

Farewell, Matilda ! though I banish hope
I shall proceed more fully into this.
The Germans though too slow in action may
Be sure, and in their overtures correct
All that upon an undue estimate
Proved false to eagerness and vanity.
If fresh experience cannot turn the scale
Then War must be their future game not Love,
Where principle and practice often separate.
To you, so much having bestowed of the last,
Good Fortune, to propitiation true
To overtures more prudent than they seem,
May now, perhaps, not ultimately give
All estimable satisfaction in the first.

ACT V.

SCENE I.—*Canossa. The outer court of the Castle.*

HENRY, EMPEROR OF GERMANY.

Behold the vision of my Years and Life
Upon the flood of all uncertainty !
And many dread anxieties, welcome borne,
Thrice welcome !   What has hollow Hope but this,
When to the cold terrestrial sphere it sinks
A victim to unenvied martyrdom ?
The loss of popularity and power,
The cold, unquiet fall unsanctified
Of elevated wide authority
Into the monstrous catalogue of woes
That now and here shall surely terminate.
Some spell has bound me, aye, and binds me still !
Some malediction of an unknown foe.
Is it my Bertha's spectral visiting ?
Is it the remnant of her successor that
Gravely betrays the spirit of predominant
And hitherto successful dignity
Of one that brooks not man's or woman's will,
And calls the world to its obedience

' ' Where former emperors have vainly trod?
Is it the virulent opposition Conrad gives
By aping rule where he can never reign?
I will demand a blessing from the Pope
And cancel all unnatural prodigies,
Born of contentious vice, inherited
Through ages of dissimulated love
Of things they know, while others only fear.
The asp of Royalty will court all change,
Negotiating with the giddy world
That with an undeviating simplicity
For the exchange of social intercourse
Has no possession of the current coin,
But substitutes the paper cheque instead.
When rivalry like this beyond the fanciful
The core of the heart absolutely penetrates,
No barrier puts a limit to its bold
And unabashed, unblushing experiment
To clutch the prize or phantom as may be,
Through all the common agencies of art '
Which never can supply what they have lost,
While covetousness uncovenanted for succeeds
In making many miserable for one hour
Of selfish individual independence,
Which feeds on poison that is in itself
Either a poison or no food at all
Unless it find incredible support
Of those whom Fortune jilted from all stock,
And sowing seed in the once wilderness acquire

A contradiction to an ancient rule
Which being baffled straight the prize withdraws
On principle, and leaves the bright base sub-
    stitute
With nought to emulate but to substantiate
The broken reed of proved unsubstantiality.

Enter MATILDA OF CANOSSA.

MATILDA.

My royal cousin and imperial friend !
Although Italian hearts some wound has touched
Until they vibrate sadly inefficient
Their grandeur and old honour to retain,
And regulate and rectify the world
Beyond as well as within these barriers,
Formed either as a conqueror to crush,
Or else in acquiescence to preserve
Amalgamated honours once its own,
So that at will, but not by impulse driven,
As of a wild unnatural career
Either to bless what it takes, or give consent
To blessings granted greater than its own,
In this constrained, conditional attitude
I cannot hospitality refuse
To one who braves the refractory elements
Which Fortune only holds so dear as I
For making wealthy, happy, and content
This heterodox and haughty Universe.

HENRY.

Your hospitality and generosity
Is not one-half, Matilda, that I claim.
My German subjects have deserted me,
But this fond genial soil on which I tread
In the reflection of good management
And answer to my diligence is my own.
Could I but be content with Italy
I would not at Canossa be your guest.
But the domestic virtue has been aroused
Within the Teuton heart that always lurks.
Their sense or their ambition should have spurned
The poisoned sting of subtle calumny
Concealed within the moral head of Rome.

MATILDA.

The secret of their grief is that the soul
Joyfully and abundantly issued forth
Is lost in the vain tumult of desires
Stirred by the dissonant spirit of rivalry
Into a claim of that not wholly theirs.
Civilisation and authority,
Principles and practices we deem our own,
Could here both introduce themselves at once,
The wedding guests in wedding garments clad.
Yet for my part, as an impartial judge,
I should be led to wink at the deceit
By fancy filling up the void of truth,
Not urge them on to desperate designs

Without any reactionary reserve.
Not that you grant them a new covenant
In the detachment from your worthy cause,
But to their ill-advised and sudden stroke
A lenient interpretation due.
Conciliation, then, should be your care,
In explanation striving to avoid
Allusion to such errors not your own
And therefore charitably pardonable
Unless they had all choice as not their own.
Refer their wild rebellion to some cause
Distant, obscure, impersonal, and vague.
The bold ambitious scheme of William of Blois
Might from reflection call out action straight,
Might animate it with a red-hot fire
Unquenchable and inextinguishable,
Whence drawing out an incendiary's rod
With a counter-irritant they all might scourge.
Should you decide on war with such as these
Before the Truth stands upright in their hearts,
Before all eloquent illustration first
The nature of your bond with them suggests
And where all disputation though not wrong
Should it in consequences culminate,
Disastrous to their merited success
Which well attuned would treason dissipate
They might from argument forcibly repressed
In consciousness of Nature's banishment
Imagine some false phantom had arrived

To plunge them into internecine war,
Without a substitute for home disowned.

HENRY.

A century behind as some folks think
But still a century before some mark
These aggravating wild Teutonic knaves
Have still a chord of sympathy below
The feature of their social lineaments.
Together close in solemn unison
Binding Life's dissonant ingredients
Till the first advocated cause becomes their own,
Or in rejection of false sympathy
A cause the best becomes no cause at all.
Then what directs their choral eulogy,
Or elegy so turned by a direct necessity
As though the passions of an hour perverse
Not the direct incline of positive fact
And shadowy motives of an ambiguous dye?
The sacred patriarchal Crook of Rome !
Whose grave decree they hold inviolate,
Nurtured by good they know not to attain
According to universal utterance.
And by a short step to the common goal
This singular and monstrous prodigy
Reciprocally for confession made
Reveals to them the essence of our worth.
Should this great oracle unimpeachable
Place all my doings in an odious light,

Enlarge upon base sinister reports,
Engraft credulity upon the stem of belief
How will their voice and heart be ready then,
The one inhaling slander's baleful breath,
The other lit with feigned conviction's spark,
To cry ' Long live Henry our Emperor '?
No ! They will follow denunciation's beck
In heedless and unapologetic tone
Till the provoked fury finds them ready arms
That thus has wound them in a long embrace
Soon my destruction and the world's disgrace.
Nerved by no blessing can I meet this force
With the sole vigour of an arm accursed ?
Its energies completely paralysed
By moral neutralisation that must arise !
Then let not Gregory's persistence in
The exercise of this iniquitous stroke
Hardly justly incurred disarm me here.
Then where Italian sanctity is not,
Where lips profane in accents different
Discourse the inmost secrets of the soul,
Where eyes weep tears for sorrows never yours,
Where joy felt but for happiness their own,
Where kindred chords of social harmony
That binds the heart or else releases it
Accumulate their injuries on my head
I may feel staggered by the assassin blow.
So let me have your heart-felt sympathy !
Encouraged by a forlorn hope gratified.

When I return to defeat Germany
With a direct and terrible effect
The reconciliation will alarm
The renunciation of a single sentiment
Which has to treason animated them,
And the repudiation of a bond
Which their crude faculties expended out
Of a meaningless and intolerable void
Into a jealous fan to expiring flames
Be civilisation's beacon well relumed.
For without us, say, what is Italy?
The hollow vapid shadow of a past
That has volcanically burnt itself out
And left a common moral to be read
By everyone around it to its cost.
Then let its last departing throb and thrill,
Bind it once more to the substantial
Sinews and thews of an embodiment
Which shall an untameable spirit perpetuate
And lead it through the story of the world
Invigorated and remodelled thus
Till the last moments of our glorious life
Rally to compliment its origin.
Matilda! as an intercessor then
Between myself and astute Hildebrand
Revive my claim to crush a rebellious race!
Restore my arm to quell a refractory son!
Grant to successful dignity prolonged
The simple yet substantial means to fix

For ever on its head the imperial crown
That hesitatingly lingers to desert
For childish passion and superfluous zeal,
Myself its strength, as you its ornament.

MATILDA.

Your shortest way would have been to besiege Rome,
And so possess the stronghold of the Pope.
You could have easily then supplanted him
And seated firmly in St. Peter's chair
A pliant substitute for Hildebrand.
He is a person of decided views,
Has bound the clergy to celebatarian laws,
The princes and the citizen body syndicate
Of the right of election has deprived
To the possession of the papal throne,
And so discharging them of that onerous right
Has to the spiritual and temporal head
Of the divine and apostolic Faith
Not only centred in the Church its power,
But all her avenues and approaches to that Crown,
From the State's influence haughtily preserved.
So to a heart so cold and cloister-like
Whether it be infatuation or devotion,
Adherence to old rules from natural taste,
Or a desire to implicate others therein,
In answer to compulsory adherence
To rigid systematic ordinances
Which vainly thus have blighted early youth

A warm appeal from me would be in vain.
My terms with him are recognition frail,
So long as he connives at feminine rule
Over the Tuscan and Lombardian lands,
Of papal bulls, decrees, and regulations,
Whatever their direction or their scope.
The writ of excommunication seems
A method of conveying a rebuke
And not involving further punishment,
And this to be redeemed by abstinence
From such mistakes and errors in his life
On whom the retribution was provoked.
The German States have been too sensitive
To evils common in a lower grade
This mere injunction to have interpreted
Into a reversal of your Divine Right,
Which cannot err we know within due bounds :
Protected by inherited reserve
Both of omission and commission too
In preservation of acknowledged rights,
In furtherance of views approved,
And in extension of immunities
A latitude of action guaranteed,
A laxity of principle allowed
Which will reform to better discipline
That discipline wherewith they are endowed.
In this much I perceive you have been wronged,
And victimised to unfair calumny.
Therefore, but with a certain doubt implied

As to the end of such an enterprise,
I will attempt your pardon from the Pope.
Hildebrand resides within these walls,
He is an old and frequent guest therein.
A home usually his own as much as mine
He in my confidence and I in his.
Perhaps he will absolve you from this ban :
I know not for he is most obstinate
In imminent and imperative design,
In interference irreconcilable,
In opposition unconciliatory,
Fond of himself but fonder of the Church,
Whose dignity and power he lives to raise
High above every earthly potentate.
However, I will attempt it. If I fail,
In strange state matters should I not succeed
I will not ask your generosity.

[Exit Matilda.

HENRY.

The Sorceries of Rome thus negatived
Unfriendliness and disobedience,
Wastefully and wilfully encouraged thus
Within the cold untutored Teuton heart,
Shall sink to sacrificial rectitude :
And in the principle which they prefer,
But which they cannot count on as their own,
Nor that of Heaven but of middle birth,
A meteor that delights but cannot kill,

Support the plan which I esteem the best,
Or Conrad could not ape my sovereignty,
Nor, more, I be set aside to make room
For Rudolf of Suabia a stauncher candidate.

Enter AZZO, DUKE OF BRUNSWICK.

AZZO.

Can I aught offer to your majesty
To make your residence here agreeable?
Outside a palace is a prison oft
Wherein few comforts balance those too many
Which the luxurious accommodate
Until they have no feeling left at all,
And neither can be surfeited nor starved.

HENRY.

I ask no carnal consolation here,
The solace of the soul is what I seek
In its external ceremonial aid
That makes plain mortals happy, kings divine.
I have a crown and armies, what are they ?
One gives a sort of hollow consequence
When care the viper coils itself within
And eats the brain the other fails to shield.
The others if they fight win but a chance,
For an impetuous conflagration fires
The hapless cities they had elsewise won.
The sword is by the crosier broken up,

And the brave mortal race who bowed to me
Stoop lower now to the more impotent wand.
'Tis no good being refractory to this
Absolute and actually recognised medium.
If nations bow to it why not a king,
Unless he would no more be emperor?
Call it a reconciliation if you will,
I wish to come to terms with Hildebrand
Who has stirred up my German feudatories
Until rebellion ploughs up all my land
And sows renunciation of my rule.
Who fights against a vision only flies :
Then exorcise this most disastrous vision,
And I will take fresh arms 'gainst Germany
And beat it as an angel or a saint.

AZZO.

Whether upon so wide a ground as this
You and I stand upon familiar terms
Is only to be judged of by those facts
Which placed around them circumstantially
Considerations form of impartial minds.
But I would never see my country torn
By civil commotion to a thousand shreds
And this without a struggle on my part,
Or any acquisition to myself.
Then as to any influence with the Pope
I stand but as a temporal potentate,
Although not quite a sinner like yourself.

Morally approved then but indifferent
I bow to no particular sanctity
Which would enable me to interfere,
And for the performances stands security
Of virtues that I also emulate.

HENRY.

Security for what ? does he expect to take
The North of the Alps, and leave the South to me
Who all its arts and sciences would drive
As loadstone iron to himself to cheer
Not man in his industrious hearty work
With luxuries that lengthen out his days,
But in a weak effeminate attitude
To warn his chill emaciated frame,
As judges do convicted criminals,
How near the end is of his earthly hopes.
Politically I must rule the two
In unrestricted, unrestrained control,
One both the hearts and minds of those I rule.
But in the circle of domestic life
Children and women find an echo of
Their puerile and pusillanimous chimes
In the scholastic head of holy Faith.
To have the revocation of a ban
Which paralyses my attempts to rule
I must make treaty for indulgences
Which hitherto I have not recognised
To those about my table and my bed.

A monarch has too many solicitudes
To add one more to an unwelcome home.
He cannot lose by making that his care
That cherishes distress and leads regret
By higher and by lower means than ours
To simple extirpation once again.
Therefore in those lesser domains he may devise
Some petty conciliation to maintain
A general happiness in its little realm
Which fills so small a part in our concern.

Enter EPPONE OF ZEITZ.

EPPONE.

My welcome, Emperor, to your new estate !
Within the borders of your territory
You stand a suppliant to our Oracle
Which should it all your temporal potency
Couple with its divine authority
Might captivate the world it seeks to win.
Let us review the subject-matter then
Which all our difficulties involves in one.
You seek a crown as we solidity
Under whatever guise we compass it.
Solidity when strengthened by itself
Lives in a banquet on one dish alone,
But grade on grade piled one over another,
As different prismatic tints a rainbow make,
Adds elasticity to solidity
And the transformed mass so invigorates

That it can take whatever turn it likes,
Resolve itself into a thousand different shapes
Exposing each some new ingredient,
Assume an attitude hostile or pacific,
Control, advise, suggest, or reconcile,
And its own friend make all the world its friend.
So you, the head, are now in front of all,
All present and all similarly situated.
Now I do not deny your right to this
Because I own myself in point in turn,
Nor does the German nation generally,
Each section hoping to achieve its turn,
Still you must have agreement with the Pope
Who with his stern morality controls
The hidden current of our secret lives.
Without his benediction good is bad,
It reconciles the traitor to the axe
And gives the axe more than a traitor's doom.
I cannot therefore think thus seeking the aid
Of such a sacred stay as Hildebrand
The dignity of your state is compromised.
Necessity they say rejects all law,
Therefore if law should be by itself upheld
Absence of law is your necessity.
Therefore your deference is justified
To one who a companion by your side
At first only inclined your mind to good,
Then counselled you to every rectitude,
Additionally pointed out to you now and then

Irregularities that lower a man
Below the estimation of his sphere.
This should perversion diligently bent
On satisfying some intrepid boast,
Some fond conceit to carry out beyond
The edge of popularity or support,
Invest you with a cold indifference
To virtuous reputation of good deeds.
Now lest this first commencement of disease,
Innocent in one stage as easily cured,
Should visit life in every other stage
And make creation one vast hospital,
One half incurable, the other physically ill,
Prudence suggested to his Holiness
To crop the growing evils at the root,
For each misfortune turns the world upside down,
And which is then the head and which the heel?
Pardon me then for illustrating thus
The character of your complexity.
I blamed not Gregory at first, and knew
How much he sought in good for Germany.
Now I will no longer blame yourself,
For still I know you live for Germany.
His condescension claimed will rescue you,
And from disunion rescue Germany too.

HENRY.

No good is gained by a dissentient law
Which overreaching good itself overreaches.

The elements of statecraft now inherited
By me are better justified in rule
Than is a boon to morbid sufferers
The best approaching estimate
That mere self-elevation can produce.
Does Hildebrand believe that temporal power
Based upon spiritual unworldliness,
And therefore free from the taint of nominal sin,
To such a style of treatment will accrue
That kings dishonoured by his abjuration
And nations into perfidy betrayed
To passions which cry civilisation down
Will lend him aid to be an autocrat?
Or furnish him with subjects to o'erwhelm
Easy dependencies with alarm and dread?
The head of an elective monarchy
Must be the most capable of all mankind.
Should one less gifted than any other claim
The sceptre that his predecessor leaves,
Or should his subjects in collision fail
To place a stamp superior on the age
Which from some motive calls him to account
The spirit that has hitherto preserved intact,
Be it for a day or for a thousand years,
This imitation of our sovereign mood
Must sink into the spiritual, and lose
At once and for a time all temporal sway.
While Hildebrand thus accuses such as us
Of not confessing virtuous essence a rule

Beware lest we some day fallacious prove
All virtuous essence without inherited
Incontaminate, unimpoverished blood
From sire to son that hands experience down,
Sympathised with by races similar
Of every creed and any locality.
Perfection flies aloft on seeing itself
Reflected in the history of its deeds
But imperfection slumbers on, the child of chance,
Finding it has no glass to measure in
Its steps whether they prosper or else retrograde.
Its very cunning that intoxicates
Presumed it is distilled from common stuff
Cannot split opposition like the wedge
Because it has no sterling force behind.
I would that help were given me like his,
That of infatuation not philosophy,
In one sole reign I would accomplish more
Than papal rule under one hundred Popes.
Call out more science for sound purposes,
Diffuse more learning hid from jealousy,
Bestow fewer dignities with as much success
As many with less judgment and less skill,
And circulate more social happiness
Within and far beyond my boundaries
Than rigid asceticism with but two aims,
One to reclaim the guilty criminal
The other to assure him when reclaimed
His Life and Home are at his patron's will.

Enter ODONE OF SAVOY.

ODONE.

Your Majesty ! I greet you in a home
Vaunted before all others in Italy
For optional examination of
Discursive and original ideas
Which prevalence, result, and issue seek,
Encouraged by the nature of their growth
Not here alone, but everywhere around.
Within the vortex of so many schemes
Before they are drawn out and tested in
The patient crucible of analysis
You would suppose the atmosphere above,
Rent into pieces by anxieties,
Would frown upon adoption and approval
As soon as they proceeded to fish out
Plans, views, plots, and designs available.
But through Canossa's walls, and on its hopes,
Intentions, inclinations, and desires
The scented aromative vital breath
To satisfaction all that dedicates
As her soft zephyr of a summer's day
Breathes hostile agencies to reconcile.
So spirits are aroused to sleep again
Born for the fitful strange emergencies
That men and nations hurry to their end
Through motions strange to insignificance.
And those that close enlist all sympathies
For better ends and purport exercised

Unangered by unfair discouragement
Awake and are invoked to testify
The base disorders that they haste to quit.
I hear there lies some difficulty between
Yourself, the Emperor, and Gregory, Pope.
However grave the nature of the case
How deep soever the solution lie,
However twisted out of reconcilability
The dissonant and discordant points may be
On which you stand to differ or to quarrel
Disorganised and reunited here.
Into a question comprehensible
Not only to the more discriminating
But to the thoughtless, undiscerning world
They may happier solution claim
Than mystery all hopes which paralyses.
Let not despondency that spirit check
Which under less embittered impulses
Plucking a brand from Fortune's sinking fire
With all the motives of a righteous cause
Had lit a beacon that had summoned man,
No more the image of escaped decay,
No more the grain ripened but to produce
A sheaf of grain as innocent as himself,
No more the sealed impression of a right
His moderate abilities never justify,
Nor fill the void with exultation's shout
From age to age dissolved in apathy,
To prove his right to invert the poison cup

Of faculties enthralled till musty hate
Announces bad ingredients the best,
And aided by the spirit of reform
On old conditions of more varied views
At a just moment to save and secure
The promised satisfaction long desired,
Evident after now and seen before,
From seeking straight a grave solution thus
Of complications leading to alarms
Already at this crisis prominent.
But by Canossa's renovating glance
Renew attachment to and then record
Alliance with insulted and vexed friends
With whom all friendship for a moment lost
Have buried and obliterated all goodwill.
But hesitating to forego the chance
Of lifting civilisation from the dust,
Its home for ever if consigned there now,
The features of dispute unrecognised
For hearts unstained by animosity,
Revoke at once the blow discouraging,
And to the social constitution give
That tone which self from selfishness discards
And makes all happy on remotest gain.

HENRY.

All Europe now is centred on my acts !
The world itself recoils from a mischance
That might have been incurred by wrathfulness,

Of mere uncompromising feeling the result
And not the due of my extensive aim
To carry Italy and Germany
Through ill report and good report to Fame,
Faithful in process, faultless in result.
Therefore I have entrusted an appeal
That I may be reinstated in Heaven's wish
For my success and Earth's prosperity
By a kind benediction from the Pope,
Excommunication's ban expunging thus,
To our good cousin Matilda of Canossa.
Strange that man's hate may be appeased by this
Accommodation vague and undefined,
And all the pleasures I can offer him
Are offered some one else for peace of mind !
But what is conquest but a hollow word
That, bellowed from a herald's hollow tube,
To the vain auditors that catch the sound
And echo it till it builds up their home,
It matters little whence and how it comes?
So if this remedy heals all my wounds,
Why test the compounds of the precious balm,
Or ask who stands its surety for success,
The registered student or the *nostrum* quack?

Re-enter MATILDA.

MATILDA.

Henry, your mission has been well performed
With all the plausibility honour lent.

To Gregory I set forth your request,
Portrayed your imminent loss and his false gain,
And for the satisfaction of an untried world
Required him with ineffable desire
To place the Crown your ancestors wore well
With his approval thus within your reach.
He is in some staid humour mortified
For cases whose lost thorn I cannot probe.
And then he said to me in dignified pride,
With yet a touch of sorrow in his voice,
' Matilda !   Not all the world, yea ! much less thou,
Gregory the Seventh shall move from his decree.'

HENRY.

Matilda, my fair cousin, recollect
All that you know of Earth's expedients
This obstinate priest to alter from his mood.
I have for this forsworn my dignity,
Endured improper insults from my friends,
And sacrificed accumulated praise.
Say, shall I claim a personal interview,
Acquaint him with the value of my cause,
And backed by every unusual argument
So paint the altitude of my predicament
That he will be reconciled upon the spot ?

AZZO.

Ugo of Clugny best had intervene
As 'twixt belligerents with a flag of truce.

There are more currents in philosophy
Than the first tempter of its stream may thwart
If it be full and headlong hurried on.

MATILDA.

Nay, woman is surely cleverer than a monk !
I will to Hildebrand again repeat,
Fashioned with more variety of skill,
Arguments I may have used too hastily,
And so fill up inadequate desire
With charity to consecrate the world.
                    [*Matilda re-enters the castle.*

HENRY.

What vanity exists in all below !
That phantom cruel and irreproachable
To which we point when all our theories sound
We cannot turn them to a good account.
Is Adelaide of Susa of your guests within ?
If so, the accents of a resentful wife
To the more sensitive side of Hildebrand's heart
The other has hardened to vindictiveness.

EPPONE OF ZEITZ.

Her thoughts are less of this world than his own.
She only lives for charitable good,
And gratifies an original tendency

To live for others more than for herself.
And urged by wisdom of superior mould
She speeds the passage of a spirit pure
As that of any disembodied saint.
If there were many others such as she
The subtlety which undermines all hopes
And renders expectation null and void
Ambition's crown would wear more brilliant gems.
The cowl would not resort to artifice
Unworthy of its conscience to adopt.
And merit in composition would acquire
A carnal satisfaction in this work
Which would reluctant energies stimulate
To services for each appropriate,
To his own end accommodating each
Till everybody would astonish all,
This universal world one harmony.

HENRY.

A fortunate voyage made without a chart.
May Providence send the right indemnity !
There are who count on the end to be attained
Thrice valuable because improbable.
You hence enlisted then in the vague course
Hildebrand watches over without effect,
Because effect can never be produced
Without its type fulfilled here upon earth,
A pliant sample of imperiality !

Why does he make his proselytes of those
That have no elasticity to shake
Infatuation from mere acquiescence
In principles that in themselves are very well,
But are in application the reverse
For want of judgment some do not possess?

ODONE OF SAVOY.

Emphasis in expression realises more
Than the unturned assertion can achieve,
And gives a point to deeds proceeding thence.
I wish I could in Italy foresee
An outlet to its moral rectitude
That would to its own integral success
At any future period redound.
Otherwise the particular germ of virtue dies
Of virtuous redundancy of thought.
I do not include your new embellishment
Of our unrolled and unapplied decree,
These are resources for the wide world's use
Hid in the forest haunts of Germany
Which may prove some day to both speculants
The truth of facts they did' not care to solve.
Innate ambition in us and the good we have,
As if with that attainment satisfied,
Is but a spur to further enterprise
Than we at present care to venture on,
Since failure a grave reprimand implies

That us would lessen in the world's esteem.
But when from all this hazardous risk to-day
The ultimate account some morrow brings,
And Europe stands aloof at the recoil
Of misadventure by disaster foiled,
And ruined practice turn to theory bent
With fierce recrimination, taunt, and scorn,
Unless the Germans are more cordial .
Within and without in their aspiring views
Italy guided by a watchful star
Which sheds on all around a jealous light
Will seek as you the price of all its worth,
Like you will ask a blessing on its head
That had consoled and comforted the world.
But then new realms attention may divide
Interests now centred on a moderate sphere,
And thus harsh, bare, and undefined ideas
And those corrupt from continual exercise
May purify this home as absentees.
Diminished thus our area where we are
We shall increase divided nationality
By supplemented land where we shall be,
And neither hurt our state nor our ideas.

HENRY.

If commerce is this secret to disclose
Let us prepare to teach discovered lands
All that we should have learnt when in the bud,
Or else the flower will nourish such sour fruit

That they will curse the planter of the root,
And not the gardener who neglected it.
Disunion here to difficulty refers
Sciences which agreement leads in advance
Of expectation of all luxuries
That prosper health and lengthen out old age.
Then let us reconcile conflicting doubts,
And smooth the way to a superior grade
Of thought and action, sympathy and design
Before we venture to enlarge our sphere.
The future will not thank us all the less,
And as it reaps our creditable fruit
Their filial attachment we shall gain.

Re-enter MATILDA.

MATILDA.

Pope Hildebrand at last is reconciled!
Whom Earth has chosen Heaven has ratified.
In spite of one impossible demur
To precedents which I hastened to overrule
In this precise position of affairs
Involving imminent and deadly hazard and risk
To your design and his utility
Hildebrand accords you a special interview
To take place now at once within these walls.
In preparation of this point conceded,
Let me advise you to place confidence
In the general use of authority spiritual

Over the particular sphere of private life,
And over public management as well :
Accommodating these with your own views
The excommunication he will then revoke
Which has decided Germany to revolt,
And more, all purposes you may propose,
Which you insist on the fulfilment of,
However startling or presumptuous
In aping the Divine as mortal man,
He will, obtaining first a guarantee
From present princes, and my friends within,
That you will recognise in domestic life
Practices both of us are aware must be,
Prosper with a new blessing, and bestow
On each cordial assistance and support.

HENRY.

Now to the castle let us all adjourn !
Where to negotiation shall succeed
The triumph of my famous family.
Dear to the annals of the past, and hence
Dear to the hearts of all futurity,
Whose fealty shown to neither in old time
In future shall be rendered to us both.
To all who have assisted this great end,
My gratitude and confidence I extend.
You, Azzo, Duke of Brunswick, you, Eppone of Zeitz,
Ugo of Clugny, and Odone of Savoy,
Henceforth I call my warmest, worthiest friends.

My palace is your home, my court the sphere
Where you may exercise familiar rights,
As in my heart your names will ever live.
You cannot fail to render back again
This solemn obligation held in trust.
To you, Matilda, who may well expect
Some confidential and conventional grant,
To give something more than a name and shade
To reciprocity's ambiguous link,
Here and upon this spot I now confer
Over the large province of Liguria
The absolute and supreme protectorate.

MATILDA.

Henry ! the re-establishment of dominion old
Perhaps by libellous calumny o'erthrown,
Perhaps by woman's pique or young disdain,
Is more to me than all Liguria.
However, grant that this success may register
Italian virtues in the book of Life !
That when the Germans recognise the fact
Of your redemption in this joyous land,
If on some future day we make a claim
That southern hearts may make on northern heads
They will, on precepts that to-day they boast,
Rome, Italy, and Canossa recollect.

SCENE II.—*Hall in Castle Hofenstaufen.*

THE MARQUIS OBERTO.

It is a cherished vision that we love
In youth to our maturer years to lead
The care-united point of harmony
Between the probable future and sure past,
And in the voluminous ocean of excess
To steep the hesitating, anxious soul
Till it be one with both, and it with them.
Irrelevant concerns enter not then
With a too plausible and passionless face
To shock the cold, unknit, irregular sense
With a frail ladder to the realm of bliss,
Which when after a thought he steps upon
His hasty, lingering foot descends to earth,
Buoyed by the worth of its experience
From all the horror disappointment brings,
And mortification fathered by repulse
Has straight Life's riddle untwisted to the end
Without a single hitch or catch to check
His expectation's thrice enamoured grasp,
And leave men pondering for a helpless age.
A soldier's life is full of these, and when
His discomposure acquisition seals

The valuable becomes invaluable
That in its measureless extent is a prize
Worthy the military destiny,
Sparing no life and forfeiting his own,
Unless the bargain is bought up at once.
Then should not Fortune smile on such a Fate,
Which Fortune should be glad to patronise.
How Love returned returns the compliment
So unaffectedly to courage paid.
Upon this spot I parted years ago
With the fair maid Ethelga of Hofenstaufen.
She wore the bloom of youth upon a brow
That stirred my nerve to deeds imperishable
That shook the centre of the social world
With the convulsion of an untold aim,
And passed my glorified name from lip to lip,
And many ventured to prognosticate
More than a coronet was shadowed forth
In the watched mirror of Futurity,
Some sphere of exercised authority
That in the apposite opportunity,
Would prove my enterprise was capable
Of rapid transfer of enduring modes
Of consolidation bidding conflict sleep
With ashes smouldering in unconscious heat.
Whether ingratitude is the traitor thief,
Of the obliquity of diets and congresses
From the right object of their confidence
Their deferential judgment turns

We have their unrecorded leave to guess.
But in the arms of her we love we sink,
And steep ambition in oblivion
That long of failure otherwise would prate
Or by some reckless deed amalgamate
The soul with all the sorrows of unrest.

Enter COUNT HOFENSTAUFEN.

HOFENSTAUFEN.

Marquis ! a single day later had you arrived
My household would to Paris have adjourned,
For we have had enough of agitations
Which while they national differences solve
No satisfaction bring to me and mine.
Perhaps 'tis better here in Germany
The little matter now to rectify.
You well remember the old proverb says,
' Blest is the wedding the sun shines upon ; '
Let reconciliation then the clouds disperse
That long have overshadowed our best hopes
And left us dark despair, which is a robe
The cause of disappointment to conceal,
And so to encourage unnatural happiness
With otherwise unbidden sympathies.
But now in our true colours we will emerge.
I hear you have been fortunate in arms,
And now the world re-echoes your applause
Which you rejected as equivocal

When last you in my castle were a guest,
And flattered German hospitality.

Enter ETHELGA HOFENSTAUFEN.

OBERTO.

Your warm acknowledgment of my poor deeds
The praise of Kings and Emperors puts to shame.
But first I must your daughter recognise.
Ethelga, you cannot but remember when
Surrounded by the simplest circumstance
That ever youth has summoned to his aid,
When with a few trustworthy friends alone
He sows the seeds of future happiness,
Forlorn, reckless, and improvident
At the bare chance accorded everywhere
To find a footing in the rough ascent
The only road to ultimate success,
Dismay which slender expectation soothed
Your Father's kind reception chased away,
And soon the unison of your life with mine,
The rides and rambles we together took,
The tender perils of domestic life,
Which though they do not for the world prepare
Prepare us for the result of its applause,
If the Heart is to have a place at all,
Or gives futurity one single thought,
The Head by heedless circumstance gratified,
You extended to me promises that if

I some day graced the Emperor's hero-list,
Before the night of the evanescent day
Against all importunity shuts the door,
I might unite with you the nuptial knot.

ETHELGA HOFENSTAUFEN.

Marquis ! the great impression you first made
Has never vanished from my altered sense.
For woman is a metamorphosis,
Dissimilar from a weather-vane, changed from
        without,
For the head takes impressions from the Heart,
And so opinion as to those we love
Varies with that imagined in the Heart,
Or true or false, having always, nevertheless,
Some basis for its unsubstantiability.
So you have some important conquests made,
Establishing our rule in Italy.
And now the twofold giant is at rest
And folds his arms in soft complacency
He may look round and firstly turn his glance
On the strange enterprise of Normandy
Which may be our instructor in the game
Which nations for their independence play.
For nations are not individuals,
Asking for station that they cannot have,
And therefore, as their days and years are few,
And a full century's life is twice a life,
Their greater hopes and views they sacrifice

To a straight boast of wealth or poverty,
Esteeming neither and deserting both.
But choice is a fulfilment in itself
Of what is chiefly valued finally.
Looking beyond to general principles,
A trial then of general happiness.
A nation with an age for its career
To barter present principles can afford
Till certain arms shall justify their use.
At present, therefore, national jealousies
Their supersession of use may well forgive,
They are retrieved, and you are welcome then.

COUNT HOFENSTAUFEN.

A boar-hunt for to-morrow is arranged,
A hawking party the day after starts ;
The wild fowl on the lakes are capital sport
For those who with the cross-bow are expert,
Offer the hills the chamois and the bear :
The mountains shall amuse you with the feats
That men of peace pretend not to possess,
But they shall take your warlike skill to task
With strokes of courage, strength, and hardihood,
In test and trial of true manliness,
That would with you the championship dispute.

OBERTO.

The Fatherland will always be a treasury
To those renewing these desirable gifts,

But due approach to those true principles
That lead to the development of points
Which bind Creeds most repugnant to their
    course
With yet more pleasure leads me to their home.
[Hofenstaufen departs.
Ethelga, now my welcome is assured
Which I had feared in war might not be so,
For Italy has yet no cordial union
With tribes and territories beyond the Alps.
It would be wrong in me, advantaged thus,
Not to explain the views which brought me
    here,
If possible our alliance to secure
Before the general agreement is disturbed
By oscillations of a discordant tone,
Which seem to prophesy the universe
Is personally centred in our general march
To that perfection which we must attain,
If from the child we emancipate the man.
Within the circle of a soldier's sphere
There are no symptoms offered, or but few,
Of changes that his consequence portends.
But I, a man of birth as well as war,
Feel confident that the sooner we make up
Our national, social, and domestic cause
Within the barriers and without the walls
Of Germany, as a social polity,
The happier and the safer we shall be.

Normandy does not invade England as a joust,
As an assault-at-arms in chivalry.
If once the two united people turn
Again to the East our end is visible.
So much for nations.   From your own account
You seem to think a man must quickly give
Indications necessary to a short career
In a fulfilment rendered readily
Of theories he cannot justify
But sees their inclination at a glance.
From the broad outline of the technical law
With agreement to the individual turned,
Let us then, doubting theory lost in time
Unite in preferential practice now.
It is not for the dangers I survive
To place in contrast with a holier life,
It is not to subdue your social views
To the bare test of my experience,
But that I hope by giving a fresh turn
To courses that in each our separate lives
Delusive or disastrous may have been
The tenor of our happiness to string
To one the most harmonious chord of all
Attachment based on mutual interest,
In ultimate alliance to result.
And whether we perfection reach or not
So to have thus sought out more intelligibly
The secret our forefathers never knew,
And which few now lead on to their success.

ETHELGA.

I would that all Italians thought like you !
They have a soft temerity their own
Which leads them to dissemble with their worth,
And place the work of others in a light
Which renders it but a contrast due to crime,
While crime is necessarily balanced worth.
If I could but rely that time would teach
So keen, ready, and comprehensive a mind
A more accommodating charity
For those who life esteem a sorry task
I should not question my sincerity
In advocating the best principles
On the best basis for their inculcation
By changing this my home for Italy.
But if associations that betray
Institutions only calculated
Unsteady aims to guide and to direct,
Persuade dissatisfied spirits to absolve
Them of their natural or acquired views
And undermine the line they might direct
Of an advancement which we falter in
Compared with their appreciation quick
But never contradict or disconcert,
How can I trust myself within a sphere
Of energies misdirected purposely,
And with all insight into things remote
Render their utilisation farther still ?

Perhaps the spirit of investigation sleeps
In Germany, because, having woke in Italy ;
It seems to behave as if truth were fallacy
And deviations should assist a law
Which, plucking principle from sophistry,
Should make direct philosophy a sin.
Embittered by internal agonies
Which not the natural fruit of Time
Only by healthy reaction can be cured
The intonation of ennobled thought
Which is the nurse and tutor of the sublime
Innate within its limited area
From dread, fear, jealousy, doubt, or false
    surmise
Twists that especial faculty, and misdirects
Its haughty aspirations to penetrate
The origin of emotion, thought, and deed
With a strange curiosity unnatural
For the too definite purpose of affront,
As if its glorious fount of victory
Over the obstacles against us hurled
Were to be slighted, since their obstacles
Are different from those of races round.
Then having discovered secrets, for their good
And not their injury, hid in mystery,
Both to each other and their distant friends
The apparent principles of right and wrong
Inverting they directly so apply,
As to mock Heaven without inviting Hell.

That so without a standard of appeal
The passions which they labour to arouse
As if for some desirable object in view,
Through unconscientious deviations turned
Abandon rectitude and veracity,
And crossed by a too lenient destiny
In methods of voluminous abundance
That every illustration reiterates
Of its generosity and your great gain,
Intention alter by unjust opinion,
The very advocated deeds disown
That would add present proof of past success,
And by perverted truth and sophistry
So check the spirit of advancement there
That here and in remoter distant lands
They hesitate to assume civilisation's robe,
Though ready proffered to their pliant tastes.

OBERTO.

We do but administer poison to ourselves ;
One of the lessons science teaches us
Fancying that in exuberance of thought
Its elevation and profundity
Vivid perception and immediate
Adaptation of the sublime and beautiful
Appreciated emanations of the Divine
We shall outrun the pace of mere success,
And be a standard, not of its attainment,

But in the breathless haste of our career,
Of the proficiency by which it may be lost.
But with liberality we circulate round
The measure of our liberal receipts
Wherever no acknowledgment is due—
Of liabilities which I have described
To those whom accident or life's requisitions
Naturally place us in connection with.
And Germany ! so proud and prompt to seize
The changeful, dictatorial challenge cup
And prove itself the chosen recipient
Of all attested suffrages around,
It differs from us but in tardiness
For the attainment of all politic ends,
For general advantage universally
Ostensibly paraded to our view,
Yet laying by a separate store of wealth,
Some day to use against us and the world,
A calculating, careful, thrifty enterprise
Which while it would achieve what others lose,
Thinks not that in a passion they will revoke
The value of the prize that they have lost
And so disturb the line you have marked out
As to make progress hazardous and vain,
A passage through a defile without arms,
Around you and above you and behind
A foe with every instrument supplied,
To mock and harass all you care and toil,
Until you never reach the promised Land.

ETHELGA.

You would deter us then, in being the head,
And therefore in administration sedulous
Our own importance firstly to maintain,
Of these two nations, Italy and Germany,
From the fulfilment on our part of that
So prejudicial in the end to you
With less of judgment, more of spiritual gifts.

OBERTO.

The contrast of the two will ultimately,
Whichever power may at first preside,
The prominent mistake in each destroy.
Suspect not yet this individual heart
Vibrates with any disingenuous stroke.
I am as honourable to you as the dawn
Which promises the mid-day summer heat,
And will not hear the Italian name aspersed,
Unless by your acceptance of my suit
You now acknowledge it is possible
At this emergency to have obtained
A creditable champion for its cause.

ETHELGA.

Consolidation is the statesman's aim.
Trouble yourself no more upon these points.
Your Italy is worthy of my faith.
It will restore to it that hopefulness
That as its skies are so it will be pure.

It will accomplish proof as its right aim
In the field of spiritual exercise
Of moderating passions I despise,
And which have not had birth in Germany.
And those tumultuous emotions which offend
The shrewd well-wishers of the public good,
And will divide and subdivide your soil
Into volcanic craters gushing forth
With the hot pestilential fumes of wrath,
All practices prudential to entomb,
Assisted by fresh charitable acts,
Into a broader basis will expand,
Where all degeneracy laid to sleep
Into a realm of wide philosophy
Where the rare monuments of ancient date,
In correspondent grandeur shall demand
Your acquiescence to a fealty thus
In their day as in ours devoutly sworn
To some divinity not all their due,
And with the symbols which we have possessed
Of truths our own, now turned to our account,
You may in Italy be a pioneer,
Ourselves the light to guide you on your path,
To glad solutions of the mysteries
Which now perplex, but never can disturb
Realms or individuals closely knit
By appreciations of, then association with
The brighter Idol of pure rectitude
Long hid, but now revealed, and now adored.

Enter COUNT RINALDINI.

RINALDINI.

Ethelga ! how is this ?   Another here !

OBERTO.

Begone ! you have no right now on this spot.
There are strange rumours of you in Italy.
You cannot here explain them, so begone.

RINALDINI.

I thought you were in the conspirator's cell
At Pforzheim, on the charge of robbery
At Mâcon of the future crown of England !
How came you to evade the warder's eye
And play the libertine and robber here ?

OBERTO.

Couple not crime with my victorious name.
Your deeds mysterious of diplomacy
Are brimful of iniquity and vice.
A soldier boasts a plain unsullied shield,
Untainted by base sinister designs.

ETHELGA.

This quarrel more befits the court or hall.

My father shall decide before us three
On this point what is right and who is wrong.

RINALDINI.

I shall not ask your father's confidence ;
He cannot give it to a man like that,
For he has been the witness to the fact,
As far as circumstantial evidence can prove—
Nay, more, what all suspicions justify—
That he committed this felonious crime.

ETHELGA.

They said that you had married an Italian girl,
The daughter of the jeweller Sasselli !

RINALDINI.

You would not see me here if that were so.
Then for this prudish moody jealousy
You would my honourable suit refuse,
Renounce connection with a councillor
Full of the secrets of our separate lands
In which your father's honour is involved,
And drive me from your hospitable home !

OBERTO.

Break off !   Count Rinaldini, draw your sword !
Firstly you accuse me of that, the account of which,
Blazing from tongue to ear, is all I know.
Then you proceed to intimate your love

Of one I now assert will be my wife.
Revoke your accusation and depart,
Or else prepare and stand on your defence !

> [*Draws his sword.*

RINALDINI.

Out upon crime ! and sudden readiness
To seize on things you never should possess !
Honour when lost creates false dignity.
With wit to penetrate such sophistry
I haste to punish thy temerity.

> [*Draws his sword. They fight.   After a sharp
> contest Rinaldini falls.*

OBERTO (*turning to Ethelga*).

Ethelga ! Rinaldini, who seemed to exercise
Some potency over your forgiving heart,
Was a designing knave, and now has paid
The price of treachery to eternity.
A man whom I have known and you have loved,
Whose deeds bore no resemblance to his face,
Whose cold significance of others' faults
One half the world has long compelled to live
On the dishonoured name of the other half.
Whose deep domestic plots marring the conscience
With truth and perjury too strangely mixed,
Had he lived undiscovered and unmasked,
With just as much of artifice as guilt,
More happy homes had ruined than the sword.
I now give you my oath it was not I

Who stole the future King of England's crown.
Banish suspicion and credulity,
And having been my love become my wife.

ETHELGA.

Believing in your oath I will assent.
When first I heard this charge of felony
I shuddered at my precipitate hastiness
In listening gravely to your proffered suit.
Unquestioned guilt will tarnish any name,
No matter how ennobled or enriched.
The soldier's life the State's necessity
Frees from all charge of rash extravagance,
Since that the evil he may perpetrate,
And this within the circle of design,
Is counterbalanced by the good attained.
This not for his advantage is, you say,
And therefore his a virtuous sacrifice
Of self and the eventual acquisition.   Then
What in a nation is advisable,
As I have said, is reckless in a man,   .
Nor do I at this juncture, criticised
In general international settlement,
Believe the warm impetuous fire of zeal
Has found in you an instrument to abstract
For this especial injury or some good
The entrusted crown of William of Normandy.
Therefore I will consent to be your wife,
Averse to crime, but not estranged from strife.

OBERTO.

I am myself one of the adventurous
Whom Providence and honour have long upheld
Free from iniquity to aid the Right.
Italy by some judicious enterprise
Will some day rival Norman chivalry,
Our race will guide it then as I have now.
Embrace me then, Ethelga ! let us live
Happy together, and our years employ
Dividing sorrow and uniting joy.

[*They embrace.*

SCENE III.—*The Castle of Canossa.   A large
sitting-room.*

An Arm-chair.   The Appendages of an Invalid.

BUONVICINO.

The Hour has come, and it has passed away !
The grim possession of Eternity
Has a percentage interest on its sum,
And this is what is paid us as our Life.
It is so balanced, if we but fulfil
The whole exactions of the close demand,
The interest is equivalent to the sum.
I will now reckon up my whole account
And tally principal with interest.
Prosperity has offered me its cup,

Pleasure at the brim, and poison in the dregs,
So I have gravely presented it all round,
Tasting alternately with those that drink.
And some the poison has annihilated,
Thereby attesting Providence's gift
By the too liberal encouragement of
Joint infatuation and credulity.
Can Mortal put on Immortality
Too slowly wheresoe'er his tent be pitched ?
His speculation in a worldly guise
For six days' service saves a Sunday wear.
Then what accomplishment can do is done,
Giving the opportunity for the unperformed
Of a reserved amount of spiritual aid.
Whether we chose at first our situation,
Or not so doing have a larger choice,
Relieves us with an option here or there,
So that we are not the tool of circumstance
In the adaptation of all principles,
To all the practices inherited ours,
In independence every man has a claim
To make some clumsy idol with his art.
Is Life the keynote of Eternity,
Or that of this our regular mortal strain ?
It matters not if each be equal each
And we have by penurious dealings here
So far invoked the spirit of Old Age
That our Eternity we can surprise
With an ascertained exact equivalent price,

Its value and our own importance sure,
Our own necessities and its requirements
Paraded to our more inquisitive sight,
Of cautious steps the sad emolument,
The grave return of countless sacrifices,
The bond contracted indissoluble now,
Every condition equably fulfilled,
And to our hot imagination, sobered now,
What once presented an impossible feat,
The series of our years half hidden by
The application of this visible end,
Is but the plain natural and sound decree
Of hardly uninvigorated Life.
Curious or simple, innocent or compound
To others, of a fixed character to me,
Is this solution of a monster trick,
This interpretation of a paradox!
Which closed round by a court's emblazonries,
Or chequered by vagaries of hid thought,
Is a career of wide philosophy
That draws to its termination.　I must yield
A haughty deference to a Power I know,
But cannot regulate in its exercise
Of that mysterious authority he apes
Who seeks mankind to school to discipline
For purposes that are not theirs but his.
Hushing wild dreams of that intemperance
From inexperienced sources which arise,
And giving solace to the tried and tired

Victim of bootless incapacity.
What spectacles of disproved philosophy !
Of ventured sympathies what reflection sad !
What devious paths that lead to nothingness !
What strides and springs to sudden victory !
Could I but chronicle ten single instances
Of variable courses to one end
What a fine lesson to futurity,
Who else have all to study o'er again,
Unskilful, and for such improvidence
Unrecognising probable results,
And entering on a struggle obsolete
With such endeavour as I chronicle.
It would have been with them as 'tis with me,
But it is better for individual enterprise
That I should be remembered, they remote
From all the causes that have made me so.

[Sinks into the arm-chair.

Enter MATILDA.

MATILDA.

Repose, Buonvicino, from all thought.
Too much the world in boisterous alarm
At this pervading crisis of your date
Has vexed your spirit with cross purposes.
The contradictions that you have supplied
To propositions of unnatural aim
And purposes iniquitously wild
Has made my Lombardy a monument

Y

Of your sagacious and attentive skill.
My dignified position contrasts well
With the fierce agitation seething round,
And stirring up commotion everywhere.
A hundred years since Sigifredo ruled
A monarch in Canossa's capital,
And spent his time in adding territory,
Increasing the extent of his domain.
Azzo Alberto followed at his death,
And just in time Canossa fortified,
For Berengaria then three years and more
Its bastions threatened pertinaciously
And tried and tested the new rampart's strength.
Tedaldo next succeeded, marquis styled
Of Modena and Reggio.   Effort laudable
And energetic for a southern soul
Enabled him eventually to annex
Ferrara, Brescia, and Mantua.
My father Bonifacio was a Prince
Whom everybody feared and no one loved.
He had two wives, as you can recollect,
The first Rechald, who an unusual grace
To the demeanour of a goddess joined,
The daughter of Count Gualberto was,
But dying early by a fever smitten
To Bonifacio left no successor.
A temporary gloom Canossa sealed,
Wrapt in the mood of an' uncertain aim,
And vexed the tract of land its main support.

At that time Frederick of Lorraine possessed
A fair and lovely daughter, Beatrice.
My father heard of her and pleaded suit,
And won her heart, and she became his wife.
A threefold produce was the timely result,
Two timid daughters, and an only son.
But Frederick, of frail and fragile strength,
Survived his father but a single year.
Shortly one of the daughters followed him,
And I alone, the other, represent
The family pedigree and the family claim :
Rich Tuscany and Lombardy are mine,
Mantua, Modena, Brescia, and Parma,
Reggio and Piacenza, and the land
Dividing sage Bologna from Verona,
And all from Camerino to Viterbo.
I hold Ferrara and the Quadrilateral.
Now Buonvicino, reputed thus
To be the wisest man in Italy,
Let me remind you again of what you sought
Just when about for Tribur to depart,
The second end of inherited domains
Which shield a trouble that they early give.
My husband, the Duke Gobbo of Lorraine,
Killed in a sortie at the siege of Antwerp,
A widow left me, first disconsolate
When youth had sealed my wishes with success,
And fortune elevated all its hopes.
But has Canossa not the art to find

In the wide world of untried enterprise
A nobler, better, wiser man than he?
Who from his birth gave no security
Of age with military proficiency
That taught him Life was but a sacrifice
To others' good, not ours, so lost his Life.
With due precision I informed you then
That to connect my states with Germany,
That wins without the counsel of the heart,
It would enhance my fortune and my name,
And your possessions turn to good account
If I allied myself with Guelfo d'Este,
The present Duke of Bavaria's eldest son.
The arrangement was successful for a time,
And all went happily between us two,
But in the varied stages of matrimony
Before the last fulfils the boast of the first,
When faltering intrigue has just performed its
    part,
And varied opposition to desire,
A quarrel will with pettifogging art
The tenor of the union upset,
And calling into play hid devilry
Strangles the soft emotions that, unfelt,
Concord to differences had supplied,
And breaks the spell that forged the mystic ring,
And hurls to ruin hopes it had enclosed.
So we two rivals, with disordered views,
A more severe disorder met to choose.

BUONVICINO.

Then marry Conrad, Henry the Fourth's successor.

MATILDA.

He is a rebel, and prosperity
The unfilial adventurer cannot surely grace.
It is one thing ambition to encourage,
Another thus to reap untimely fruit.

BUONVICINO.

A month since he proclaimed himself Emperor
With quite as many friends as Henry had.
'Tis three weeks past he was at Milan crowned.

MATILDA.

What ! with the imperial crown of Germany ?
   [*Buonvicino is seized with a fit of coughing.*
Excuse me ! I perceive I have overwrought
Your patient mind with my sincerity
As to my union with Guelfo d'Este.

BUONVICINO.

Conrad, the probable German Emperor,
Joined to the spirit of his ancestors,
Has the warm briefness of Futurity.
He wildly seeks no universal rule,
But, with a patience that I emulate,
Watches events that rival his career,
And unless Henry is successful soon,

The German princes, for the furtherance
Of their resolve to arbitrate between
A cruel husband and a wondering world,
His name will whisper for the sovereignty ;
And it is heard in cottages in the Alps,
And as you utter it avalanches fall,
And nature in convulsions must be true.
Neglect not this grand opportunity
Of succouring our Italy by one stroke
Of self-invited natural policy.
You know that I am older than I seem—
Indeed, I linger on Death's precipice.
To such the gift of prophecy belongs ;
To such the opaque veil the Future lifts.
I could not speak suggestions sinister,
And with my last and most extended breath
Remonstrate fiercely with a double tongue,
For your advantage one apparently,
For my own character the other reserved,
Aware of both positions absolutely,
And with eyes turned to one result alone—
Italy's welfare and your happiness.
I conjure you to wed the Emperor's son,
Whether he be discarded or be safe.
I see already distant Germany
Under these auspices small dependencies
Into a glorious whole will amalgamate
To startle the world with a capacity
For sound internal and external rule,

And the false Light, just now its Regent Light,
Before a brighter luminary be extinct,
Which then in efforts comprehensively,
So with a centralised essential point
Creation's extended energies cumulatively
Consolidating into one closely woven
Embodiment of our creation's aim,
Will so accomplish universal rule,
If not politically, spiritually.
Controlling all with an invisible wand,
Suggesting where coercion cannot win,
From passion free our race, from prejudice theirs,
On this side and on that side of the Alps,
And Europe loose from cavernous deceit,
All civilisation's ruin and defeat !

MATILDA.

Think you then unassisted in its aim
By friends of disposition different
Whose methods of comparison alone
Would furnish every lost ingredient
Italy or Germany would achieve
The full perfection you anticipate ?
I could not marry one already my lord !
If you think Conrad has alarmed the Diet
Into base acquiescence to his claim,
Bavaria stands on terms equivalent
To my Italian provinces around.
It is a match of happier incident,

Offering more regularity of thought.
Further than this the Pope approves of it.
You wanted his opinion on the point.
As for the crown with which they Conrad crowned,
A jackdaw dressed out in a peacock's plumes,
Unripe credulity softened with flowers of thought
That it will never live to eat of the fruit,
How I shall laugh if Guelfo eat the fruit !
And he or some one else first strip the daw !

BUONVICINO.

Matilda, you remind me of my youth,
But even then I could not have assumed
And partially feathered such a pointless shaft.
View with discretion this complexity.
I feel my frame grow faint, my eyes grow dim.
If in the mirror of insincerity
For the best purposes and gravest ends
I have the artificial web of life
Peopled and filled with frothy fallacies,
In this last moment when we thus must part
I will one solitary truth reveal
To your deep heart and educated mind,
A pattern revelation of the rest.
William the Second, Duke of Normandy,
Having in fancy seized on Britain's isle,
From a jeweller in Rouen ordered a new crown,
A copy of that worn by Charlemagne
When Roncesvalles placed it on his brow.

Unwilling or unable to set forth
In mould equal to the original
Symbol of European pride and pomp
This delicate and difficult design
He sent the order to a Tyrolese,
Who had a reputation long achieved
For ornamental rich gilt jewel-work.
Herein the business lacked Italian art,
Carved intricacy, and curious workmanship.'
Florence promised a skilled artificer,
A master in this branch of heraldry,
So trusting in the methods he had acquired
Referred to him the stones the Tyrolese,
And in three weeks the crown was furnished forth,
Sent on to Innspruck to the Tyrolese,
Who, in delight at the accomplished feat,
Seems to have thought mankind had halted here,
And so could not retract the fact fulfilled.
He was no politician, and the gems
Which did not circulate circumspection's light
Within, gold not resembling our support,
Instead of carrying on to Rouen himself
He sent by an untrustworthy messenger.
For travellers unwary Mâcon placed
To be a lesson the ' Rouge Dragon ' Inn
And a probation for all honest men,
The one themselves and all that they possess
By life's intoxicating current caught,
Engulfed a moment in the tempter's snare,

They forfeit all they have, yea ! be released
By incapacity and want of wit,
Oversight or inadvertency,
By wanton murder's poniard unseen
Their griefs they drown or joys they ridicule ;
The other life easily so resuscitated
By moderate draughts of potent Burgundy
More easily lean to balance life's account
And make themselves respectable at last.
Having received of this arrangement note,
The copy of the crown and its intent,
Seeing the house of Blois was going to offend
The house of Capet in new dignity,
I had a third crown made, so similar
To the other two in character and design
That none by assayers and lapidaries could
The possibility of a cheat discover.
I then selected a skilled Bolognese,
In secret service that I oft employ,
Directed him to choose a hunter's guise,
Acquainted him with all the current facts,
And gave him my fresh copy to exchange
Under the influence of a sleeping draught
For that with which the trusting messenger,
Thinking that Providence was to be bribed with
    what
Conciliates and controls inferior man,
The Norman capital intended to reach.

                  [Sinks into a chair and coughs.

MATILDA.

Had not the Florentine jeweller a daughter?
Antonio Sasselli was his name.
Count Rinaldini fondly loved Theresa,
But she liked Johann Chemnitz better, because
He understood and helped her father's trade.

BUONVICINO.

Exactly so! hence jealousy arose
Between Rinaldini and the Tyrolese.
My Bolognese dispatched his business well,
Chemnitz's messenger liberally entertained,
Infused a strong narcotic in his wine,
And when sleep seized on his unwary limbs
And turned a life of toil to misery,
He changed the crowns beyond discovery,
In jovial humour paid the messenger's bill,
And passed him off to Rouen silently,
With wondering wink and gesture dissolute
As if he were as innocent as snow,
And in the other smouldered guilty fire.

MATILDA.

What then became of the crown you thus procured?

BUONVICINO.

This is the point I wished to lead you to.
Firstly the Tyrolese was placed upon his trial
At Rouen in the court of justice there

Together with the hapless messenger.
Indignant at the theft and looking at
The instigation of the felony
Suspicion on Count Rinaldini fell.
Chemnitz avowed the firm belief in this
Too probable Italian conspiracy.
One lover with those means all lovers find
To prove the other is a criminal,
Then by the regulations of the law
The jealous interference to withdraw,
And the first dame without a rival wed
Beyond restraint of option or free choice.
The Count's arrest the Norman judge decreed.
For all I know in gaol he lingers yet.
The stream of freedom blocked flows far and free.
Then comes the use I made of my possession,
Which I determined in antipathy
Should not the King of England's brow adorn.
When you discern the secret of my plot
Adopt the plain fulfilment of its aim
And marry Conrad, the new Emperor!
Before a crowd of Italian dignitaries,
Applauding followers of his great success
In turning arms against unnatural art,
In the cathedral at the altar stone
Where Milan rears its consecrated fane
The crown, not William of Blois', though
    Charlemagne's,
I placed upon victorious Conrad's head.

MATILDA.

Did you not know that Henry the Emperor
Had in your absence from Canossa claimed
Through me an interview with Hildebrand,
In which excommunication was withdrawn,
And thus from German superstition freed
The provinces rebellious had returned,
And Teuton allegiance by this trick regained
The rather had set Conrad's claim aside.
Therefore my mind is made up in the search
Of present difficulties for due remedy.
I will not sacrifice my hopes for yours,
And temporisation prudently denounce
Which in the modification of enlarged decrees
Prefers adjustment to wrong rectified
Finally and for ever by my plan.

BUONVICINO.

Which is to ruin all for your renown !

MATILDA (*rising from her seat*).

Buonvicino ! this is all too much
For due subservience to my dignity.
You have supported young rebellious blood
And compromised parental priority !
Have you no mercy to extend to one
Who sued for mercy to our high oracle ?

Then she who bore thee, therefore, has no more
Affection for thee left within her heart.

> [*Buonvicino rises from his seat.*

BUONVICINO.

Away ! recrimination's bitter tone
Had better come from other lips than thine !
Know I have laboured all my life in vain
For benefits never to be mine or yours
If you are to direct their tone, not me.

> [*Approaches her with threats.*

MATILDA (*starting up*).

Miscreant !   Now Canossa fears thee not ;
I love thee not.   Passion is principle
With me, who am not so unprincipled
As thus to sacrifice the means to the end,
Knowing that end cannot be so secured.

> [*Rings a bell.   Courtiers enter.*

Seize and disarm this criminal infidel
Who seeks in feeble measures to reproach
As woman's weakness wisdom's second wit,
And will not have what Providence decides
Stands for Canossa's good, and yours, and mine.

> [*The courtiers press Buonvicino into his chair.*
> *Matilda unwinds her scarf, and passes it*
> *round his neck.*

Now, traitor to Italian hopes, and all
That earnest wish for earth's expected gain

And rival agencies for common weal
Have placed upon the balance of design,
The penalty of guilt and treason pay
At the great altar of immortal day!

> [*She strangles him.*

SCENE IV.—*Sasselli's house in Florence.*

Enter CHEMNITZ.

CHEMNITZ.

She is not here! Theresa is not here!
Then Rinaldini must have married her!
That twofold villain, deeper in intrigue
In life domestic than diplomacy!
Then off to Innspruck I return alone.
But first of all my accounts I will make good
With old Sasselli, her laborious parent.
They have been standing over a long time.
Remorseless fiends these politicians!
Business stands still and commerce never thrives
Soon as they put their finger in the pie.
No more the labourer is paid for toil,
No more the artisan for exercise
Of talents that each century subverts
With rare productions of another date,
Which other disconnection certifies
In the lost harmony of devices rich,

And eschewing relief to the far distant hope
In revolution of art excellence
That breathes for breathless praise, then sooner dies,
To show disapprobation may have breath.
Then why reveal the secrets of the mine,
If from the very bowels of the earth
A gloomy vault we carve out for ourselves
And write upon the lid *OBLIVION?*
The mitred superstition of the Church
Brings us its proselytes, but the supply,
Ransom of sorrowing souls is not enough,
And the Iron Rod reviles the twisted Crook
Till in course juxtaposition places both
In rapacity of unsatisfied desire
The victim of two disappointing schemes
Calculated to have made them prosperous
If either of them liked prosperity.
But what we most admire they hate and fear,
Lest accidentally they being one with us
Intentionally they may be compelled
The burdens that press on us to relieve,
Or foster in us similar principles
Than would permit imprudence unprovoked
To summon with pretended injury
Such dissolute sympathies to their assistance,
Diseases providential that must deprave,
And dislocate the motives of all right,
Till all the remedies we can discern
For all the contradictory confluences

Of mischief and distress that circumvent
The round of happiness that time would unfold
Is called the intolerant chafing of disturbed,
Unhealthy mechanism of too subtle a mind,
Having no nutriment to its palate natural,
But yet a most unnatural appetite,
No longer pleased with what it seems to wish,
But irreconcilable, and unconciliatory.
Thus pleasure dies, and failing is no good,
And the world vanquished by its favourite thought
Lives to find out that thought's unworthiness :
Then in a sudden agitating fit
Either its rash existence terminates,
Or, not the final upshot relishing,
Overturns everything and begins again.

Enter SASSELLI.

SASSELLI.

Good morrow, Chemnitz !   What an unusual hour
To strike the rest from an old jeweller !
I am not all I was when youthful fire
Awoke the cold perceptions of the world
To that prosperity we then cheered on
With our glad tokens of encouragement
From dark through dawn to a most glorious day.

CHEMNITZ.

Then trade is flourishing in Italy.
In Germany we are at issue yet
With manor-rights and royalties and laws

Directly or indirectly which affect
Discouraged ingenuity for the worse,
And censures independence in the test
With quarrelsome materials for the rule,
As if being so subdued was to subdue
A nature more refractory than us,
With us unnatural, since they increase the price
Of valuable creations that they wear.
Export and import dues we must evade
If we intend to live on moderate gain.
Can wealth pressed from a straight to a devious path
Do aught but stagnate in unhealthy nooks?

SASSELLI.

Here the assayists seek to interfere,
And analyse the crucible's returns.
And then to fill the cup of impudence
Comfort me with the brief acknowledgment
That current coin should be debased below
The moderate standard of our working gold
Till friction cannot lineaments erase
Which they say gives the metal all its worth,
Although the manner of the secret is
We thus substantiate their tyranny.

CHEMNITZ.

Succession of their currency but announces
In local and individual difference
How vague each tenure, and how short each claim.

Now to resume the business of our class,
Which has stood still between us a long time.
It was a crown you last set up for me,
For which I gave the stones, and you the gold.
The world has not yet lived quite long enough
To tell us the result of crowned heads,
But my good head has ached for many a day,
In the first process being so utterly condemned
That the last product must be equally so.

SASSELLI.

Gems give unnatural lustre to all things.
You look at events through a prismatic light.

CHEMNITZ.

Why, you were burnished gold when first we met,
And now, you dead and unreflecting gold,
Hatefully insusceptible of Life,
Have neither feeling, heart, nor sympathy.
Or else you know not of man's suffering.

SASSELLI.

With ignorance or incredulity
I never taxed you, Chemnitz, on my part
I have not uttered to you a single word
Of irritating taunt or cold reproof
For difficulties I have undergone,
For which you chiefly are responsible.

CHEMNITZ.

I paid you down three hundred marks at once,
You had only to deal with the workmanship,
As the result was wholly fathered upon me,
Who has a piteous, lamentable tale
Firstly of incarceration, then *perdu*
To temper to your acrimonious ear.

SASSELLI.

The money you paid first was not enough.
Full many an ounce of metal purified
Into refined gold of the highest test
I worked into the crown at my own risk,
Thinking that when you had presented it,
For purposes of doubtful character
Enough to have disqualified my skill,
And remuneration adequate received
The additional expenditure of mine
Joyfully you would directly have repaid.

CHEMNITZ.

Money ! the round world is not one of gold.
Believe me it is one of liberty.
And he alone is rich who freedom knows,
And by close cunning the false stroke evades
Which tears him from himself and happiness.

SASSELLI.

But I have paid that other penalty,
For you and for your debt I lingered months
Incarcerated in the city gaol,

And but for a good friend more staunch than thee
There I had spent the residue of my days.

CHEMNITZ.

Sasselli, when I parted from you last
You gave me your Theresa for a wife.
It is some years ago since first we met.
She was a girl of artless innocence.
I found I was upon untrodden ground,
And I aroused that early confidence
Within a woman's untried heart that springs
When she beholds a stranger and a man.
And she and I measured Futurity
Carved to include our mutual Happiness.
The second time we met, a certain count
Had biassed her opinion, and laid claim
The matrimonial knot to justify,
And I was told at once I had no chance.
Therefore to Innspruck I, plain lapidary,
Returned on fallacy to meditate.
A Count Rinaldini one day came to me,
And from a tray of diamonds chose a stone
To be enclosed in chased gold, and despatched
Unto Ethelga of Hofenstaufen.

SASSELLI.

                  · Ha !

Theresa wears the gem upon her breast,
In token of an agreement with her made
To cancel all the debt upon the Crown,
And so to free me from imprisonment.

CHEMNITZ.

On what condition was the agreement based?

SASSELLI.

What? when it frees your liabilities?
Unless you wish to have me lock you up.

CHEMNITZ.

I now have come to pay you the amount
And take Theresa back to the Tyrol.

SASSELLI.

Count Rinaldini is your creditor,
And as Theresa was betrothed to him
You my descendants pay instead of me.

CHEMNITZ (*drawing a stiletto*).

Then they are married! before this it confess,
Sasselli, I will confiscate the breath
That would my downfall and defeat proclaim.
The mercenary treaty they two signed
Shall be washed out by thy impatient blood!
　　　　　[Seizes Sasselli and lays him on the floor.

Enter TARCHETTI.

TARCHETTI.

Hi! Murder, Fire, Confusion! Stop thy hand.
This in the Capital of Tuscany?
　　　　　[Drags Chemnitz away, and shakes him.

CHEMNITZ.

Who, and what stranger are you, I demand ?
This is a quarrel on a financial point
Between disciples of a special trade,
And neither brigandism nor housebreaking.

SASSELLI.

Upon my person this is an attack
On no trade differences pardonable !
Make your peace with the banker, not with me ;
I now have done with you, and know you not.

TARCHETTI.

Business is not improved by taking Life.
Its usefulness deserts us with our Life.
This was not a financial interview :
You must account for the attack at once
Or I the guard shall summon from without.

CHEMNITZ.

I came to pay a debt and found it paid.
If the vain god you worship sent but this,
A gilded pill royal headaches to cure
And it was palatable to my illness,
I then had asked Sasselli for the receipt
And vanished a dishonourable knave.
But he who paid it sought for in return
Union on his part by that solemn link
Never to be broken by a wiser world
With her his only daughter, only child.

TARCHETTI.

Let that alone ! it was a Father's will.
He wished to have a noble son-in-law :
A natural mode of showing gratitude
For liberty decreed and life preserved.

CHEMNITZ.

But only known to the mother of the girl
Her love before the Count I had secured,
And only put our marriage off until
The German states, in revolution then,
Had given my business that stability
On which a happy union depends.
I carried on my business as before.
A crown was ordered just a year ago
From Bonnières of Rouen, Normandy,
Who sent it to me, coupling an order for stones,
Of nature rare, and cutting to the shape
Of an old pattern crown legibly defined.
Secretly the transaction was to be managed,
And all within a period specified,
With money to make and set the crown complete.
Not being in precious metals an artisan,
Carefully having cut selected stones,
I took them with the pattern to Sasselli,
Enjoining him to use his famous art
In unusual skill of mould and tracery.
For no one was if possible to discern

The copy from the fine original.
Sasselli executed his share well,
The crown returned defied all scrutiny.
Having some business for the Pope at Rome,
A shrine to jewel for his holiness,
I sent the crown by a trusty messenger
To Bonnières of Rouen, who received
The order in a manner indirect
From William of Blois, the Duke of Normandy.
A week had passed away when I was seized
On accusation of a treacherous deed.
The crown returned was of false gold, false gems,
Instead of rivalling as the direction meant,
It ridiculed that worn by Charlemagne
Of which a copy had been sent to me.
On this charge I to Rouen was transferred,
And led before the Prefect, who declared,
The pattern and my copy before him laid,
That I had taken Bonnières' honest gold
That would have made their duke the English
   king,
And in a moody hatred of that cause,
Its dignity and quality to o'erthrow,
Had on their judgment vanity imposed,
And lessened Conquest in their childish eyes.
That sacred oracle of Equity,
Seeing no more than simply he could see
With both eyes shut by servile loyalty,
The obvious deduction would not make

That some one had transposed two similar crowns,
But locked up both myself and Bonnières.
In the meanwhile Count Rinaldini sought
With all persuasion and kind promises
A matrimonial union with Theresa, whom
He found distracted at her Father's debts.
His liberty, that for which I was a petitioner too,
Was bought at the price of Theresa's hand, not heart,
For that I know that she could never give.
Then when I offer to repay the debt,
And different engagements would fulfil
Sasselli coolly says I am too late.

TARCHETTI.

There has been a disclosure of the robbery,.
And a discovery of the trick so played.
An agent from Bologna stole the Crown
For Buonvicino, the Countess of Canossa's Minister,
Who with it crowned Conrad, the Emperor's son,
Who since has perished on the battle field.

CHEMNITZ.

Ha!   What a world of base iniquity.
Who then is in possession of the Crown ?

TARCHETTI.

You might have known all this had you returned
As soon as all in Europe knew this fact.

SASSELLI.

And then I would have turned the Count away,
And if you loved my daughter, as you say,
Well, I might have consented at the last.

CHEMNITZ.

Of the solution not a word transpired,
So I abode in prison many weeks.
But ingenuity that never tires,
But racks man's brains for some impediment
To mere mechanical regularity,
Suggested to the Duke of Normandy
That to increase the already elated force
Impetuous to descend on Britain's Isle
And make him monarch of the two-fold realm
Every state prisoner of whatever crime
Accused, either on remand, or guilty proved,
From Rouen city castle to release
And add their number to his warlike ranks.
This hardly came within the sphere of Law,
And as a German I could not consent
To act in arms against the Teuton Race.
So in my prison cell I lingered out
As long a period as time sufficed
To clear up all the doubt upon my case,
A Patriot and a Martyr to the right,
When weariness and disappointment lent
A scheme for my delivery at last.

I with a diamond carefully concealed
Within my llama girdle's eastern fold
The turnkey of the Rouen prison bribed
To let me have a blessing from a priest
And free my soul from all impurities
Which bar the passage to the outer world.
Good men that listen to the warning voice
Of those rejected by unworthy laws
Shall never now lack proselytes and friends !
At my suggestion we exchanged our dress :
I left him kneeling at a Crucifix
And sought the Monastery at Lisieux.
For nine months I performed those offices
Wherewith holy devotion consoles the world
For those who in its game do not succeed
Or reach prosperity beyond their meed.
One day a letter reached me from without,
The wording written in Italian, thus :
' Carl Johann Chemnitz haste to Italy,
The daughter of Sasselli, whom you loved,
To whom the contradiction of the World
Denied all access and accomplishment,
Expects you in Florence at her Father's
  house
A matrimonial union to complete.
Witness my seal and signature to this,
Matilda, Countess of Canossa, Sovereign
Of Tuscany, Liguria, and Lombardy.'

TARCHETTI.

You certainly deserve some recompense
In suffering for another's fraud and guilt !

SASSELLI.

Rinaldini has not married my Theresa.
The ceremony will take place on his return
From Fladenheim, where he led Emperor's troops
Against his enemies the Suabians.

TARCHETTI.

A letter here from Wurzburg yesterday
Upon financial business, most of it,
Contains a fact I should reveal to you :
' A duel on the plain without the gate
Was yesterday fought between two noblemen,
The Marquis Oberto, and Count Rinaldini.
The meeting ended fatally.'

CHEMNITZ.
                                Who fell ?

TARCHETTI.

After a contest where ambiguity
Could not from observation be dispelled,
And triumph leaned to this side, then to that,
Concealing the result in clouds of doubt,
Through the Count's heart the Marquis ran his
        sword.

CHEMNITZ.

Then dear Theresa is at last my Wife !
Good banker, give me joy !   Sasselli, you.

TARCHETTI.

Excuse me ! I have lost a noble friend.

SASSELLI.

And I an aristocratic son-in-law.

Enter THERESA SASSELLI.

TARCHETTI.

Signora, let me introduce you to a man
Who half an hour since in this very room
Had very nearly you an orphan made,
And now he offers you his heart and hand.

THERESA.

Carl Johann Chemnitz, welcome back to Florence !
You must have made your fortune in the year
Which has played me and my Father many a prank
Yet leaves him still a miser, me a maid.

CHEMNITZ.

'Twas for a year upon the Brenner Pass
We sacrificed that earthly happiness
We knew the value of but abjured
Till all the world should be as good as we.
Measures and individuals unworthy us
That changed security into alarm,

Exertion ruined, paralysed commerce and trade,
And rendered all existence a matter of chance
For what sound cause we lived, and how, and where,
Like the reverberating thunder-storm
That to the unwary, only danger speaks.
But now the rainbow of encouragement
Reanimates the prudent wayfarer,
Who ventures from the Refuge he had sought,
And double reaps for all expected Hopes.
Consent, Theresa, then to be my Wife.
Heaven has given you all that I could wish,
And the good Tyrolese have subscribed for me
Ample indemnity for a loss sustained
In one of my engagements months ago.
Then let me lead you to my German home,
The brightest jewel that I shall possess !

THERESA.

Were I to refuse your offer now
Just as your Countrymen our Emperor
The shock would paralyse that industry
We brave Italians boast as well as you ;
But I, of a more liberal stamp than they,
Will inculcate conciliatory views
And so a good example be the first
Honest exertion to prosper and support.
Carl Johann Chemnitz ! with my heart and hand
Within the year that we agreed should pass
I ratify the promise that I made.   [*They embrace.*

SCENE V.—*The Castle of Canossa.*

EMPEROR OF GERMANY.

Italy has resumed his noble work
Of leading to perfection step by step
Each childlike tribe of separated Man.
It was at first an universal aim
To match the offspring of mortality
With all the value of its best result,
At once assumed in absolute effect
Without the tedious process that all time
Would naturally languidly wear out,
A lesson and an oracle to us all.
But there are obstacles which rise around
And faith's trustworthy lamp nearly obscure
Which seem Prosperity to paralyse,
And leave us wondering pilgrims doubtingly
To manifest all due uneasiness.
Now, our experiment to test again,
Again and yet again more willingly,
Whether by some ideal standard first,
And solely guided by a will-of-the-wisp,
Or waiting on the waylaid secret patiently
The dross of earthly passions laid aside
To realise the covenanted price
Of all exertion and all enterprise

By gracing the solution with support,
Or by enjoined advancement to attain
Laboriously but earnestly achieved
The fair seductive dream of this our night
We feel within the principles we love
Warmed by the genial glow of measured heat
Joyfully to develop the sure friend.
Then to increase the value of the prize
Already the sharp jar of rivalry
Warns us to flee devotion to one's self,
And zealous in each natural sympathy
To bind the stroke of that unerring date
Which slow but far from tedious by design
To our request consistent will reply,
Each in his own turn pleased and gratified,
Unmingled with the poison of dissent.
So it appears, shading all differences,
To Normandy and all such chivalrous ranks,
Whose only boast it is that, beating the world,
In eagerness they sacrifice themselves,
By summoning an earlier and later power
Germany as of original intent,
In ultimate integrity will arise.
I speak not in the mood of vanity,
Despondency has strangled vanity,
I know it is a strange eventful child,
Like the staid Sun beating a cloudy array,
Not with his own will, nor yet anyone's,
And knows not where to shine, or what to burn.

A A

And yet the Future under its considerate care
When all but insular worthiness has fled,
Through anxious doubts will look to Germany,
Its reference in experience grown sage,
Its arbiter in quarrelsome debate,
Its testing crucible of principles,
Coined as of forgery, forgery to detect,
With pattern coins bearing the true mint stamp :
Solemn in respectful assurances,
Grateful in long-accepted Confidence,
The emblem of some unapproachable type
Which in itself not prospering aids some else,
Fulfilling certainly not all man may be,
But all that sense and decency permit.

COUNT OF PIEDMONT.

To-day spreads joy over all Italy.
The universal rage of rivalry
That thus usurped too long philosophy's chair
And subjects dictated in discordant tones,
To surfeit all immoderate desires
With Truth stretched to its farthest boundary,
Gives place to views of joy and happiness,
Time, that had laid aside its olive wreath,
And grasped the sword with rabid, frantic eye,
Averse its destiny to sacrifice,
To crop up some new fungus of dispute
That had encrusted civilisation's trunk,
Steps forth to sanctify the kindlier art

Which satisfies the wonder-seeking Soul
With some fond emanation of the profound.
An age uncertain, but in this grand certainty
Which gives security to what it acquires,
Upon that gift enables man to build
Again another institution up,
The union solemn ceremonial
Of opposite sexes for fruition's sake,
So that our children blessed by the antitype,
And by the type of all security
Their Life may have and hold and exercise
In all the spleen of liberty undisturbed,
For purposes all different most manifold,
Advantages according as received,
Fashioned by rarest opportunities
The secret of all origin to evolve
Into a combination as sublime,
So that the goal whenever such attained
To the beginning may be adequate,
Life supernatural but more manifest,
Yet bearing with it an essential worth
Irradiated by joint ability
Into a thousand faults on one stone,
Whose lustre is a beacon that shall find
All satisfaction both for matter and mind.

ODONE OF SAVOY.

It is then time Fortune to ratify
By our acceptance of these overtures,

And so our gratitude will accelerate
Renewal of fresh hopes, and visions bright
Will be preceded by fresh heralds of light,
Enjoining all with attention to those truths
That we have reaped and they shall have sustained
To be biographers of our success,
The thrifty fountains of a wide domain,
Acceptance of which we later can regulate
With the parental curse or blessing that
Those deeds can grace that know how well to live
To those who know not, or to those who learn.
Sensations that can never be effaced,
Guarded from error by the accomplishment
Of tardy actions, not theirs, but our own,
By the transposition of generalship
Will strike from readiness the frequent crime,
To paralyse itself with its own dread,
That thought to have supplanted ready wit
With enmity and emulation base,
And with its practices, fraudulently obtained,
To win the rare and chance-directed prize,
To foster idleness and indolence,
And giving to Prosperity no Law,
Which law we have evaded earlier on,
Foundation to create for flippant arts,
Profounder industries and subtler thoughts
To definitions and distinctions coined
To the employment of mere intercourse.
No healthy and intuitive impetus

To suffocate new-kindled destinies
For broad and comprehensive establishment
In advocacy of measureless designs
For constant restoration to our lot
Of that indulgence which once premature
May succour us in credulous belief,
And seconded by ultimate decree
To supplication Innocence return,
Our genuine worthiness revivify,
Our absolute infallibility restore,
Over disease our triumph re-assert,
And all concurrent accidents and ills,
Extending without disintegralising sympathy,
Damning while it proposes intercourse ;
Since blended ills invite no ready cure
Which only waits on stupor and despair,
Beyond the pale of a protracting sphere
Into the region of discarded points,
Where Fallacy and Falsehood give them home.
We are ourselves again, and let us strive
For that accelerating pass of skill
Which the executive wand of perfidy
Finally and for ever may dismiss.

EPPONE OF ZEITZ.

Then something for Canossa has been gained
In the past Diet's self-solicitude,
For honour to accrue to Germany,
And latitude in doings they dislike,

In feigned devotion so to please the Pope.
How seldom constituted indifference
To indirect and separate ways and means
The satisfaction of that object proves
For which the independence was assumed !
At first who louder swore than Suabia's duke :
In declaration of presumptuous rule
Principal of Germany, Patron of Italy,
Joining Contention, Compact, Cause and Creed.
And then he thought Cisalpine territory
So worthless and so valueless would be
That he believed in Conscience it was dead,
Or like the Satellite fulfilled a round
Of duties to his most superior orb
To which it could not if it would object.
To-day his condescension is complete
In his reluctance finally to agree
With principles he could not but admire
Worthily by conclusions, not his own
But of his friends, who lend him all their eyes
To scan the features of the visible day.
And all the force that he should have possessed
To break the moody barriers of his heart
Has so subsided that, the object, lost
By old Bavaria to Suabia, will
By new Bavaria have been ably found.
So Circumspection baulks itself and flies
In the face of its advantage to relent
When disadvantage is too imminent,

Its measureless dominion overspread
With clouds that to a moderate demand
Had not from thrifty Providence been provoked
Thus for a compromise to be exchanged
For something antagonistic virtually
To all that its integrity aroused,
And raised it to a level with its date.
Experience makes a wise man many friends.
Which theories of pretended purity,
Adhered too long and pertinaciously
Unwillingly but positively debar
In the final prosecution of those claims
Which most careers irreverently absorb,
From sharing grave responsibilities
Too many for the shoulders of one man.

AZZO, DUKE OF BRUNSWICK.

Then let us heal up all our differences
And at Earth's holiest altar grace the day,
Since this alliance from all opposites strained
Has every contradiction put to flight
That has the narrow-minded lately fed
Till the improbable became impossible,
And nature in reflection of itself
Died like Narcissus of its loveliness.
To venture such a supposition frail,
And full of consonant redundancies,
As a panacea for ills redeemable
By superstitions plain relinquishment

Of infidelity to infidelity
Would rather have evoked the qualities
Which on mistaken ground are not mistakes,
Nor proper reformation have provoked
Without some insult to the honest heart
Which either from susceptibility drew fruit
Or from inaptitude, superlative consequence.
By proud Correction in its counterpart
Of errors which have crept in unawares,
Or offspring were of inborn fallacy
That grew unnatural monsters to disprove,
We had not sank into chaotic infirmity,
Or grasped the secret and been stung to death
As adders sting when seized too hastily.
Looking with an undeviating glance
Into that troubled sea Futurity
This coming marriage will be found the Fount
Of good alternate with Catastrophe.
Not Europe only in the crash involved
But tribes and territories yet unknown,
Yet recognisable to the curious eye,
Of undeceived inquiry guided home
By profitless desires, requiring a light,
Natural or supernatural as may be.
That corner-point to give to obscurity
More certain truth than we are truth ourselves
Will to our cordiality testify,
To future experimentalists a proof
Of foresight and foreknowledge singular

In sacrificing base and meaner thoughts
Of passable and profitable views,
Delineating to the external eye
Fulfilment of a rational decree,
Proof in the length, and breadth, and depth of Change,
Weeds wafted on the sea of circumstance
That indicate a further wider sphere
Which those who seek to value will expect.
Assimilation wins expectancy,
Aggrandisement and elevation lift
The veil before our vision, and make known
New worlds and hidden treasures all our own.

MATILDA OF CANOSSA.

Your majesty, princes, and territorial dignitaries,
Companions of my former lonely state,
I hasten to acquaint you of my wish
For the immediate consummation of
The marriage of myself with Guelfo d'Este.
It is a measure wherein those difficulties
That clouded its result foreshadowed here
So far that in obedience ominous
Futurity the present distanced on a par,
With pointed thorns strewed Concord's rosy path.
But cold suspicion has given way to Hope
That energy and zeal will counteract
On our part and on yours impending woe.
Accept my gratitude for past support,
And here to-day assist me to cement,

In cordial agreement on your part,
The union of Bavaria and Canossa.
It always has been said, and lawfully,
That long accumulated internal wrongs
Destroy the immediate efficiency of kings,
And make external gain impossible.
My provinces, so loyal hitherto,
Mantua, Parma, Modena, and Ferrara,
Lately forswore allegiance to my rule,
But in a vigorous war which I declared,
Unmannerly rebellion I have crushed
That else had trod on civilisation's bud
And pressed out future good for present ill.
Futurity's protection and defence
Attracts ambitious man to weigh it well
In the just balanced scales of rectitude
And indecision as to what betides,
From past and future on the stepping stone,
The passing moments' requisite resource.
But more immediate and anterior destiny
A strong temptation held to enterprise,
A fulcrum whence to lift or lower mankind,
A Fountain's orifice whence Fortune flows,
Which the wave returning meets again
Refreshing redundantly its origin
With all that it has gathered in its course.
Whoever in its spacious halls resides
Will either dictate to the world around,
Within the pale of purity enthroned

And warned by its condition to be true,
Or fall the victim of conspiracy,
On vanity self-engendered falsely poised,
To fiendish machinations which exist
An undercurrent of the tranquil stream
The semblance of whose virtue it reflects,
But caverns animosity in those depths
That the Sun's searching eye never explores.
My individual solicitude
At present would determine all things well.
The close assistance of religious aid
The fury of my enemies has disarmed.
But when resources straight to mine reveal
With what a parsimonious liberality
In points which are of vital interest
Our hopeful Italy has been supplied
It seems most natural somehow to secure
By Treaty, War, Trade, or Diplomacy,
The absent happiness with which ours mixed
We may seize hold of the Cup Prosperity
And quaff it off, draining it to the dregs.
Guided and animated then by this
Profound but ever too perceptible
Solution of the situation grave
In which with many others I am placed,
But yet more singularly so than they,
Moreover viewing your Majesty's success
With that approval which Pope Gregory
Impartially determines it deserves,

I have determined on the politic step,
Set forth in stately guise as best may seem
All those desired objects to secure,
Of matrimony with a ducal house
Equal in dignity, as great in difference,
Like me possessing power of control
Over all neighbouring rival potentates,
Gifted with an imperishable name,
Gratified with the unbounded confidence
Of others in a patriotic creed
In preservation of irregular rights
Inherited in understood bequest
From a wise patriarchal ancestry,
Whose prophecies have fanned a natural wish
To enrich, and rule, and rectify all round
Sooner or later or at some special time,
When we and other nations are at fault.
Each community expanded from a tribe
To form a sound and proper polity,
As such, or with which, or a part of which
Promotion to success we may attain
And all erratic jealousy control.
Bavaria's Duchy being such an one
With this then in the person of Guelfo d'Este
I pitch the hazard of my experiment,
Two nations, by your Majesty's power joined,
And under your wise head concentrated
By your connivance and the Pope's consent,
From this day forth as long as Time shall last

Shall form an integral and solid State
From its own evident boundaries measured up
Not trammelled and encumbered by a trick
Mistakes and superstitions to unfold
Within the shroud of their own craftiness,
And with corruption stimulating Life
Before it had attained maturity,
But adding to the certainty of Good
As fitter unexceptionable Good,
And from the bud unworthiness neutralised
By undesigned entanglement with worse
That thus excluding the incurable
And so all quarrelsome elements refined
Into agreement of no common kind,
We may by our discoveries regain
The lost Elysium all have sought in vain.

EMPEROR.

Good promises of fruit often attained
Who love to essentialise in the result
Exertions in the outset laudable
Are apt by estimate and encouragement
Upon the way to vex and dissipate,
And there are serious obstacles opposed
To mar and blight ends hastily obtained.
Then time should soothe every solicitude.
But you have tested unity and amity :
If 'tis a coin passable join the sides
And put the stamp at once upon the gold.

AZZO.

You have no enemies, Matilda, in this suit.
It offers many sound advantages,
And in the outset surely prospers much
Complicate difficulties to alleviate
Which Time tries to increase, not to diminish.
But there are clouds more grave than these around
Which will disturb this early happiness,
Which seem to convey under its genial mark
Destruction to good Fortune later on,
When Time shall have deluded us with joy
Into some confidence in its promises.

MATILDA.

I cannot, Azzo, from this suit withdraw,
The Pope has countersigned the settlements.
The Emperor here, in the presence of us all,
Considers it for my especial good.
Good for the union of our rival races,
And likely to produce to all Mankind
Emolument, Accommodation, and Goodwill.
But if you think the alliance insecure,
A present happiness to be overthrown
By elements of discord now unseen,
One half the Italian territory I own,
Saving the other for my son and heir,
To Gregory and the Church I will bequeath.

EMPEROR.

Enough !   We are not all astrologers,
Baffled in contradicting destinies
That would political experiment preclude
Lest they interrupt the mapped out certainty.
· There is less venture than is usual,
If more than one is on one end agreed,
This confidence in the Future thus displayed
Will never by that Future be disowned,
Nor they from filial piety deviate,
And change a benediction to a curse.

Enter GUELFO D'ESTE.

GUELFO.

Your Majesty, and princes, prelates, and potentates
Standing around in solemn girdle now,
Pillars of uniformity of thought
And principles by ages satisfied,
Whose only dream has been to further aims
Beyond the natural turn of wilful man,
And place him on that present happiness
Beyond the reach of his ulterior star,
I now require your witness and support
To my immediate matrimonial union
With Matilda, reigning Princess of Canossa
Consolidation, also with your individual aid
And joint co-operation of a design
In confirmation at this rising date

Of passions drained of due philanthropy
Which would discretion prejudice, wisdom pervert,
And level a dishonourable path
For you and I and all of us to tread.
It has been difficult to render long
In definitions and distinctions safe
In propositions for our regular use
Sound justice to all arguing disputants :
Delimitations, Lines, and Barriers
We must to some fresh oracle refer :
And what but Happiness can spring from Love?
What other virtue seeks prosperity
With half its diligence and earnestness?
What other principle can all security
Discover for two rash experiments?
From its existence, lofty and profound
As ever faculty or fact announced,
All meritorious labour is derived.
Then with this Princess this my union
To such all satisfaction will decree.
Then when two rival races join in one
Collision that had stolen all good fruit
Shall to co-operation yield it up.
Each stake in either hazarded or both
Shall to the Speculator be returned
In every separate case an hundred-fold.
Then all that undermining dissonance
And innate volume of external hate
A force more natural shall interdict

As nature's most unnatural aim and end,
As savouring of unfathomable desires
That culminate in wickedness and wrath,
Not soothed by individuals but aroused
 To stormy rage of irritated wills.
So by joint compliance and comparison
Inaugurated thus by our two selves,
The bond of all exertion thus enlarged,
We may build up a stately edifice
In its importance so far guaranteed
As to determine all yet undefined,
Give to the future more than we can claim
But less than we might earlier have achieved,
And with vague circumstances ratify
A Treaty of expectancy and hope
That, while securing them an indemnity
In labour and exertions all our own,
By an adoption instant and precise
Of those advantages we offer them
We trust them with a broad inheritance
Beyond our tenure but within the view
Where verifications of an outline drawn
Impartial, absolute, and incorrupt
Shall prove ourselves in occupancy them,
They guardians to the fulfilment of the Bond.

MATILDA.

Witnesses here to my agreement now
To this approved and acceptable union,

Henry the Fourth, Emperor of Germany,
And you Princes of Piedmont and Savoy,
You Duke of Brunswick, and you Eppone of Zeitz,
And you the pious Prelates of our Church,
Its terms and treaties sign and register.
Enlarging an infirmity of doubt
By holding great improvement in reserve
But balancing their failure ultimate
By recognisable prosperity,
And then by our example reassured
Securing the furtherance of the design
To change close and restricted sympathies
For a more broad and comprehensive line,
In which experience easily will reduce
Plain truths that never should have been concealed.
Happiness and misery are not for ourselves
Nor all we individually do
Or suffer in this pilgrimage of Life,
But in forbearance, faith, and charity
Perceptions of a day relinquishing
Imperfect visions of a mind obscured,
And of a heart susceptible of wrong,
And deeming wrong is something from without
And not a foul conspiracy within,
Which, with a false deduction of all art
Misdirected ingenuity and skill,
Evading all but natural enmity,
And persevering in the development
Of impulses of staid antipathy,

Leads us from ourselves to ourselves, while
  starts
Enterprise on its glorious march elsewhere.   ·
Let us now, therefore, train our destinies
In odious fetters from ourselves released
In all we know to agree to as much
As will in reciprocity return.
That so by joint exertions profiting
Yet leaving originality intact
We may with confidence each has in each
Those means and opportunities extend,
The avenue which opens to results
Which otherwise we labour for in vain,
Disclosing further fields for speculants,
And adding, more, a reason to that space
Wherein that high perfection not our own,
But ours if we but recognise the want,
We shall advise, suggest, and in inheritance
Of which we know the value, they not yet,
Possessions due to all of us acquire,
Enhance, and to Futurity bequeath
Without a jealous sorrow or regret.

EMPEROR.

Matilda of Canossa, and Guelfo d'Este,
In the fulfilment of this union,
By all the world and by myself approved
As the solution of a paradox
The past and future centre on ourselves,

And in a paroxysm of circumstance
Which renders all solution difficult,
The attempt hazardous as the end envious,
You have the cause of Otho based upon
Something more serious and significant
Than Papal blessing or rebellion's curse.
Civilisation had no centre-point
When first it started on its famous march,
And edging points of unembarrassed land
Teeming with soft fertility its own,
A mere circumference to our solid strength,
Advanced the interests of all mankind,
And bought their admiration in return.
Mankind will some day have a debt to pay
For the amalgamation by my race
Of the prospective abilities, which, spent
Wherein they started on the vantage ground,
Could never have consolidated in return
Fulfilment of wide advocated views,
For which no other sphere of equal stamp
In prosecution of our great device
Will in remote discovery be found.
Therefore, in your union you have bid
A higher price for the return of merit
Than for its dispersion our fathers bid.
The woes that some of you have announced
As being the last fruit and most probable
Of corresponding Love and Policy

Will shake the object of enquiry and research
Till the applied points of opposite impulses
Will fuse encouraged energies into distrust
Of Providence, the Church, themselves, and us.
But whenever we have all those secrets gained
Which prompt us to concentrate advantages
Finally to their attainment and their cure
It will be necessary to reconstruct
Upon the basis of Earth's infancy
A fit arena for maturer work,
And so exiling all irregularity
By the spontaneous action of all minds
Germany will be at once the home and rest
Of spent Philosophy and Philanthropy.
So far our joint exertions will achieve
A double triumph and a twofold gain.
Expand around our profitable good
And in affection to those principles,
Which others to preserve will learn too late
As having been too late in learning them,
To value left all value gained restore.
With this ring then, from the imperial treasury,
Through five whole generations laid in store,
Render your Compact holy and secure.

  [*Guelfo and Matilda advance and take the ring.*
And to the generations summoned thus
Let it be a bequest from sire to son,
To children pious in performance of

Great duties to a parent, I for one
Political, to whom afresh is due
More obligations of a filial kind,
Stranger but nevertheless as natural,
This law fulfilling, as I now fulfil
A Sovereign's pleasure and a Father's will.

> [*Guelfo places the ring on Matilda's finger.*
> *Trumpets sound a nuptial strain. The*
> *Curtain falls.*